starting
OVER

starting OVER

Joanne Wilson Meusburger

Ambassador International
GREENVILLE, SOUTH CAROLINA & BELFAST, NORTHERN IRELAND

www.ambassador-international.com

Starting Over

ISBN: 978-1-62020-936-3
eISBN: 978-1-62020-962-2
Library of Congress Control Number:2019947184

This is a work of fiction. Names, characters, and incidents are all products of the author's imagination or are used for fictional purposes. Any resemblance to actual events or persons, living or dead, is entirely coincidental. Any mentioned brand names, places, and trademarks remain the property of their respective owners, bear no association with the author or the publisher, and are used for fictional purposes only.

Cover Design & Typesetting by Hannah Nichols
Ebook Conversion by Anna Riebe Raats
Edited by Daphne Self

AMBASSADOR INTERNATIONAL
Emerald House
411 University Ridge, Suite B14
Greenville, SC 29601, USA
www.ambassador-international.com

AMBASSADOR BOOKS
The Mount
2 Woodstock Link
Belfast, BT6 8DD, Northern Ireland, UK
www.ambassadormedia.co.uk

The colophon is a trademark of Ambassador, a Christian publishing company.

CHAPTER 1

TED WOKE FROM A SOUND sleep to the wail of sirens. The clock on the bedside table registered midnight. With a sigh, he rolled out of bed and crossed to the bedroom window. All he could see were the snow-capped peaks of the Rockies under a plethora of stars, in peaceful contrast to the blaring intrusion.

He turned and saw Diana pulling on a robe over her pajamas. "What is it?" she asked in a fearful voice.

"Must be somewhere on the other side of town," he mumbled, heading back to bed. "Maybe at that subdivision that builder abandoned . . . some poor jerk trying to collect on insurance."

Diana crossed the room to peer out a window in another direction. "Can't see anything. Must be north somewhere."

They went back to bed, but Ted could not sleep. When the doorbell rang, Ted checked the clock beside him. *Four a.m.* He grabbed his handgun from the bedside table. "I am not taking any chances this time of night."

He slid his feet into slippers and padded down the stairs. Through the peephole he saw a badge with the fire chief's insignia. The chief spoke as soon as Ted opened the door.

"Mr. Rutherford?" The chief looked very tired, almost haggard. "Are you the owner of Hometown Furniture?"

"What happened?"

"Sorry. It burned to the ground. Nothing left. You'll be sent a copy of the fire marshal's report."

Ted's shoulders slumped, the sidearm heavy at his side sending a dark shadow across his feet.

Diana clutched his arm. "What will the insurance cover?"

Ted knew at that moment that the fire had consumed their last hope of financial recovery in the growing recession. "Only the contents. Couldn't get insurance on that old building."

Diana had handled their situation better than Ted, saying things would work out. Ted had told her the only thing working out was the money in their meager saving's account. The classified ads weren't helping either.

"For Pete's sake!" He crumpled the newspaper to his lap. "A calling? Sounds like a monastery."

"What does?" Diana took a sip of her coffee.

"This ad in the paper. Listen. W*anted: Married couple as resident managers for charming, turn-of-the-century apartment hotel. Free living quarters. Commission. Must love people and regard the position as a calling. Contact James Toos, Owner.*"

Diana laughed. "You have to admit it's unique. Besides, I like the part about free living quarters."

"We're that desperate?"

"You know we are." Ted didn't want to hear that, but it was true. Since the fire, their savings had dwindled, becoming so small the amount could no longer be considered savings. During the past six months, Ted had pursued every possible lead, but to no avail.

The July sun bore down from an azure sky as Ted climbed the stone steps of the turn-of-the century mansion. A plaque beside the entrance designated the structure as an historic landmark. Ted raised the brass handle and let it fall. The sound reverberated deep inside.

A wet ribbon of sweat traced down her spine. She had chosen the yellow silk because it complemented her naturally-curly brown hair and amber eyes. It also reminded her of the "golden days" she wanted back, when their business prospered, and she could afford a dress like this to wear to dinner parties or a dance at the country club.

She straightened her back to hold the fabric away from her skin. The dress was a poor choice for such a warm day. Judging by the refined voice on the phone, Emma Toos probably didn't have sweat glands.

Ted patted her shoulder. "Don't worry, sweetheart. If they don't like us, it's just as well. This whole idea is crazy."

She shrugged and moved a few inches away. "You've been unemployed for months." Her words hung stark. "As you've often told me, people won't say it, but your age is against you. If we're offered this opportunity, we need to consider it."

But she stopped when the lines deepened around his mouth. Her handsome husband worried more than he let on. Then why couldn't he just say so? Wouldn't it help to worry together?

At length, they heard the slide of a dead bolt. The large door creaked inward.

"You must be the Rutherfords." The elderly gentleman extended a thin, bony hand to shake Ted's and then hers. "I'm James Toos."

Diana looked for a cane—he was that bent—but he stood sturdy. His small head was completely bald, but clear eyes met theirs from behind steel-rimmed glasses.

"You're right on time, I see," James continued. "Punctuality is rare these days. Come in, come in!"

Into the twilight zone. Diana fought the nervous impulse to giggle. As her eyes adjusted to the dim light of the foyer, she stepped onto the Persian rug and noted the rosewood paneling and marble fireplace. A huge grandfather clock standing in one corner chimed two o'clock.

"Please follow me," Mr. Toos said as he led the way down a long hallway and into a paneled dining room. "May I present my wife."

Emma Toos sat at a long oval table. A Dresden teapot on a silver tray waited in front of her beside four fragile teacups so delicate the candlelight cast shadows through them.

Her skin was almost satin smooth except for crow's feet bracketing brilliant blue eyes. Her steel gray hair was pulled back in an attractive twist at the base of her neck. Perhaps in her late sixties, she appeared some years younger than her husband. When she rose in regal fashion, spine erect and head high, Emma stood at least four inches taller than James. She wore a flowing gray skirt and a pink silk blouse that complemented her ivory skin.

"Welcome," she said, her smile gracious as she extended her hand. Diana fought the absurd impulse to curtsey and found her hand gripped in a firm handshake instead.

"We've awaited this meeting with great anticipation," Emma told them. "As you can see, Consuela has prepared tea."

She directed them to their seats. They followed her lead, taking linen napkins from the white tablecloth and placing them across their laps. Diana noticed how uneasy Ted looked, but he squared his shoulders and managed to smile.

Up to this point it was more like an audience than an interview. Diana almost expected a footman to appear in the doorway. Instead, a young girl with coal-black hair and large dark eyes appeared. She would have been lovely minus her sober, almost sullen expression. Dressed in a black uniform, she carried a crystal plate of petit fours that she placed in front of Emma.

"Thank you, Consuela."

The girl cast her eyes down and backed from the room while Emma lifted the teapot and poured the tea. An amethyst ring glittered on her ring finger as she directed Diana on her right to pass each cup and saucer around the table. The crystal plate followed the last cup.

Diana reminded herself that Emma was, like herself, a wife and homemaker. The surroundings might be different, but her role remained the same. She took a deep breath and willed herself to relax.

"If I remember correctly, you live on the western slope and have two college-age children?"

Emma looked toward Ted, but Diana jumped in to ward off a long explanation.

"That's right," she replied. "Our son, Brad, will be a junior this year at the University. He's in summer school now." She clutched her hands together to avoid twirling a curl around her forefinger—a nervous habit from childhood. "Laurel, our daughter, just enrolled as a freshman."

"That's wonderful!" Emma said. "You must be very proud."

James cleared his throat in a series of small dry coughs. The sound startled her, and she turned to his end of the table where light from the crystal chandelier gave his sunken cheeks and slanting forehead the translucent quality of mottled parchment. What odd bookends the couple made—one a regal, commanding presence, the other frail and hunch-backed.

His keen gray eyes peered at Ted. "I'm impressed by your resume, young man." His voice gained strength until it found its measure. "Even though you have no experience in hotel management, your business background constitutes a definite asset. Many young people jump from one job to another these days, but I see you stuck by your furniture business for twenty years. Commendable. We're very sorry concerning your tragic loss."

The gold chain that crossed the vest of his dark suit swung away from his concave chest as his head bobbed up and down. "As an attorney in practice for fifty-one years, I applaud your sense of loyalty and purpose."

"Thank you, sir," Ted replied. "I appreciate that. However, Diana would be the one to assume the manager's position—with my support of course. When I'm available, that is."

Diana saw his fair skin redden beneath his sandy-colored hair, making his freckles more prominent so that he looked even younger.

I'll look old before he does.

Ted continued. "I hope to find another position to benefit from my previous experience."

Emma took a lace handkerchief from the sleeve of her blouse and pressed it to her throat. The gesture covered the cameo Diana had noticed at her neckline, reminiscent of Olivia DeHavilland in *Gone with the Wind*.

"We sympathize with the reversals you've suffered, young man."

Forty-five wasn't old but it wasn't a good age to be starting over.

James cleared his throat again. "We prefer a couple to bear joint responsibility, even if the man pursues outside employment. Hartwick House needs the stability of managers who love it as we do and treat its residents as their personal guests."

Emma turned back to Diana. "We've read your statement of experience, my dear." She paused as if mulling it over once more. "In your own words, what qualifies you to be the new mistress of Hartwick House?"

Of course, she lacked Ted's business experience, but Diana resented being thought of as his appendage, somehow needful of male authority. She glanced in Ted's direction and found his raised eyebrows and slight smile infuriating.

Clearing her throat, she answered. "I view management of a hotel as similar to the organization of a household. It would require one to wear many hats, and I'm experienced in that."

"Well put." Emma reached to refill Diana's cup, the gesture putting her back in control. "Please excuse my rather blunt approach. You see, we've been in an untenable position the past few weeks. Our former managers left on short notice and Cloomer, a young man we know in the neighborhood, offered to fill in until we found suitable replacements. He turned out to be totally devoid of the necessary skills. It's been quite distressing."

James pushed back his chair and rose to his feet with a sudden agility Diana would not have thought possible. He inclined his head in deference to his wife, but his tone left no room for argument. "Let's not burden these young people with our problems, my dear. It's time to take them next door . . . on a guided tour of Hartwick House."

CHAPTER 2

EMMA LED THE WAY NEXT door to the three-story structure that loomed over Humboldt Street. James followed behind. The gray stone edifice sat on a high, grassy bank held back by a stone retaining wall. Several blocks away, Diana saw the gold dome of Colorado's state capitol glittering in the sunlight.

"Capitol Hill was once *the* place to live. Grand structures like Hartwick House lined the streets at the turn of the century." Emma's broad shoulders propelled ahead of her narrowing body and small feet.

"I remember when doormen stood at apartment house entrances and maître d's greeted patrons at fine restaurants. Then automobiles replaced streetcars and many residents moved to the suburbs. Such a shame!"

She'd given this spiel more than once it seemed. She looked up at the hotel's peaked roof and third-floor dormers which had the look of a medieval castle. They fit perfectly with James and Emma, as if packaged together from another century.

A police car streaked by, siren blaring. For a moment Diana relived the fire siren and reached for Ted's hand.

Emma paused, but then continued. "The streetcars disappeared, and many lovely homes were torn down and replaced with storefronts in the name of progress."

An ambulance wailed to a stop somewhere close by. Emma waited for the noise to subside and then continued. "Hartwick House was built to provide gracious apartments for its occupants. In fact—Cloomer! For heaven's sake!"

A German shepherd skidded to a halt so close to Emma's feet that she almost stumbled. A muscular young man wearing striped running shorts, but no shirt, held the long leash—his features partially concealed behind the bill of a navy blue cap, bushy black brows, and a tangled beard. Swearing, he stumbled to a stop.

"Cloomer—really now!" When Emma grabbed ahold of the leash, the dog licked her hand, his long tongue going well up her arm. She bent to stroke his head with her other hand.

"This is Henderson," she told Ted and Diana. "And this is Cloomer Dooley, the interim manager."

He tugged the bill of his cap in a brief salute before bending double, hands on knees, to catch his breath. His back dripped sweat.

"Cloomer," Emma continued in a formal tone, "I'm pleased to introduce Ted and Diana Rutherford. We're about to take them on a tour of Hartwick House."

"Who's tending the desk?" James asked, his tone forceful.

One hand lifted in a vague gesture. "Left a note," Cloomer panted. "The place is all but empty."

"All the more reason to tend to business."

"Henderson needed a workout." Cloomer reached for the dog's leash and gave it a sideways jerk to maneuver around them and set the dog off at a run.

Emma's cheeks grew spots of rose, like those on the face of a Dresden doll. "Well, I never!"

James motioned her on with a flick of his age-mottled hand. "Never mind. He'll soon be replaced."

Emma nodded, her face grim, and resumed her monologue. "Mother and Father Toos raised five sons here. The place is named for her—Edith Hartwick Toos. When she died, she left James the hotel and the mansion."

She paused, then added, "The other sons inherited controlling interest in the Texas oil field."

"Stay on the subject," James said from behind.

Diana glanced at Ted, but he pursed his lips and refused to meet her eyes. Oil fields in Texas?

They approached the front entrance of the hotel. The huge stone building was imposing; the stained-glass window above the entrance was truly beautiful. The sun reflected lavender, rose, and azure hues against the stone exterior.

At the curb a wooden signpost framed in wrought-iron proclaimed *HARTWICK HOUSE - AN APARTMENT HOTEL* in black script against a maroon background. Diana thought the sign unique and well-fashioned. It created an impressive effect and Diana's spirits lifted. Maybe this wouldn't be so bad. She looked at Ted, but he looked straight ahead.

Emma mounted the curved cement steps, took a ring of keys from her skirt pocket, and unlocked the heavy oak door. Then she stepped back. With a sweep of her hand, she motioned for them to precede her. Pink wallpaper flocked with green vines adorned the walls of the entry foyer above white wainscoting while red roses patterned the pink plush carpet leading up a short flight of stairs to the lobby.

Diana tried again to gauge Ted's reaction from the set of his mouth. If they hadn't driven so far to get here, she could imagine him leaving right now.

Four numbered doors faced the circular lobby. On a fifth door, MANAGER was imprinted in gold on the frosted glass door panel. In front of it, a high desk held a leather-bound registration pad. Beside the pad rested a feathered pen in an ebony holder and a leather-framed sign in gold letters read 'Please Register Here'.

Propped against the placard, a torn scrap of paper yielded the scrawled message: "Running the dog. Back soon. Wait."

Emma crumpled the note in her hand. "As long as Cloomer is absent we might as well view the manager's apartment first. I told him I'd be showing it, but I can only hope it's presentable."

She unlocked the door and preceded them through a short entrance hall into a good-sized living room. A large middle-aged woman busily swiped a grimy rag across the top of a small television set. A magazine lay open on a nearby wing chair, a page still lifted.

"This is Hattie, our weekday maid." Emma's emphasis on *maid* managed to convey her disapproval. "Hattie, this is Mr. and Mrs. Rutherford."

"Pleased to meet cha.'" Hattie ducked her head and resumed dusting. Her round face and rounder body looked mid-thirty.

"Cloomer said to spruce up his place 'fore I left," she muttered to no one in particular. Her eyes narrowed, and one shoulder rose higher as she turned away.

"Heaven knows it needs it! I can't see that you've made much progress." Emma waved the back of her hand in a gesture of dismissal. "Scrub the entrance floor before you leave. It looks as if it hasn't been mopped in days."

"Yes, Ma'am." Hattie sidled from the room, the gray dust rag trailing behind her like exhaust from a dirty tailpipe. She looked back with a smug smile as if to say, "See, I do what I want."

Diana despaired. How would she manage with help like that?

Emma directed their attention to the small, U-shaped kitchen. "Compact, but efficient," she pronounced. "Everything you need within reach. The step stool allows for that."

Cupboards reached to the ceiling around three walls. The refrigerator stood on the left, the stove on the right, the sink in the middle with drawers on each side below the counters. Beside the sink was a dishwasher. *Ugh, no windows.*

"And of course, there's a garbage disposal," Emma continued. "We aim to provide all the comforts of home." Her manicured fingertips trailed the countertop as the blue flash of her eyes turned back toward the living area.

"We know the wallpaper is outdated. It will need to be replaced— and we most definitely would have the carpet cleaned before you moved in." A grimy traffic pattern criss-crossed the cement-looking carpet. Magazines littered the sagging cushions of a dark brown sofa and a large ashtray on the scarred coffee table overflowed with cigarette butts.

Emma sighed. "I'm afraid Cloomer is accustomed to squalor."

Ted's brow knitted into a deep frown that he made no attempt to disguise.

The place was a disaster. The hideous wallpaper Emma so casually referenced had a deep brown background scattered with large pine cones in shades of gold and tan. Heavy floor-to-ceiling mustard-colored drapes hung in limp folds at tall windows that fronted the street and circled the dining alcove. One could imagine the gloom when they were drawn at night.

The sofa, a plaid wing chair, and a fairly modern television provided the only furnishings. In the dining alcove, a card table with two folding chairs stood forlorn.

Right then, Diana expected Ted to take her by the arm and walk out the door. Instead he turned on his heel and strode across the short hallway that separated the living room from the bedroom. Emma gestured for Diana to follow, as if Ted deserved the right to take the lead. James brought up the rear.

The bedroom quarters appeared somewhat less depressing. The space would probably accommodate their king-sized bed and dresser. A windowed alcove, identical to the one in the dining space, remained bare except for a pair of jeans pooled on the floor in side-by-side circles of faded denim. A guitar propped against the leg of a straight-backed chair.

Opposite the unmade bed, a white, wood-framed fireplace lined with green tile centered the wall. It held a glint of promise as Diana pictured a basket of flowers in place of the grate and family pictures on the mantel shelf. The flowered chintz drapes and apple-green carpeting created a more cheerful appearance.

As Emma's monologue continued, it dawned on Diana that the bedroom floor plan replicated the living room in reverse—a bedroom instead of a living room. The alcove matched the dining area and a room off to one side with cupboards, counter, and sink replaced the kitchen.

Obviously, this end of the lobby had once housed two apartments. Separated by the side entrance hall before the building became a hotel, the two apartments had been combined into manager's quarters.

Emma flicked her hand dismissively. "Cloomer's here only temporarily, of course. The furnishings are castoffs from the basement storage. With your own things in place, I'm sure the apartment will be very comfortable."

James cleared his throat. "Mr. and Mrs. Rutherford know the possibilities, Emma. The apartment is easily worth a thousand a month, not counting the utilities, cable TV, and daily maid service included."

Emma smiled and nodded. "So true, dear. Now please follow me as we show you the rest of Hartwick House."

Sure enough, another short hallway led past a second bathroom, the same as on the other side. Diana caught sight of a claw-foot tub with a faded plastic curtain trailed inside it. Ted cleared his throat, but she refused to look at him.

As they toured the three floors of the hotel, Emma pointed out the doorknockers: a woodpecker, a deer's head, a bust of William Shakespeare, a bucking bronco, a French hen, a Model T Ford, a saxophone, the Hartwick coat-of-arms, and even a pair of kissing cupids.

Emma smiled. "We call this our honeymoon suite," she told them.

Intricately fashioned in dark bronze, each doorknocker would make a unique statement in a different setting. The garish wallpaper and stark wainscoting, however, overwhelmed their impact.

"We've collected them from all over the world," Emma said.

"Emma loves doorknockers—until they knock," James observed as he trailed behind. "She somehow assumes guests will only admire them and never actually use them."

"Some don't," Emma replied with her usual calm. "Others need a reminder now and then."

Ted hadn't said a word during the entire tour. Now his eyes failed to meet hers again.

By the time they reached the third floor, Diana expressed her confusion. "This room is Number Thirty-One? There can't be thirty-one apartments?"

"No, dear. The numbering starts over on each floor," Emma said.

Of course. Diana blushed.

The floor plans of the vacant apartments Emma showed them varied from spacious and airy to cramped and crowded. Each contained a small kitchen with refrigerator and apartment-sized stove —hence the term "apartment hotel." The furnishings appeared adequate, in some cases quaint, but overall shabbier and more utilitarian than "charming and unique"—words used by Emma.

Diana tried to listen, but as she followed Emma's halting steps back down the staircase, she experienced a sudden panic. Could she really live here? Do this?

On the second-floor landing, Emma paused and directed their attention out the large window to the scene below. "This is our secret serendipity," she said. "Everyone is surprised by it and many guests return because of it."

Diana gave an involuntary gasp, bringing her fingers to her lips. Below them was a formal English garden, hidden from the street by a high stone wall upon which grew a profusion of ivy and white clematis.

Akin to spotting a violet in a crack of a concrete parking lot, the discovery proved totally unexpected. The space it occupied was rectangular, shadowed by a huge oak tree. The fence concealed it from both the street and the alley.

A flagstone path meandered from the front gate to a bricked area with wrought iron benches situated on either side. At the foot of one of the benches appeared a small bronze plaque with lettering. From that distance, one couldn't read what it said.

Branching off, another path wound through a series of carefully tended flowers and shrubs. Diana recognized daffodils, asters, and cyclamen. As Emma led them down to the first floor, she sought the view again, this time over red geraniums that filled the first-floor window box.

"The garden was designed by a landscape artist," Emma told them. "The plaque reads, *'Best of Show—Garden Club—1999.'* Mario, our gardener, tends it weekly. Isn't it beautiful? A respite from the outside world and no one passing on the sidewalk would ever guess it's here."

"We would like you to take the position," James told them when they reached the lobby. He named a salary. "If you do the job I think you will, there would be a sizeable bonus at the end of sixty days."

Diana said, "We'll take it" at the same time Ted said, "We need some time to discuss it." What was Ted thinking? But she smiled and added, "All right if we get back to you tomorrow morning?"

"Of course," the elderly gentleman agreed. "We'll look forward to hearing from you."

CHAPTER 3

TED AND DIANA SETTLED INTO a booth at a Chinese restaurant down the street from the hotel. Diana said she couldn't eat, but Ted insisted. "It'll be late when we get home," he told her.

Conversation and the clank of dinnerware competed beyond the lacquered screen placed for privacy. Just as well. It put off the outburst Diana feared coming. They ordered and ate in silence.

At last Ted asked, "Why did that Cloomer guy have Henderson?" He poured more tea in Diana's cup. "Emma talked like he was their dog."

Diana shrugged. "Maybe he was on loan."

The lame joke received no comment. Not even a smile.

She tried once more. "The doorknockers were unique . . . as well as Mr. Toos' comment that Emma was 'into' doorknockers."

"I do admire the old man. Lets Emma run the show but reminds you he's the one that finances the production." The waiter arrived with the bill and Ted added the tip.

They rode mostly in silence, separate in their thoughts. At last Ted spoke. "Is this something you honestly want to consider?"

Expecting argument, defiance, even outright refusal, Ted's quiet inquiry brought tears to Diana's eyes. What made her so sure this opportunity provided the solution to their problems? Would the shared responsibility of managing the hotel limit Ted's future as well as quench any talents she had of her own? If they waited, would they still have other options?

Several moments passed before she replied. "All I know is that it is something available. My friend, Dorothy, always says, 'God opens doors.'"

"Ah yes . . . Dorothy." Ted's tone bore no malice, just resignation. It scared her that Ted seemed so distant, so removed.

Towards midnight, Ted pulled into the driveway and turned off the ignition. They sat for several moments. Diana stared at the *For Sale* sign illuminated by the porch light.

Ted spoke into the silence. "It's our life, Diana, our future. What will our kids think? What about your career in home decorating? That was just beginning to take off. Or the years I've spent in retail? I'm not sure it's possible at this point to start over doing something so radically different."

Diana turned towards him. "It's a respectable position, Ted. How hard can it be? When you find another job, I can run the hotel during the day. Basically, all that's required is checking guests in and out and seeing that the maids do their job. Besides, as quaint as they appear, James and Emma Toos are respectable people. The apartment is grim, but I sense they might be open to improvements if we do a good job and they want to keep us. They're getting old. I think they truly want someone to take charge and relieve them of the responsibility. It's a six-month contract, subject to renewal. That's not forever."

Ted levered the door handle and pushed the door open with his foot. "We have a week to decide. I'll have to find another job regardless. It's you who would be stuck there, so I guess it's really up to you. Just don't shut your eyes to the realities."

Bitterness laced his voice. "I realize only too well that our options are limited but don't lay a Pollyanna act on me, pretending everything is 'sweetness and light.' If we take it, we go in with our eyes wide open."

In other words, if she made the decision, she could take the blame if it didn't work out. That was the distance that separated them. Tears filled Diana's eyes. She and Ted were becoming strangers. Because of the fire, they had lost the social standing and financial security that seemed so important. Besides their children, what did they still even have in common? Could they weather the realities of moving and making a new life for themselves?

She opened the car door and stepped onto the wide driveway, her body stiff from the three-hour drive. The wording in the newspaper ad came back to her: *Consider it a calling.* What did that mean?

Ted went into the house ahead of her, leaving the front door wide open. Often in the past she walked through it with a warm feeling of pride and satisfaction in the home she herself had designed and decorated. Now it would be sold, and she felt as if already it belonged to someone else.

As she packed boxes for the move, Diana dwelled on the morning several months before when she had knocked on the door of Ted's den. It bothered her that he kept the door shut, but after the fire they had installed a private telephone line and the den became Ted's home office to accomplish what had to be done—absorbing the final report from the fire marshal, collecting on the insurance, meeting with their former employees. At least she knew those people and could commiserate with them—their floor manager, Jake, the salesmen:

Bill, Henry, and Frank, and their longtime bookkeeper, Barbara. She and Barbara remained good friends, sharing the mutual shock of their circumstances. Ted made sure all the final paychecks contained a generous bonus, but still.

"Come in," Ted said as she opened the door carrying a cup of coffee.

"Have a cup with me?" she asked.

"I think I will."

Pleased, she placed the cup in front of him, went back to the kitchen and returned with her own mug to sit in a club chair and cradle it in her hands. Ted swiveled his chair to face her.

"Time to face facts, Diana. The insurance covered the building and inventory, but we still owe our creditors."

"Creditors?"

"Electric, water, phone bill, radio and TV advertising, sublet furniture repair, customer financing, the list goes on."

Diana tightened her grip on the coffee cup. "How will we pay them?"

"I'll find another job. You may have to as well. At least Brad and Laurel's college funds are safe. But as for us? We're starting over. We could declare bankruptcy, but my parents raised me the old-fashioned way—'Pay your debts.'"

Ted brushed his hand through his hair and Diana noticed the dark circles under his eyes. Since the fire, they both often lay awake.

Diana looked around the room Ted called his refuge. She had decorated it herself. The masculine colors—sage carpet and rust-colored drapes patterned in sage and gold complemented the mahogany desk and chair as well as the rack of smoking pipes that had belonged to Ted's dad.

Her eyes filled with tears. Setting her cup down on the end table beside her chair, she stood to wrap her arms around his shoulders, her cheek next to his.

Ted's father died trying to land his small plane in a snowstorm soon after Diana and Ted were married. "I know my dad was disappointed that I had no interest in ranching myself," Ted told her. "After high school, I left for the city with my 'pipe dream' of playing a guitar for a living."

In fact, he was playing with a group in a Denver club when he walked into the jewelry store and smiled at Diana. It was her first job, just out of high school.

"May I help you," she had asked the young man with the muscular build and the whitest teeth she had ever seen. Probably because he was so deeply tanned.

"I'm looking for something for my mom for her birthday," he told her. "Can you describe her for me?"

"Well, she's small . . . delicate almost. Gave me her blue eyes."

And they *are* blue—like cornflower, Diana thought. She reached for a silver chain set with delicate blue stones. "Do you think she would like this?"

"Perfect! You have wonderful taste. May I take you to lunch?"

The question took her aback, but she answered 'yes' and, as they say, 'the rest was history.'

They had married so young—each an only child. Their parents told friends it was 'love at first sight,' but it wasn't really. They had the same interests, were attracted to each other, and saw no need to look further.

"A good fit," people had said. And it had been true.

The band gigs petered out. After his father's death, they moved back to buy the store with money Ted's mother insisted he take as his share of the estate. The former owner was retiring and sold it for a fair price. Ted had worked so hard to learn the business and make a comfortable living. Now it was gone, their dream literally gone up in flames.

Diana picked up the guitar and placed it with care in the last box, marking 'Basement' on the lid with a black marker. She thought of the hours she spent at tables in bars listening to Ted play, waiting for the intimacy of the glances he sent her way.

Good thing the hotel basement provided a storage area. Who knew when or where all their things would be in place again?

CHAPTER 4

TED PARKED THE U-HAUL TRUCK as close to the hotel's side entrance as he could. James Toos had given him the key the week before when they returned to sign the contract. Now he climbed the steps and inserted it in the rusty lock. He wanted to check and make sure the apartment was cleared out before they unloaded their furniture.

When he pushed open the door, he saw the pansies—then more pansies: in bowls, dishes, pie pans, atop the window sills, the old-fashioned radiators—even in strategic locations on the carpet. Their smiling faces stared up at him—white, yellow, blue, orange, and purple.

"What on earth?" he stammered.

Brad and Laurel followed him in, their arms full of bedding. Laurel dumped her load on the clean carpet and turned in circles to view the panorama of pansies before breaking into a cascade of giggles.

Brad's face, however, maintained the scowl that Ted had witnessed on most of the ride. He backed up, leaning against the wall to balance the load in his arms.

Diana came in last. She'd ridden with Brad, who made little or no response to her efforts at conversation, only grunts. Now she heard Laurel's giggle and Ted's remark. When she saw the pansies, they became the last straw.

"They must be Emma's doing." Her cheeks flamed. "I'll take care of them." Fighting tears, she hurried to the kitchen in hopes of finding trays, cookie sheets, or pans—anything to gather them up. Behind her, she heard the calm, modulated voice that could belong only to Emma, probably entering the apartment from the lobby.

"These must be your lovely children. I've been waiting to welcome you to Hartwick House, but I wanted the pansies to do it first."

Diana heard Ted introduce Brad and Laurel. When she felt composed enough to reappear, Emma greeted her with seemingly endless grace. If she saw traces of the tears, she didn't show it.

"What fine young people." Emma wore a flowing, black wool skirt with a cream silk blouse, the cameo again at her throat. Low-heeled suede pumps completed Diana's previous impression that Emma always dressed for the day, no matter what.

"The pansy faces are saying 'Welcome.' It's an old tradition that pansies bring prosperity. I picked them myself."

While Diana found it impossible to picture Emma at such a task, a closer look revealed the uncut pansies simply plucked by the handfuls. Probably Consuela had stood nearby with trays to collect them.

Laurel saved the day. "I've never seen such a riot of color—like sunbursts!"

Emma beamed. "Exactly. Just as you are—rays of sunshine in answer to our prayers. We hope to see you often," she told Brad and Laurel, "but for now I must leave you to your labors."

She turned to Diana. "I'll come by the desk at nine o'clock tomorrow morning to go over the things you'll need to know." She turned to leave, giving them a bright smile and that signature wave of her hand above her shoulder. "Welcome! Welcome to Hartwick House."

The door closed, and Laurel burst into a fit of giggles. Her brown eyes danced with merriment.

But Brad's face remained fierce. "Mom! Whatever you plan to do with these flowers, do it," he said. "What a dump. Do you guys have the slightest idea what you're doing?"

Laurel punched him in the shoulder. "Oh, come on, everybody," she pleaded. "It's not so bad. Rise to the challenge."

"Let's get this over with," Ted agreed, his voice flat, resigned. "Come with me, Brad. I'll get the dolly out of the truck and we'll start with the dresser. It's at the front of the truck."

Diana knew Brad wouldn't stick around a minute longer than necessary. Since the day she and Ted had sat down and explained the situation to their children, Brad had distanced himself from its reality.

Laurel helped her carry the containers to the kitchen where Diana forced most of the flowers down the running disposal. The white Formica countertops struck her as so stark compared to the dusky brown of the granite counters left behind. But then nothing remained the same except maybe Laurel, who stole up and hugged her from behind.

"Did you see Brad's face?" Laurel asked. "He's furious, but I think it's a hoot. Oh, come on, Mom. Don't be so glum. You'll have this place fixed over in no time. All Mrs. Toos needs is a nudge. It's easy to see how far she'd go to keep you here. The pansies say it all."

Diana saw a tiny bit of truth in what Laurel said. The fact that Emma had gone to so much effort to welcome them seemed out of character for her.

Later she would unpack a rose bowl, fill it with water and float the remaining pansies on top. She would put it on the front desk where

Emma would see it tomorrow—when she came back for Diana's "indoctrination," or whatever she'd called it.

"Thanks, sweetheart," she told Laurel. "You always look on the bright side." She hugged her daughter's straight back, the strawberry-blonde ponytail tickling her arms. Then she opened a cupboard. "Want to wipe off these shelves? I saw a bottle of ammonia under the sink. They look clean, but I don't trust the maid."

Brad and Ted leveraged the dresser over the threshold. Brad's dark brows remained knitted into its deep frown. When they returned from the bedroom, he went to the curtained French doors against one wall, jerking them open to expose an upright springs and mattress.

"What in the . . . "

Ted came up behind him and reached to pull the springs and mattress down a few inches. "That, my son, is a Murphy bed—circa 1950."

"Maybe we can take it out, Dad."

"Maybe."

"You could make it into a recessed bar. Serve the guests martinis."

Ted grinned for the first time that day before dragging the dolly toward the door after another load. "We welcome all suggestions," he told his son. "A Murphy bed in the living room and a fireplace in the bedroom—how's that for a switch?"

Beds made and furniture in place, they ate pizza from cardboard cartons before Brad and Laurel left for Boulder. Dusk approached as Ted and Diana stood on the stone steps to see them off. Laurel smiled and waved out the open window, but they could see Brad's scowl as he made some comment and fired the engine to take off in a spurt of gravel by the curb.

As they turned to go back inside, Ted asked, "What do we do now?"

"Guess I'll know after Emma comes over tomorrow morning. All I want to do now is fall in bed."

She jammed the pizza box into the trash can before the bell rang at the front desk. Ted set the tone. "Your call, Babe."

And so, her new career began.

CHAPTER 5

PRECISELY AT NINE O'CLOCK THE next morning, the desk bell in the lobby rang.

"I see you're making progress," Emma observed, peering past Diana when she opened the apartment door.

If she's waiting for an invitation to come in, she'd best think again. They were in no way settled yet.

"We'll manage," she told Emma. "As you predicted, with only two apartments rented, things were quiet." She knew her voice sounded stiff and formal, but she hadn't slept well and wanted to get this over.

"Good. Then we can get started." Emma came through the swinging gate that hung between the registration desk and the wall. She smoothed the back of her navy-blue skirt with both hands and seated herself at the desk. "You will need to bring out the reservation book and another chair for yourself."

Diana felt like a child on the first day of school.

Seated side by side, Emma reached over to place her own hand on Diana's. She looked into Diana's eyes with what Diana recognized as sincere compassion. "You're very brave to undertake this, my dear."

Diana hadn't expected the tenderness in Emma's voice. Looking down, she fought back the hated tears.

Emma's blue eyes sought hers. "I'm sure it hasn't been an easy transition. These times are grave, but you can make a new beginning here."

Taken aback by Emma's obvious sincerity, Diana thought perhaps she'd been too quick to judge. "We hope it will buy time for Ted to find other employment," she answered. She needed to make it clear that Ted was the 'breadwinner' and would find work that would enable them to leave. "But we promise to do our very best while we're here."

"I'm sure you will." Emma turned back to the registration book. "Now, as to the registration process . . . "

Thus, Diana learned the procedures involved. With only a few apartments, nothing was computerized; but the bookkeeping looked simple. Emma told Diana that guests at Hartwick House found the simplicity part of the charm. It cast Hartwick House as belonging to another era.

When Emma left, it was time for lunch. Ted had made a trip to the neighborhood market and now had soup and sandwiches prepared. "How did it go?" he asked.

Diana slumped into a chair at their dining room table. It barely fit in the small alcove.

"Emma surprised me. She's actually very nice. Very patient. She made it clear she wanted to be available for questions or to help in any way—except on Wednesdays." Diana crossed her arms and rested them on the table. "I don't know what she does on Wednesdays, but she sounded very emphatic about that. But it's not the Hilton, you know."

"I should hope she'd be nice. After Cloomer, they must be ecstatic to find us. And as we speak . . . "

Diana followed his gaze out the window. The aforementioned Cloomer now approached the side entrance. "Oh no," she moaned.

Ted crossed the room even as Cloomer knocked.

"Hello, Cloomer." Ted stood in his path, but Cloomer, sweating from his run with Henderson, maneuvered on past him. Ted looked to make sure the dog hadn't followed.

"Hey! The place sure looks different. Expennnsive! Guess you came from a better lifestyle 'fore you landed here."

Ted's expression hardened, but Cloomer continued before he could speak. "Thought I'd stop by and maybe help you out with a few pointers."

"I'm sure we'll manage just fine."

Nevertheless, Cloomer forged ahead.

"It's not much of a job, really." He flopped himself down on their expensive Thomasville sofa and draped his arms over the back. Sweat soaked deep swatches in the underarms of his sleeveless jersey. "Anyone could do it. Keep track of who comes and goes—tell the maid. How hard is that? Bet this put you back a bunch," he observed, patting the flowered upholstery on either side of him with the palms of his hands. Then he reached one hand into his shirt pocket. "Got an ash tray?"

"We don't smoke." Ted's words came out curt, but Cloomer didn't appear to notice. He crossed his hairy legs again and replaced his arm on the back of the couch.

"I guess I should have known from the start that they considered me a stop-gap until they found another sucker—uh—manager. My room-mate and I rent a place down the street. James Toos met me out joggin' one day and hired me to take Henderson for runs. Now ain't that a name for a dog? Always on the lookout for ways to 'one-up' everyone. Anyways, when the last couple left—or got fired maybe—they asked me to move in. Sure didn't fix it up for me like you have it now." He craned his head around to peer toward the bedroom. "If all this stuff is yours, you sure must be makin' a comedown to land here."

Ted remained standing. "That's none of your business, Cloomer. Sorry, but we're busy now. It's time for you to leave."

"Well, excuse me! Just tryin' to help out—see if you have any questions and offer my help." Cloomer stretched his legs out and crossed his ankles. "The old man will tell you to call Hack Cummings when you need something fixed. Hack Cummings is a worthless drunk. I'll work for less and do a better job." He reached into his shirt pocket and dug out a scrap of paper from behind the square package of cigarettes. "Here's my number. Leave a message and I'll stop by."

Ted took the paper between two fingers and walked ahead toward the door. "We'll call if we need you. Or maybe catch you as you run by with Henderson."

"Yeah, Henderson—what a privilege."

The door closed, and Ted turned the lock. "Hack Cummings can't be any worse than him. I'm sure we'll find out soon enough. Without a doubt, this place often has regular need of a handyman."

The outside buzzer announced Hattie's arrival—late of course. Over the past two weeks, Diana learned that Hattie used a long list of excuses—the bus ran late, her alarm didn't go off, her cat ran away, she broke a shoestring, her arthritis slowed her down. Diana kept a log of Hattie's "misdoings," as Emma put it. Probably to no avail, but just in case.

Poised to replace Hattie that first day, Emma enlightened her with the realities of unemployment compensation. "Our insurance rate is already sky-high," Emma said, "and you can be sure Hattie will run her payments out to the limit. I've never seen a lazier girl. The former maid quit when your predecessors left without notice. In desperation, we hired Cloomer and he up and hired Hattie before we knew it. The temporary service sent her over and he hired her that same day. Anything to avoid the possibility of having to do the work himself."

"A bad situation all round," Emma continued, "but in order to avoid paying unemployment, you'll have to prove sufficient cause to get rid of her and that isn't easy. Documentation is required, and laziness and insolence are matters of opinion. You'll need hard facts of something substantial."

So Diana gritted her teeth and kept Hattie on a tight leash, hoping that alone might cause her to quit—which she doubted. She wasn't sure Hattie even noticed one way or the other. She whined and complained, but quitting didn't appear a likely scenario.

No rational person would look at Hattie and think she could do the work in the first place—climb three flights of stairs without an elevator; four counting the basement. Hattie waddled when she walked and held her arms out to the sides to carry the caddy of cleaning supplies and maneuver the vacuum cleaner. Hattie was fat. No way getting around it.

"Got checkouts?" Hattie asked as she stashed her oversized black handbag in the hallway closet and scribbled on her time sheet. Diana looked over her shoulder. As usual, she fudged on her actual time of arrival.

The hotel should have a time clock. "Three checkouts. Twenty-One and four are already vacated. Thirty-two is the other one. The guests in that suite stayed a week, so pay special attention to the kitchen. They told me they ate in quite a bit. Liked to cook their own meals."

"I know, I know. Don't need to tell me. I got eyes. Been here lots longer than you have." The woman jerked the ring of room keys off the hook by the door and used the front bathroom. At last she left through the swinging gate and trudged down the hallway to the supply closet.

Diana hurried to catch up. She'd try a different approach.

"You're right, Hattie. I have much to learn. Suppose you show me what cleaning supplies you use. If you should call in sick someday and I have to call the agency for a substitute, I'd need to show that person where things are."

The swaying hips stopped moving as Hattie cast a suspicious look at Diana over her shoulder. "I ain't plannin' on being sick, but you do need to fetch what I need when I run out."

"Of course. All the more reason to take inventory." Diana felt less and less in charge, but she trailed after Hattie nevertheless.

The first-floor closet faced the stairway. Hattie jerked the keys out of a pocket of her super-sized trousers and unlocked the door. Standing behind her, Diana viewed shelves of linens, towels, and extra blankets. On the floor below the shelves sat an upright vacuum cleaner, a broom, and a green plastic caddy with cleaning supplies.

Hattie grunted hard as she bent over to retrieve the caddy. "This here's the cleaners I need," she said. "Have to make more trips back for the linens and vacuum cleaner." She heaved a huge sigh as if exhausted by the thought of it.

Diana saw Windex and Pine Sol bottles, a large sponge, and some dirty-looking rags. "Aren't the cleaning cloths washed every day?" She knew linens were picked up by a laundry service, but Emma said towels, throw rugs and such should be washed and dried in the basement.

Hattie scowled. "Big enough loads every day as it is," she huffed. "I throw rags in on Friday 'fore I leave."

For Margie. The weekend maid.

"Thanks for showing me," she told Hattie. "Let me know when you need something."

"No problem." Hattie hoisted the caddy onto one hip and headed into room four.

Diana called after her. "Seems like you should also need toilet bowl cleaner, furniture polish—"

But the door closed, leaving Diana face to face with the deer's head doorknocker. She remembered Emma warning her to always have her own set of keys with her and to keep the apartment door closed. Now as she crossed back to the apartment, the door was open, and her keys still hung on the hook.

Would she ever feel at ease here, let alone in charge? Right now it didn't feel remotely possible. She felt like a captive within stone walls—at the mercy of people like Hattie.

"Of *course,* you must get away at times," Emma told Diana. "Please forgive me for not making that clear from the start. Any time you want or need to leave Hartwick House, call Cousin Fanny. We call her cousin because we've known her forever. She's like one of the family. Knows all the ins and outs of running the hotel and can handle the maids as well as the guests. You can depart knowing Hartwick House is in capable hands. Her fee is ten dollars an hour, so you can judge your time away accordingly."

In other words, your free time isn't free. Nevertheless, she would call this Fanny person to come the following Friday when Laurel came to spend the weekend. Laurel's Friday morning class had been cancelled and her roommate had offered Laurel a ride. Ted would drive her back up to Boulder on Sunday.

Time away with Laurel would be well worth the money. Only three weeks since the move, but it seemed twice that long.

She'd hoped Ted might step up, but he'd said he needed to finish his job in the basement.

Diana dialed the number. "Known her forever" made Fanny sound as old as Emma. Older maybe.

"Good morning!" a perky voice answered.

"Fanny Mason?"

"Speaking."

"This is Diana Rutherford. My husband, Ted, and I are the new managers at Hartwick House."

"So I hear! You're an answer to prayer, according to Emma."

"I hope so. Anyway, I need someone to watch the desk Friday morning. About eleven?"

"I'll be there with bells on."

That expression sounded like something her grandmother might say. "I'll look forward to meeting you," Diana told her.

"And I, you," Fanny answered, her voice more like a child's than belonging to a senior citizen. "I'll knock three times and you'll know it's me."

"Goodness," Diana moaned to herself. Could this Fanny person handle Hattie, let alone whatever else might come along?

Diana still felt so unsure of herself that she woke up each day wondering what unknown might happen next. Nevertheless, nothing must keep her from time with her daughter. Laurel would be just what she needed.

Oh yes, Laurel chattered on the phone and Facebook concerning her classes and professors, the awful dorm food, and the foibles of her roommate. But a mother needs to assess things for herself without the assumption her daughter is simply putting up a good front. There were many questions to ask.

When Friday arrived, three taps sounded at the side entrance door promptly at eleven o'clock. "It's me," the tiny person announced as she took a high step to cross the threshold.

Diana stared. Fanny Mason couldn't be more than four foot nine—if that. She probably weighed ninety pounds at most. She wore a powder blue pantsuit to match her eyes and wore her white hair pulled back in an old-fashioned topknot that emphasized her fine features. Diana felt she should sit this person down and wait on her rather than leave her to fend with Hattie and any unexpected circumstances.

"H-hello," she stammered. "I'm Diana."

"Figured. My pleasure." Fanny looked her up and down, but mostly up. "Just the sight of you is a deep pleasure after what came before. Besides, you're downright pretty!"

"Why thank you." Diana found herself twisting a curl and recaptured her fingers to clasp Fanny's small outstretched hand instead. "Please come in."

After taking a big step to clear the threshold, Fanny stopped still and looked around. "My, what have you done with this place? No wonder Emma's pleased."

"We haven't done anything but move in our furniture," Diana said.

"That's what I mean. Do you mind?" Fanny pointed to Ted's plush burgundy recliner.

"No, of course not." Fanny walked past her.

Fanny backed up to the chair, put her hands on the arms, and achieved a sizable hop to settle onto the seat and work her way back. Then she reached over the side to grasp the handle and recline. "Ahh," she sighed.

Diana remained speechless, but another knock on the side door revealed Laurel's face in the glass panel.

"Hi, Mom." Laurel burst into the room like sun through clouds, just the way Diana anticipated, and clasped her mother in a mighty hug. "I thought I'd never get here."

She let loose and looked around. "Oh Mom. What a difference your furniture makes now that you're settled. Don't you feel better about things already?"

Fanny propelled herself out of the recliner, landing nimbly on her feet. "This must be your lovely daughter."

"Laurel," Diana said, her tone formal. "This is Fanny Mason. She's here to watch the desk while we're away. Fanny, this is my daughter Laurel."

"Now isn't that a funny expression—watch the desk? Watch *Oprah*, more likely. Anyway, it's a pleasure, darling. I understand you're attending my alma mater."

"You went to the University of Colorado?" Laurel's animated response caused her cascade of reddish-brown curls to bounce on her shoulders, her voice mingling astonishment with delight.

Fanny let out a deep laugh that couldn't possibly come from such a tiny throat but did. "Yes, dear. In the dark ages. Studied literature. Taught it for many years."

"There's a girl on my hall majoring in Classical Literature. She's a real brain. Comes from a wealthy family in Texas."

Diana blinked. Laurel hadn't shared that information with her and she was suddenly jealous of this knowledgeable stranger who knew just what to ask. She considered herself and Laurel close, but now Laurel lived in another world—one this Fanny-person knew better than she.

Diana picked up her purse from the table. 'Out of prison' she had thought of it. "We should go now," she interrupted.

Cousin Fanny reached out to put a hand on her arm. "But of course. I didn't mean to detain you. Forget this place and have a wonderful time. I assume Hattie is here?"

"Yes, as well as my husband, Ted. He's doing some sorting down in the basement. I left him a sandwich in the fridge, so you needn't bother about fixing anything for him."

"Bother? It will be my pleasure to make his acquaintance. Just tell me which apartments are open and then run along."

"Four and twenty-one are vacant," she told Fannie. "Both are 'check-outs', so I told Hattie to do them first. I only hope . . . what I mean is . . . I haven't found her very reliable."

"Hah!" Fannie rolled her eyes and clicked her tongue. "That girl doesn't know the word reliable, let alone its meaning, but you two run along. I'll see to things here."

Diana harbored not a doubt in the world but what she would. Fanny settled back in Ted's recliner, but Diana now knew she could climb back out if so required.

As mother and daughter walked the three blocks to the restaurant, the beautiful fall day set the mood. Rust and gold leaves shimmered in the slight breeze and fell to the sidewalk as Laurel chattered on about the campus, her professors, and what a treat this would be after days of dorm food.

Ushered to the canopied patio as they requested, Laurel chose a table with a view of the distant mountain range. Once seated, she shrugged out of her jean jacket, twisting sideways to drape it around the back of her chair.

"So, Mom," she began. "I've done all the talking so far. Now tell me every little detail about Hartwick House. Do you see much of Mr. and Mrs. Toos? What sort of guests stay there? Just think—you've embarked on a whole new life. I'm so proud of you!"

To her dismay, Diana felt tears sting her eyes. Leave it to Laurel to affirm her instead of the other way around.

"It's not a career, silly." She busied herself with her own coat as an excuse to turn away and regain her composure. "It's just a job until Dad finds something else and we get back on our feet financially."

"Mom, people get degrees in hotel management." Laurel put her elbows on the table and leaned forward to place her chin on her fists. "Besides, Hartwick House isn't just any hotel. It's a romantic getaway— listed in guidebooks."

"An overstatement if I ever heard one." Diana laughed at Laurel's unfailing exuberance. "Not exactly your dad's description, though we do have respectable guests. Yesterday a young woman told me she's on the road much of the time for her job. Said she likes the intimate feel of Hartwick House over a big hotel. She wore a jacket in that latest puffy sleeve fashion and a designer purse over her shoulder. And her nails looked gorgeous—orange and pearl-colored to match the jacket."

Laurel nodded, her dark eyes sparkling with interest.

Diana continued. "Said she loves Hartwick House for its quaint charm and because she can cook her own meals once in a while. Then guess what she said."

"What?" Laurel leaned closer.

Diana loved the way Laurel's eyes grew darker when her interest in something intensified. "She said, 'Mrs. Rutherford'—I always give my name that way, more businesslike, I think—'how lucky you are to live here and get paid for it. What a dream job, and what a smart choice you made to drop out of the rat race and make this your career.'"

"See, Mom, what did I tell you?" For emphasis, Laurel smacked the table with the flat of her hand. The waiter arriving to take their order took a step back.

"Oh, excuse me," Laurel said, and the waiter's admiring smile revealed that he would.

Drop out they had, Diana agreed to herself; but not by choice.

While waiting for their food, Diana breathed in the scent of the honeysuckle growing beside them on the patio fence and relaxed her shoulders for the first time in days. "Now tell me about your roommate," she said.

Ted sat hunched on a low metal stool in the middle of the cavernous room. Gray cement walls and high barred windows surrounded him like the prison he felt it to be. His knees almost reached his chin as he sorted the piles of dishes arrayed at his feet.

His dark mood matched the grim set of his face. At least here he could be alone with whatever thoughts he cared to harbor, not upstairs where he forced a smile in front of hotel guests as well as his wife. Especially today when Diana's plans would have required him to stay there alone. What a drag that would be, just sitting around and dealing with Hattie.

He placed dishes in boxes to his left or to his right, depending on whether they would go or stay. It wasn't rocket science, just whether or not they were chipped or discolored or suitable for the hotel kitchens. Sort of like furniture stacked in the back room of the furniture store—too much damage or could the piece be restored to be sold in the Bargain Corner? Of course, it wasn't the same at all. How does a chipped dish compare to a fine piece of mahogany?

After they felt somewhat settled in, Ted set up his computer in the bedroom alcove to read the want ads and churn out resumes. Only two led to interviews where people complimented him for being overqualified for the position.

"You wouldn't be happy here for long," they told him. "Best you seek something more suited to your managerial background."

So, after seeking permission from James Toos, he retreated to work in the basement. The day they moved in, he and Brad shoved things aside to make room for boxes and extra furniture unloaded from the U-Haul. He needed to bring back some order, but it went beyond their things.

"That basement is a fire trap," James Toos had told him. "Should have been cleared out years ago, but Emma's a 'saver,' so it stayed as it is. Whatever you decide is junk, the trash collection people will take. Have our handyman move it to the curb for pickup. And what is usable can go two blocks over to Goodwill if it can't be utilized somewhere in the hotel."

"Yoo-hoo!" The high-pitched voice echoed down the hallway. "Lunch time, Mr. Rutherford."

Ted hadn't met the esteemed Cousin Fanny, but he retained a mental picture of her—old, slow, frumpy perhaps. As a friend and contemporary of the owners, wouldn't she likewise be at least somewhat eccentric?

"Coming," he called, pushing on his knees to stand. Because of the long session in a cramped position, his lanky body unfolded by increments.

He passed the laundry room and furnace room and climbed the flight of stairs to the front entrance hall. Bright sunshine met him there and it took a moment before his eyes adjusted. Then he locked the door behind him and proceeded up the three steps to the lobby, turning left toward the front desk and their apartment.

There he found Fanny to be the direct opposite of his expectations—small and spry with piercing blue eyes and a broad smile.

She bounced out from the kitchen when he entered the apartment. "I'm Fanny," she said, her smile crinkling the crow's feet at the corners of her eyes. "After glowing reports from Emma, I'm so glad to make the acquaintance of Diana and your daughter and now you." She motioned him toward the table in the alcove. "Diana left you a sandwich, but I was in the mood for pizza, so I called Pizza Hut. My treat."

Ted saw that their Ethan Allan table was set with paper plates, napkins, and glasses filled with ice. A tall bottle of Pepsi stood in the middle as well as a platter heaped with sausage and pepperoni pizza slices.

"Looks mouth-watering," he told her. "I hadn't even thought about being hungry." He grabbed a chair, motioned for Fanny to join him, and pulled the first slice off the pile.

They discussed the stalled economy and the Denver Broncos with Fanny voicing informed opinions on both. When Ted polished off the last slice of pizza, he found himself reluctant to leave.

Leaning back in his chair, he patted his stomach. "Thanks, Fanny. That was great."

"Well thank you for keeping me company. I get so tired of dining alone. Now I think I'll sit back in your lovely recliner until Diana and Laurel return. If the hotel remains this quiet—I suspect I might even nap a spell."

"Sounds good," Ted answered, chuckling at Fanny's forthright honesty. "Take one for me." When he returned to the basement, he found himself in a much better mood.

Laurel and Diana entered laughing over some remark one of them made.

"How was lunch, you two?" Fanny asked.

"Great," Laurel answered. "I had a delicious Cobb salad and the weather proved divine for eating on the patio."

"And for being with my daughter," Diana added.

"And I had the pleasure of eating and conversing with your handsome husband and father," Fanny told them. "We discussed everything from the sad state of the economy to the football team. He keeps up on things right well."

"As do you, I would guess," Laurel told her.

"What else is there to do? That's why I like coming here. Keeps me from vegetating." She turned to Diana. "The hotel is quiet, and Hattie has left for the day."

Three hours and thirty dollars well spent.

Fanny picked up the small leather purse that swung on a gold chain and headed to the door. "I'll just let myself out, so you get back to business."

Laurel went into the bathroom and Diana opened the wall closet to pull out the Murphy bed and made it up. When Laurel came out, she placed her hand on her mother's arm to stop her.

"Don't do that now. Take me on another tour of Hartwick House. Things were so hectic the day you moved in that I barely remember our brief tour."

So much for more girl talk, but Diana obliged her daughter. They headed upstairs, and Diana unlocked the doors of unoccupied rooms they passed.

"The architecture is really unique, Mom." Laurel pointed to the bay windows and corner alcoves. "Start your creative juices flowing. You must have a slew of ideas in mind already."

"Not really. I've thought of a few things, but Mrs. Toos needs to approve the expenditure and more than likely she wants everything left the way it is."

Diana led the way up to the third floor where she unlocked an unoccupied suite and showed Laurel the contents of the kitchen cupboards. "Of course, the larger suites have more pans and utensils. They also have dishwashers."

Thirty-one and thirty-two faced the street, but on the opposite side of the hallway the ceiling sloped downward, following the roofline on the back of the building. At one end, a paneled door led to a fire escape, a glowing sign above it reading, "EXIT." Next to that door, a window, then another door.

Laurel stopped. "What's here?" she asked.

"It's a tiny room, almost a closet. Mrs. Toos told me it could be rented for twenty dollars a night if guests need it for an extra adult or a teenage child. But only in conjunction with a room on this floor because they would need to share the bathroom."

"I've never heard of such a thing," Laurel exclaimed. "Let me see."

Diana took the ring of keys off her wrist and opened the door.

The tiny room measured approximately six feet by eight feet and contained a single bed that stretched lengthwise below a dormer window. A two-drawer dresser with a mirror above and a tiny closet with four wooden hangers completed the furnishings—such as they were. A crinkled roller shade covered the window.

"How absolutely quaint," Laurel breathed as she gazed about.

"More cramped than quaint," Diana observed.

Laurel leaned over the flowered bedspread and raised the shade. In a flurry of dust, the roller spun to the top. Resting her hands on the window sill, she gasped, "Oh mom, come look."

"What?" Diana peered over her daughter's shoulder and realized the tiny room overlooked the garden. The mountains to the west formed a backdrop over the rooftops for city lights now starting to blink on as gathering clouds blocked out the sun.

"Please, Mom, let me sleep up here," Laurel pleaded. "It's so private and unique—worth any inconvenience just to wake up to this glorious view!"

Diana looked horrified. "Don't be silly. It's tiny and there's no bathroom."

"I'll have a key to the apartment, Mom. I'm a big girl. I can let myself in. After all, I go down the hall at the dorm."

"Of course, you do." In spite of her clear and reasonable objections, Diana laughed. It was so like her precious daughter—all grown up.

And Diana would do whatever it took for Laurel to come back often, so she gave in.

CHAPTER 6

THE NEXT WEEKEND LAUREL WENT home with her roommate, but Brad drove up from Boulder to stay over Labor Day. Diana watched him park his car in the side street and unfold his tall, lanky frame from the vintage Corvette. Having restored it himself, he was rightly proud. She remembered the many hours he tinkered with it in their driveway, sometimes talking her into shopping for parts he needed, bribing her with smiles and bear hugs that more than made up for the inconvenience.

Diana saw no smile today. He wore a Colorado sweatshirt and faded jeans, the pant cuffs raveling over beat-up boots, but his face appeared as beloved as ever, even as he frowned and pursed his lips. He appeared to contemplate two men lounging beneath the lamppost on the corner: one in threadbare jeans, a tattered leather vest, and tattoos covering his arms and chest, the other shorter, bald and better dressed in a plaid shirt and khaki pants. They weren't talking, so Diana wondered if they even knew each other or whether they just loitered there. She hadn't seen them there before, but that wasn't unusual. The street scene varied from moment to moment.

Brad grabbed an orange athletic bag from the back seat and closed the car door. He checked the latch again after he'd clicked it from his key chain. Not that Diana blamed him, but it did seem a bit paranoid.

He bounded up the short flight of steps to the side door as she opened it for him. "Hi, Mom."

Short and simple. Brad allowed her to hug his neck and then surveyed the apartment with an air of indifference, as if her efforts to arrange their own furniture had no effect.

Poor Brad. Laurel adjusted by making the hotel an adventure. So typical of her. But during Brad's once a week duty calls, he made it clear he wanted only the basics: "How are you? How's Dad's job search?"

Period.

"None of my business," he had told them, though of course it was. The move affected his life along with theirs.

"How was the trip?" Dumb question, but something a mother says.

"Fine. Where's Dad?"

"Down in the basement—still sorting."

"Wow, what a grind. Poor Dad."

Diana pursed her lips to stop herself from the retort she wanted to make. Of course, Brad saw things from the male perspective, but how about her—in charge while Ted dawdled away on a simple task?

"He'll be up for lunch any minute. Sit down and tell me what's going on with you and college life."

"Same old, same old. Nothing new."

Nothing new all right. Laurel the chatterbox. Brad the clam.

Plunking his suitcase in a corner, Brad made for the kitchen. Diana heard the cupboard open and the faucet run.

"There's ice in the freezer," she called as she followed him there.

"No need. Think I'll go find Dad." Brad moved past her and crossed the living room again in just three long strides. His six-foot, four inch frame filled the hallway door before disappearing down the hallway and clattering down the steps to the entry landing. Diana heard the basement door open and slam shut.

So much for pleasantries.

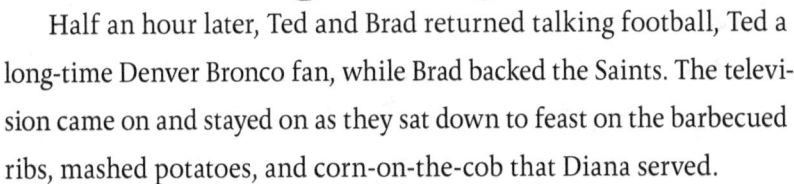

Half an hour later, Ted and Brad returned talking football, Ted a long-time Denver Bronco fan, while Brad backed the Saints. The television came on and stayed on as they sat down to feast on the barbecued ribs, mashed potatoes, and corn-on-the-cob that Diana served.

Then the men left the table and slouched in their favorite positions, ready to watch the Broncos play the Raiders. Ted dropped into his recliner and Brad kicked off his boots and stretched out on the couch.

It didn't matter that she was a Bronco fan herself. If Laurel were here, she would make them help clear the table. In a pout of self-pity, Diana picked up plates and carried them to the kitchen.

Then she heard what sounded like an explosion. Much louder than a gunshot! The plates in her hands clattered onto the counter.

Ted leaped out of the recliner, but Brad was ahead of him. He reached the side entrance in three long strides before he stopped and grabbed one foot up behind him. "It's a rock. A big one! There's glass all over the floor."

Ted rushed past him and flung open the door. "Hey you! Stop! Come back here."

Diana crunched across the glass and followed Brad into the bedroom where he had seated himself on the bed to examine his foot. She arrived as he peeled back the blood-soaked athletic sock.

"Brad!" she cried. "I'll get the first-aid kit."

"Call 911!" Ted called back as he bolted down the step. He saw the rock-thrower running fast, not looking back.

A young kid, fifteen or so, had stopped and turned to watch him flee. Ted stumbled to a stop. "Did you see him?" he demanded. "What did he look like?"

The kid shrugged. "Just a guy. Must be on somethin' to run that fast."

"When the cops get here, we'll need you as a witness." Ted bent over, hands on knees to catch his breath.

"Hey, man—I'm out of here. Didn't see nothin.'" The kid took off running in the same direction as the rock-thrower.

"What's your name?" Ted called after him, but the kid kept running.

Ted tromped back to the hotel and picked his way through splintered glass in the hallway. He found Brad and Diana in the bedroom.

"Did you call 911?" he demanded.

Brad sat on the bed with one knee crossed over the other to pick glass from his foot. Diana stood ready with the first aid-kit and a patch-sized bandage.

"Brad's cut his foot," Diana replied.

Ted snorted in disgust. He strode back to the living room, grinding bits of glass into the carpet beneath his feet. "Too late anyway," he flung over his shoulder. "He got away, but it still needs to be reported."

A police dispatcher answered Ted's call. "An officer will be there shortly," the woman said.

Ted strode to the front entrance where a blue light flashed on the patrol car pulling to the curb. Thankfully, no siren to alert every guest in apartments overlooking the street.

"Happened to be in the neighborhood," the officer, a burly, heavy-set man, told Ted as he emerged from the driver's seat. His partner, a much younger blonde female, got out her side and followed him up the steps.

"Officer Sperling. My partner, Officer White."

Ted shook their hands and led them up the stairs and into the lobby. He kept his voice low and hoped they would do the same. "We appreciate your fast response," he told them. "Unfortunately, the man's long gone."

They entered the apartment where Ted introduced them to Diana.

"The dispatcher said it was a rock through a window?" Officer Sperling asked. "Better than a bullet. Did you get a look at whomever threw it?"

"He ran fast, already pretty far away," Ted answered. "And it was getting dark. Tall, thin."

"Black? White? Hispanic?"

"I'm not sure. His face was hidden by his hoodie."

"See a weapon?"

"Just the rock."

Officer White handed Ted a form and directed him to write out a statement and sign at the bottom. "The complaint will be duly filed," she told him as Officer Sperling collected the rock and placed it in an evidence bag. Then they were gone.

Diana took the keys off the hook and headed down the hall to the supply closet. She returned with a whisk broom and dustpan and swept up the glass in the hallway. Ted picked glass bits out of the carpet and Brad limped from the bedroom into the front bathroom.

"Did you apply Neosporin?" Diana called to his back.

"It's nothing, Mom. Don't stew over it."

"But it might get infected."

The door closed, and she knew better than to hover.

When he returned, Brad held the board Ted brought up from the basement while he nailed it over the shattered window. The evening was over. Ted pulled down the Murphy bed and they said stilted good-nights.

Diana asked Brad about his foot and Brad muttered, "It's fine."

"He'll never come back," Diana whispered to Ted.

CHAPTER 7

IT ALWAYS COMES BACK TO me. I pressured Ted into coming here. He kept telling me to wait, that something else would come along. But the economy hasn't improved, and Ted is still out of work. Is that my fault?

Diana tossed in bed, attuned once again to street noises she thought she had begun to ignore. Ted appeared restless as well.

The red digits glowed 5:00 when their door creaked open. "Sorry to wake you. I'm going for a run."

"Okay, Son," Ted muttered.

The door closed, and Diana sat upright. "You let him go? Just like that? It's not even light yet."

"Whoa, Diana. He runs every morning in Boulder. Besides, he's twenty-two years old."

Diana slumped back on the pillow. "He hates it here—probably didn't sleep."

"I doubt that. He sees this as our problem, not his."

Diana reached for her robe. "We have to tell the Tooses, you know."

Ted pulled the covers over his head. "I know. I'll go over after breakfast."

Diana acknowledged the truth to herself. Ted always stepped up when necessary.

Ted climbed the steps and pushed the doorbell. Too early?

Mr. Toos opened the door fully dressed. At his knee, Henderson gave a low growl and James reached for his collar. "Come in, come in," James said. "Henderson wants his food before company. Look, boy, it's Ted."

Once inside the foyer, Ted stooped to pet the dog, who now panted in a patient rhythm, and then Ted related the incident without embellishment.

"Sorry it happened," James told him. "No one hurt, thank goodness. Call Hack Cummings to put in a new pane. He's our handyman. Does a good job for the most part."

For the most part. What did that mean? Did this Hack person have a drinking problem, as Cloomer implied? The old man didn't seem surprised by the incident but having lived in this neighborhood for such a long time, probably nothing surprised him anymore.

"Emma's Rolodex is in the kitchen," James told him. "Follow me. I'll get Hack's phone number for you."

Ted followed James as the old man shuffled down a short hallway into the spacious kitchen and stopped at the center island. Copper-bottomed pots suspended from hooks hung above the counter. James trailed his hand on the granite surface until it ended at a recessed desk. Emma was nowhere in sight.

James spun the cards on the wheel of the Rolodex, stopping them at the letter C. He plucked out a card and handed it to Ted with palsied fingers.

"I'll let you copy the number down." He motioned to a pen and paper. "Hack's capable enough—does a good job when he gets around to it."

"That's good," Ted added.

James ushered him back to the front door. "Best keep that hall light off at night," he warned, "and the curtains closed. Don't make yourselves a target."

Ted repeated the conversation to Brad and Diana, who had lingered at the table over second cups of coffee. "Now wasn't that comforting? 'Don't make yourselves a target'. Sounds like something an air raid warden would say. Come to think of it, that's appropriate, the rock being a missile and all."

"So, you're going to call this Hack person?" Diana stood to pick up plates in both hands.

"Yep. Of course, he may not work on Labor Day."

Ted dialed the number and Hack said he'd be right over. Ten minutes later, he pushed the buzzer at the front entrance. After Cloomer's description, he wasn't at all what Ted expected. Tall and muscular with wiry gray-black hair and a bushy mustache, he could be described as good-looking in a weathered, hard-living sort of way.

Ted shook his hand and introduced him to Brad and Diana. Brad nodded and went back to reading the sports page.

Hack's smile brought a twinkle to his dark expressive eyes. "Pleased to meet you," he said to Ted and Diana. "Been wonderin' when I might get the chance. Over at the Tooses last week—changin' light bulbs— Emma gushed on and on about you two. The old man called you a mighty big improvement over the last."

"You mean Cloomer?" Ted asked.

Hack snorted. "Cloomer? He don't count. I meant the couple who left before him. Only here about a month. Liked to party. After they left, the Tooses found Cloomer available, that's all."

"You work here long?" Brad asked, surprising Ted by entering the conversation.

"Yeah. Been around for years. Pick up work here and there as it comes along."

"Well, we're grateful you could come today." Ted pointed to the hallway. "A rock crashed through that window last night."

Hack whistled through his teeth. "A perfect target. Always wondered why they installed a flimsy door like that here at this side entrance."

"What type of door would you recommend?"

"A heavy solid-core door with maybe a couple of small skylight windows at the top. Might cut down a little on the light, but sure would be safer—better insulated, too."

Ted strode to the desk and picked up the phone. "Sounds good. I'll call Mr. Toos right now and see what he says." He motioned to the dining alcove. "Have a seat."

Hack accepted the coffee Diana offered him. She filled a large mug and Hack added generous doses of cream and sugar. Then he turned to Brad.

"Old man Toos said you're up at CU. Hear they're supposed to have a good basketball team this year." He pushed his chair back and crossed a leg over the other knee as if preparing for a long conversation.

Brad put down the paper and placed his elbows on the table. "Should be. They have all their starters back."

Ted got off the phone and dropped into a chair beside Brad. "Think Home Depot will be open on Labor Day?"

Both Brad and Hack answered in unison, "Of course."

"Let's go then. A solid core door should be just the ticket."

Diana watched the three men squeeze into the cab of Hack's beat-up red pickup. Wonders of wonders, Brad accompanied them without an invitation, or maybe he preferred doing so to staying behind with her.

Enough of her childish self-pity, she thought. Would she make something of this venture or not? After all, it was her urging that landed them here.

The desk bell rang. Abby Parton in number four was wanting a bus schedule. "I see Margie's here again," she commented. "I thought she worked only on weekends."

"Hattie wanted Labor Day off," Diana told her.

"I see. Well, none of my business, but I'd rather see Margie any day. She's so pleasant."

"Yes, she is," Diana agreed.

Tall and thin, her dark hair parted down the middle and pulled back into a bun at the nape of her neck, Margie reminded Diana of the African women who balanced water jugs on their heads. She stood that straight and tall, her aquiline nose and regal bearing contrasting with her soft-spoken manner. Diana knew her to be forever kind and considerate and wondered if her sincere desire to please others came from her deep faith.

In fact, Margie was so eager to please that Diana worried guests might take advantage. But Margie dismissed her warning, saying it was an honor to "do unto others as my dear Lord has done for me."

When she arrived on Sundays, Margie and her son, Sam, had already been to church. "Praise God our church has an early service," she told Diana. "I couldn't work weekends if it meant I'd miss it. The choir, the pastor's message—starts my week off right."

Sam was the light of Margie's life. Probably in his early twenties, Diana guessed, Margie referred to him as her baby. In some ways the term fit.

"Sam can't stay alone," Margie told her. "Sometimes a seizure takes hold of him and he needs his medicine, so his daddy takes care of him when I work. They play board games or sometimes they go bowling. My James is a good man. They get along just fine."

When Diana asked Margie about working on the holiday, Margie told her, "I can always use the extra pay" and Diana suspected that was true. Margie's husband picked up jobs as a laborer. Diana often saw him standing across the street on the corner, where contractors stopped to pick up short-term labor hires.

Now Diana found Margie stripping the bed in number twenty-three—moving fast, as usual.

"Hi, Ms. Diana," she said. "Ms. Gilmore left for the drug store, so I thought I'd change her sheets before she returns. Have one more check-out and then I'll eat my lunch, if that's okay."

Diana had invited Margie to call her Diana, but Margie refused. "You're my boss. Wouldn't be proper." Hattie called her "boss" most of the time, which Diana despised.

"I didn't come to check on you," Diana answered. "I just wanted company."

"Now isn't that nice! So pleased to meet your handsome son this morning. 'Round about Sam's age, isn't he? Know you love him like I love my boy."

"Yes, I do." Diana bent over to tuck under the top sheet while Margie changed the pillowcases. The cellphone clipped to her belt dug into her waist.

Now Diana could leave guests a note at the desk as to her whereabouts. The front doorbell buzzed on all three floors, so being elsewhere in the hotel didn't pose a problem for new arrivals. It also allowed her to take reservations from anywhere in the hotel and later transfer the information to her laptop instead of being tethered to the apartment.

Margie hurried to the kitchen carrying the two glasses left on the nightstand. "Mighty pleased to meet your pretty daughter last weekend, too," she told Diana. "As sweet as she can be!"

"Yes, she is, isn't she? And she liked you as well, Margie."

"Sure surprised me to find her up in that tiny room on the third floor." Margie laughed. "But then she told me to come in and see the view and what a surprise! Sometimes young folks see things we're in too much of a hurry to take the time to look at."

"Exactly. That's Laurel for you. Always spotting the violet in the crack of the sidewalk."

Margie laughed her deep laugh. "Now isn't that a good way to put it!"

Diana soon left so Margie could finish the room and eat her lunch. Margie would leave each room spotless and when guests commented the next day; Hattie would take the credit.

On the way back down the stairs, Diana squared her shoulders. Enough of feeling sorry for herself—sitting around worrying about Ted finding a job and whether or not she could handle Hattie and do a good job of running the hotel. Tomorrow she would take charge.

The men returned, stacked their purchases in the hallway and propped the new door in its carton against the wall. Diana ladled out bowls of bean soup and placed potato chips and ham sandwiches on the table and they sat down to eat.

"You're going to like the door," Ted told her. "Hack knew just what to look for and where to find it."

"By the way," Brad interrupted. "Where did you get the name Hack?"

"Real name, Elliot. Always hated it. Had someone tell me I took any hack job that came along, and I said, just call me 'Hack' then." He laughed and stroked his mustache, looking pleased with the explanation. "The name stuck, and I like it lots better."

"I agree," Brad said. "Can't imagine you as Elliot."

After lunch, Hack retrieved his toolbox from the back of his pickup and removed the old door off its hinges, smacking his gum as he worked. Brad helped, and Ted supervised. Pedestrians glanced in their direction at the droning of the drill, but then moved on.

Brad shouldered the new door out of the box and held it in place for Hack to secure. "Got an empty can for these screws?" Hack asked.

"Hey, Mom," Brad called. "Hack needs a can for the screws."

Diana washed out the soup can and brought it to Hack. "Now that's a door!" she exclaimed. "Looks a lot more substantial."

Hack put the screws inside the can and parked his gum on the edge. Then he took a can of Copenhagen from his shirt pocket, and scooping out a wad with his forefinger, placed it inside his bottom lip. "Gum works for just so long," he shrugged. "Trying to quit. My gal doesn't like it."

His gal . . . Diana mused. Interesting. The whole scene was interesting—having Brad involved and Ted joining in.

The door had a dark wood-grain interior with a white primer on the outside panel. "I'll come back tomorrow and paint it," Hack told them. "Black all right?"

"Black sounds fine," Ted told him. "Blends in. Won't attract so much attention."

"By the way," Hack told him, "you can call me anytime without the old man's say-so. He told me you're the boss. If I don't answer the phone, you can leave a message or check down the street at The Lair. Place to spend time when I'm not busy."

He crossed to the desk, tore a sheet off Diana's memo pad and wrote down the number. Then he packed up his tools, thanked Diana for the lunch, and turned to Brad. "That your silver 'Vette out there?"

"Yep."

"Mind givin' me a look?"

"I'll give you a spin if you want one."

"You bet!"

Hack followed him out the door and Brad called over his shoulder. "When I get back, Dad, let's go get a coke . . . maybe some fries."

He didn't see the pleased look on his father's face, but Diana did.

"Sure thing," Ted answered. He sat down with the paper while Diana cleared the table and when Brad returned a several minutes later, they left together.

Diana experienced a pang of jealousy, but then she scolded herself. She'd had her time with Laurel and now it was Ted's turn. Besides, she wanted to prepare a good dinner before Brad left and think of the best way to approach Hattie in the morning. She also needed to confirm something with Emma.

CHAPTER 8

HATTIE SAUNTERED IN LATE, AS usual, but Diana was ready. "I'm keeping a record of your actual time of arrival," Diana told her.

Hattie settled back on her heels and crossed her arms across her ample bosom. "What for? I come as soon as I can every day."

"That may be. However, Mr. and Mrs. Toos have agreed to a Christmas bonus based on performance and punctuality."

"What's that? Punctuality?"

"Being on time."

"Huh!"

Diana continued. "Your performance will be judged on meeting the standards I've posted inside the supply closet door."

"Standards?"

"A list of what needs to be done daily or weekly and how it should be accomplished."

Hattie uncrossed her arms and put her fists on her hips instead. "Who knows that better than me? Been here lots longer than you have."

Diana took a deep breath to temper the heat that crept up her neck. "Lots of it is common sense—same as keeping your own house. I'm sure much of it you do already."

Hattie removed one fist from her hip and put it down at her side. A good sign, Diana hoped.

"I went to the store and bought some new supplies last night," she continued. "Duplicates are in caddies in the hall closets on each floor. You won't have to tote a caddy up and down the stairs anymore."

"Now that's smart! Whyn't anyone think of that 'fore this?" Hattie actually smiled, but then the smile faded, and the frown returned. "What you mean by new supplies?"

"I'll show you." Diana took her keys, locked the apartment door behind her, and walked across the lobby to the first-floor supply closet. "Furniture polish, glass cleaner, all-purpose cleaner, cleaning cloths, and a dust cloth. The cleaning cloths go in the washing machine with the towels before you leave every day. I'll put them in the dryer and replace them in the caddies."

"Hmph."

"In addition, dishwashing compound and Clorox wipes will be restocked under the kitchen sinks as needed as well as toilet, sink, and bathtub cleaners in the bathrooms."

"How am I supposed to 'member all that?"

"You won't have to. Just look and you'll be reminded."

"Maybe. We'll see."

It was all Diana could expect for now, but at least Hattie appeared to like the idea of supply caddies on every floor. And maybe the Christmas bonus.

"Another thing." Hattie had turned away, but now her shoulders stiffened as Diana hurried on. "Except for check-outs, start on the top floor and work down. Saves you steps, and you'll have all the towels collected by the time you're back down."

"You talk like you've done this hard work yourself." Hattie's lower lip protruded.

"I have—that day last week you called in sick when it was too late to get someone from the temp agency."

"Oh." Another huff followed, but no more words.

Ted closed his phone and pumped his fist. "I got it! I got the job."

Diana threw her arms around his neck and gave him a fierce hug. "That's wonderful! Which job?"

"The small consulting firm. It's called Opportunity Knocks. They work with people who have lost their jobs or businesses to apply their skills in a new direction. Even though I don't have a degree, they think my management experience will add a new dimension. I start next Monday. Forty-five thousand."

"I'm so proud of you," Diana exclaimed.

"I know that's a comedown, but it's a start. It will probably take six months to qualify for a loan on a house, but at least we can look forward to the end of this craziness."

Diana squeezed his arm. "I know how hard it's been all these weeks, searching and waiting, but I just knew you would find something. As Dorothy says, 'God opens doors'."

"Ah, Dorothy. I thought I opened this door myself." Ted shrugged. "But if God helped, I'm not one to complain."

Diana tugged him toward the couch. "Sit down and tell me all about these people who made such a good choice."

"Let's call Cousin Fanny," Ted said. "See if she can come tonight so we can go out and celebrate."

"Oh dear." Diana let go of his sleeve. "I'm so sorry. I promised to attend that Bible study Dorothy's friend called me about. Remember? You said you'd watch the desk."

Ted's shoulders slumped. "Darn. Where is it you're going?"

"Remember? Dorothy met a woman at a Christian women's conference who lives just three blocks from here and holds a Bible study at
her home every other week. How unlikely was that? Anyway, Dorothy
gave her our number and she called to invite me to their meeting this
evening. Her name's Kate and she sounds really nice."

"I just wish it wasn't tonight."

"I know, but Dorothy has been so faithful to pray for us. I just felt
I couldn't say no."

"I understand. Dorothy's your friend." Ted didn't sound angry, just
resigned.

"And she stayed a friend when other people ran out of things to
say and found excuses to act busy," Diana added.

"I know." Ted sat down and picked up the newspaper.

"I'm disappointed myself, but I'm sure Cousin Fanny will come
on Saturday and we can celebrate then. It will give us time to make
reservations somewhere special."

"Maybe you're right," Ted muttered.

Diana planted a kiss on top of his head. As she went into the
kitchen to check on ribs simmering in the Crock Pot, she thought back
to when she first met Dorothy, a librarian in their western hometown.
Dorothy helped her find resources for home decorating and researched
where Diana could find information online.

"I mainly use our computer to email my parents and high school
friends back home," Diana told her. "Ted's the techie in our family."

But Dorothy found websites that increased her knowledge and
sharpened her skills: how to coordinate colors, utilize space, and

incorporate the client's interest and personality in making decorating choices. Over time she and Dorothy became good friends and looked forward to coffee next door at Starbucks on Dorothy's breaks.

Yes, Dorothy was prone to quoting Scripture, which made Diana uneasy at times, but when their circumstances had forced them to face reality, Diana found it comforting. One verse in particular lodged in her mind: *"God is our refuge and strength, a very present help in trouble."* Over the months, she repeated that verse to herself whenever Ted found himself turned down for a job or unpaid bills mounted. Not that anything changed, necessarily, but her mind settled when she repeated the verse to herself.

"Thanks for being such a good sport," she told Ted as she put on her coat. Diana hugged him tight. "The hotel should be quiet. Only one vacancy and number twenty-one is too expensive for most walk-ins."

She started toward the door and then turned back. "Don't forget to fix the door to number five."

"Yeah, Mrs. Talbot. What a pain she is."

"I know, but if you don't fix it, she's likely to be knocking on our door at midnight."

"Call before you leave there. I'll watch for you," Ted told her.

"Oh, come on," Diana teased. "It's only three blocks away. I could walk." She wouldn't, but she could.

"Yeah, right. Be serious."

Diana opened the new door, thankful for the substantial push it required. "I turned on the vacancy sign—just in case. Bye now."

Ted went to the window, pushed back the curtain, and watched her unlock the car at the curb to climb in and drive away. Then he retrieved his toolbox from the bedroom closet and carried it to the dining room table where he sorted through the contents. Retrieving a steel file, he slammed the lid down with a metallic clang. Should be a five-minute job at most. The Rockies game came on at seven.

Plucking the key from its hook on the board that hung in their hallway; he went into the lobby and walked across to number five. Mrs. Talbot had rebelled when Diana told her the only available small apartment was on the first floor.

"I don't care if the outside door has ten locks," she informed Diana. "People are careless. They open the door for strangers or just let others follow them in. And what about the windows? I'm sure they can be reached on a ladder."

Last night Ted had checked the window locks and tonight it was the door. Next week Diana would have a vacancy on the second floor and it would be a relief when Mrs. Talbot was settled there.

"I can't believe how much the rate has gone up," she had complained to Diana. "When I stayed here six years ago, it was expensive then—forty dollars. Looked it up. This time when I called, and you said sixty-five, I nearly had a stroke. Didn't have any choice, you know. It's the closest hotel to the clinic and my asthma has been acting up something fierce. Had no alternative but to come for an evaluation."

Ted lifted the bronze bust of Shakespeare and let it fall against the door.

"Who's there?" a shrill voice demanded.

"Ted Rutherford. I've come to fix your door."

Minutes elapsed before the doorknob turned and the door thudded open against the chain. "See how it sticks?" Mrs. Talbot called, though only inches away from Ted. "Can you fix it without opening the door? I'm not dressed."

"No, I can't." Only ten minutes 'til game time.

"Oh, all right then." The door closed, and the chain slid in its slot. When she opened it again, it stuck very briefly near the bottom of the frame.

"See?" she demanded. "It almost knocks me off my feet." The pink hairnet covering her tight gray curls matched the pink corduroy slippers and the pink chenille robe.

"I'll have it fixed in no time." Ted dropped to one knee and started to file on the spot where the door appeared to stick.

"I hope you're not going to make a mess. I'm allergic to dust."

"Then perhaps you should wait in the kitchen," he suggested.

"Oh well, I'll take my chances." She dropped into the easy chair beside the bed.

After wood had piled beneath the file, Ted opened and shut the door to test how it closed. The pre-game show would be on by now.

"Everyone raves about Denver's climate. Seems just like Ohio to me. September and cold. I've had the heat on day and night. Can hardly sleep with the noise from the radiator. Can you do something about that?"

Ted was sweating. He cocked his head to listen. "Sounds pretty quiet to me."

"Don't get smart. You're not here all night."

Thank goodness, Ted thought. "All fixed, Mrs. Talbot. I'll bring a broom and clean up these shavings."

She heaved herself out of the chair and crossed the room to test the door herself. "I guess it's better. If I'd needed to open it during the night, I would have waked the dead."

Ted found the broom in the supply closet, swept up the shavings, and started toward the wastebasket. "Don't dump it here," the woman shrilled. "I'll be inhaling dust all night!"

Ted clenched his jaw. "I'll take it with me. Good night, Mrs. Talbot."

"Good night, young man." The door shut behind him, the dead bolt thudded, and the chain slid back in its slot.

Ted dumped the shavings into the basket under the front desk, dropped the dustpan beside it, and leaned the broom against the wall. Shutting the apartment door behind him, he dropped the keys on the desk and crossed the living room in three long strides just in time to see St. Louis fans celebrate a home run on the first pitch of the game.

"Dang!" Ted kicked off his loafers and dropped into the recliner. The file fell to the floor beside him as he lifted the footrest. When the screen switched to a beer commercial, he leaned back and surveyed the room.

The ghastly wallpaper remained, but Diana's touches detracted from it—a pine wreath, a grouping of botanical prints, gauzy tie-backs for the curtains. Of course, their own furniture had made the biggest difference of all. After years in the business, Ted knew quality and Diana knew colors, texture, and what went well together. The result proved both comfortable and in good taste.

But then he recalled the hardwood flooring, the expensive drapes, and crown moldings of their former home. No way could these surroundings ever begin to compare.

Just as the Rockie's pitcher wound up for his first pitch, the desk bell rang. Ted lowered the footrest with a thud. Now what?

The two women that waited in the lobby were not registered guests. Ted was sure of that. The blonde wore her hair swept up on her head, her fair skin complementing baby-blue eyes. The other woman had dark skin, black hair past her shoulders, and smoky gray eyes that held Ted's. He would have remembered them.

Both wore full-length leather coats. Too warm for this time of year. But the nights were cooler now. He guessed the two women to be four or five inches shorter than his own height.

Ted cleared his throat. "May I help you?"

"Are you the manager?" The blonde's husky voice sounded skeptical.

Ted kicked the dustpan beneath the desk. He tucked in his shirttail but caught himself before he patted down the cowlick that always popped up when he leaned back in the recliner. "My wife's the manager," he said. "She's at a meeting."

"Pleased to meet you." The dark-haired woman extended her hand, then used the long-tapered fingers with manicured red nails to flip back the lustrous black wave that draped her cheek. "I'm Cleo Wright and this is Dusty."

"Seems we caught you in the middle of something." Dusty smiled, her pink lips parting to reveal two rows of perfect white teeth. Then her eyes rested on the broom leaning against the wall.

Heat rose in Ted's face. "Not at all. I just completed some minor repair work for a guest."

"How thoughtful of you." Dusty fiddled with her cell phone, then flipped it shut. "So maybe you can help us." She tilted her head and smiled a brilliant smile. "We're looking for something nice for a week or so—maybe longer. Depends."

Could they be models? Maybe singers or showgirls. He'd seen plenty of those when he played clubs with the band. He modulated his voice to his usual baritone. "We have one of our deluxe suites available."

"The sign out front says Apartments. Does this one have a kitchen?"

"All the suites have kitchens."

"Two beds?"

"Queens. It's one of our larger suites." He sounded calm now, in control.

The women turned and looked at each other as if some silent message passed between them.

"Could we see it please?" Cleo asked. She turned as she spoke, as if expecting compliance.

"Sure." Ted felt pleased with his salesmanship as he closed the apartment door and led the way across the lobby. "By the way, how did you get in? We keep the front door locked."

"A nice man entered with his key as we came up the front steps. When we told him we were here to inquire about the vacancy, he held the door for us."

Ted remembered Mrs. Talbot's words. "I told you so," she would say.

"How much is the suite?" Cleo asked as Ted led the way up the stairs to the second floor.

He should have stated the price up front, but now he upped the monthly rate. Diana said they should discourage monthly boarders since they had started to fill up at nightly rates. However, these women looked as if they could afford a higher price. "Five hundred a week, fifteen-fifty a month," he answered, pleased that he still had his sales touch.

"Sounds fair," Cleo drawled.

When they reached the landing, Dusty pointed to the window. "Will you look at that gorgeous stained glass?" she exclaimed. "I told you this looked like a classy place." She trailed her fingers along the windowsill and inspected them. "Clean, too."

Ted turned down the hallway of the second floor. "Where are you from?" he asked, making conversation.

"East," Cleo drawled. Ted turned and saw a look pass between the pair. Dusty put her hand over her mouth to stifle a laugh. Ted frowned.

He inserted the key to number twenty-one and reached inside to flick on the light switch.

"Oh, Cleo, look at the doorknocker!" Dusty gushed. "Kissing cupids. How sweet."

Just inside the doorway, Dusty stopped to pat the gold foil wallpaper. Her musk perfume wafted even stronger than Ted noticed at the desk. "Elegant," she observed.

"A great place to entertain." Cleo opened cupboards in the kitchen and looked inside the dishwasher. As she reached to push back her hair, an earring fell to the floor. She bent over to retrieve it, her coat falling open to reveal her deep cleavage. Feeling the heat in his face, Ted turned away.

"It even has a fireplace," Dusty exclaimed. They browsed through the suite, continuing to comment on the décor and the seating alcove in the bay window.

When Dusty gave Cleo a nod, Cleo pulled a roll of money from her coat pocket.

"We'll take it for the month," she said as she peeled off bills and reached for Ted's hand to place the money in his palm.

This wasn't the proper procedure. "You'll need to come down to the desk . . . " Ted held the money back out to her. " . . . to register and get your keys."

"In the morning, sugar, in the morning. We're dead tired. Just leave the key and put the receipt under the door."

"But your luggage . . . "

"We'll move our things in tomorrow. Anyway, we both sleep in the nude." She gave a wave of her hand as if that explained everything. "Any rule against that?"

Ted felt the warmth returning to his neck. "But the law requires you to register."

"In the morning—like I said. 'Night, handsome." The door closed in his face, gently but firmly.

Ted stood like a statue in the hallway. It had all happened so fast. What would he tell Diana? What would she say when she saw fifteen one-hundred-dollar bills? He should never have shown them the room, let alone take their money—even at the inflated price. Nevertheless, he now owed them a receipt.

Back downstairs, he made out a receipt and hurried back up to the second floor, thankful to find the hallway deserted when he pushed the slip of paper under the door. Most likely he worried for nothing. How the women dressed or what they did for a living wasn't his business. They could be topless dancers at *Shotgun Willie's* and still be model guests.

Back down in the apartment, he shut off the television and paced the floor, stopping to part the drapes and look out at the street. How late did Bible studies last anyway?

Then he remembered the broom and dustpan. He would hear about that. Grateful for something useful to occupy his time, he went back out to the lobby to put them away.

As he approached the supply closet, a middle-aged man descended the staircase. Ted didn't recognize him, but then he didn't know all the guests. "Good evening," he said to be polite.

The man ducked his head, hurrying across the lobby and down the stairs to the foyer where he pushed the crash bar on the door and hurried out. *Unfriendly sort.*

Might as well tour the halls, something he did every night—ever since a guest reported a vagrant sleeping on the fire escape. Security? He was it.

Coming back down the stairway from the third floor, he stole a glance down the second-floor hallway. The door to number twenty-one stood slightly ajar. Why? The women said they were tired and wanted to be left undisturbed. Had they opened the door to retrieve the receipt and failed to shut it? Should he knock or just close it? As he stepped into the hallway, a board creaked beneath the carpet.

"Who's out there?" Dusty peered into the hallway, clutching her coat shut with one hand. Her feet were bare, and her blonde hair now fell about her face. "Oh, it's you, Teddy!"

Ted made a sudden decision and walked up to the door. He forced his voice to a lower register to sound firm and leave no room for argument. "I'm sorry. I've checked the reservation book. There's no way we can free this suite for a month."

Dusty opened the door wide. "Cleo," she called over her shoulder. "We have a little problem." She reached out and tugged Ted's sleeve. "Step inside a minute, handsome. It's time we let you in on our little secret."

Ted glanced down the hall. At any minute a guest might appear. Light shone under the door from number twenty-three. He made sure the door stayed open as he crossed the threshold. Whatever these two were up to, he needed to set them straight in a hurry.

They stood side by side, relaxed and smiling. Then, as if re-hearsed, each shrugged her coat from her shoulders and let it fall to the floor.

Ted stood rooted to the spot as if his scalp lifted from his head— like an exploded radiator cap. The women wore nothing but skimpy bras and bikini panties.

Silence. Then Dusty collapsed on the bed in a convulsion of giggles. "What did you expect? P.T.A. members?"

Cleo sat down and crossed her long legs. "Don't feel bad, Teddy. You're not the first to be fooled. Rent us the room and we'll let you in on the fun—for free, of course. What do you say, good-lookin'?"

Ted struggled to find his voice. "Are you crazy? Put some clothes on. I'm a married man!"

"So? You're home alone tonight, aren't you? Your wife need never know. We're very discreet. Tonight we did a special favor for the man who brought us here and carried up our luggage, but we meet most of our clients elsewhere."

The man he met on the stairs. Ted swallowed hard, his throat so dry it proved difficult to do so.

"No way," he said at last. "Get out or I'm calling the police."

"I think you've forgotten something, sugar." Cleo's voice honeyed as she took his arm and steered him toward the door. "You have our money and we have your receipt."

"I'll refund all of it. Right now."

"No thanks," Dusty replied. "We like it here. Without an eviction notice, you're stuck with us, sweetheart."

The door shut in his face, the kissing cupids still kissing.

Ted felt sweat run down his ribs. The muffled sound from a television came from down the hall. What a fool he was to assume Diana had it easy here . . . that nothing unexpected happened.

Back in the apartment, Ted remembered to go the kitchen and flick the button that switched on the *No Vacancy* sign. Should he call the police? What if it got in the paper and they closed the place down? Didn't they do that sometimes?

He heard the key in the lock. "Ted?" Diana stood in the doorway. "I called, but no one answered. Where were you?" She glanced at the silent television. "Is the game over?"

Ted swallowed, desperate not to give anything away. "I was showing an apartment."

Diana laid her purse and Bible on the table and shrugged out of her coat. "Did you rent twenty-one?"

"Yeah."

"For the night?"

"For a month." She would see the copy of the receipt. "Fifteen-fifty."

"But that's great!"

"Big deal." Ted reached for the remote and flicked the television back on.

"Who is it?"

"Two women." He turned up the volume.

"Young?"

"Stop it, Diana. I did the job you asked me to do. Lay off the inquisition."

Diana threw her coat on a chair and crossed her arms over her chest. "Why are you in such a bad mood? I walked in excited to tell you about the meeting and what I learned. Now you've ruined it. I'm going to bed."

Ted waited for the bedroom door to shut, then sat down and put his head in his hands. What was he going to do? Sleep was out of the question.

He opened the French doors and pulled down the Murphy bed. What rest he got might as well be there.

But Diana came back out. "I'm sorry I snapped at you. Put that back up and come to bed. You had the wonderful news about the job and then you were busy all evening when you wanted to watch the game. I'm sure Mrs. Talbot took up her fair share of your time."

Mrs. Talbot—the least of his worries. Ted turned off the lights in the living room. He would probably lay awake all night, but he'd wait until morning to tell Diana.

CHAPTER 9

DIANA ROLLED OVER AND SHUT off the alarm just as Ted left the bedroom dressed in his navy suit, white shirt, and navy-striped tie. She hurried to dress in her denim skirt and the sweater Laurel had insisted she buy—navy with rust trim. Laurel said it brought out the amber glints in her eyes. She intended to make a nice breakfast and give Ted a good send-off on his first day at Opportunity Knocks. Already she could hear the coffee grinder start.

Ted had tossed and turned in the night, often punching his pillow. Poor Ted. Probably anxious about getting off to the right start. She must be sure to tell him how handsome he looked.

Leaving the bedroom, she prepared to do just that. But Ted spoke before she did.

"Sit down, Diana. I need to tell you something. I should have told you last night, but I didn't." The freckles knit together on his forehead.

Diana headed to the kitchen. "About Mrs. Talbot? She can be such a pain."

Ted caught her by the shoulder and guided her to a chair. "Just be quiet and listen. This isn't easy."

Diana's eyes widened, but she did as told.

Ted kept it brief. He'd showed the women the apartment; they'd liked it and gave him the money for a month's rent.

"So?" Diana interrupted. "You got a good price. Nothing wrong with that."

"They paid me then and there—in the room—with one hundred-dollar bills. Closed the door in my face without waiting for a receipt."

"Rude, but don't worry. I'll make out a receipt and see that they get it today." She started to get up from her chair.

"Just please let me finish!"

Diana sat back down, pursing her lips. How in the world could she fix breakfast and give Ted a good send-off when he was set on relating every tiny detail?

"You know how I make the rounds every night," Ted continued.

"Of course." *Do I need to give him credit for that?*

"As I came back down, I saw that their door was open."

"Get to the point, Ted."

"I sensed something wasn't right and tried to give their money back." Ted spoke in a rush now. "And then they let their coats fall to the floor and they were practically naked. There. Now you know."

Diana stared at him. "How could you be so naïve?" She moved to the edge of the chair. "I leave you in charge one night and you rent a room to hookers? Can't you tell a hooker when you see one? They're on the sidewalks every day. Take a look sometime!"

"I'm telling you, these women weren't ordinary hookers. They were well-dressed, attractive . . . "

"Obviously. They flattered you, Ted—sucked you in. I would have seen through them in a minute!" She stood to her feet and placed her hands on her hips.

"Then maybe you should have stayed home."

"And maybe you should go to a Bible study."

Silence. They stood inches apart. Then both looked away.

Ted spoke first. "I did learn something. You don't have an easy job here. I need to step up. Therefore, I'm going next door to confess the situation to the Tooses. Mr. Toos is an attorney. He'll know what to do."

"You took their money. I think we're required to give them so many days' notice, maybe have a witness."

"I said I'll handle it. Forget breakfast. I won't have time." He walked to the hall closet, grabbed his topcoat off the hanger, and strode toward the side door.

"Wait!" She reached to stop him, but he was out the door.

Diana stood at the window and watched him stride down the street and make a right turn up the sidewalk to the Toos mansion. She had to admire his courage. If it were her, she'd want to put off telling the Tooses as long as possible.

The remark she'd hurled at him about the Bible study wasn't fair. She recalled the verse the women memorized from Proverbs: "Trust in the Lord with all your heart and lean not on your own understanding . . ." Easier said than done.

As part of the evening, the women had shared prayer requests. She shared their need for God's guidance. Not that she had asked for it, but it seemed the right thing to say.

One of the women had asked, "Under so much turmoil and stress, did you ever consider divorce?"

The question rattled Diana, floored her actually. In circumstances such as theirs, did couples often go their separate ways?

"No," she had stammered. "I don't believe we ever considered it."

"Good," the woman had replied as she reached to place her hand over Diana's. "Many view divorce as the easy way out—leave the baggage behind and start over. They assume they can do better alone, but the Bible says 'a cord of three strands is not easily broken.' Strength comes when we share our burdens with each other and with God."

Diana wondered if she belonged in the group. The other women seemed to know so much more about the Bible than she did, yet the quotation made sense to her. Raised by church-going parents, she and Ted took for granted 'till death do us part.'

The front desk bell interrupted her thoughts. She wanted to stay at the window to see Ted leave, but she crossed the room and opened the door to the lobby.

The couple in twenty-three asked about tours of the capitol building. Diana showed them the brochures on the hall table and helped them find the one they wanted. After they left, the scent of bacon coming from number one reminded her she hadn't eaten and neither had Ted.

"Please God," she prayed, "don't let this spoil Ted's first day at work."

No sooner had she reentered the apartment than the desk bell rang again. Diana picked up her keys and this time stretched the pink coiled wristband over her hand. One of these days she would lock herself out.

Emma waited at the front desk. *I'm in for it now.* Diana's heart sank.

Dressed as always in meticulous fashion—the low-heeled black pumps matching her black wool skirt and black-and-white pin-striped shirtwaist. Well, she had her own maid and Diana knew Consuela did her ironing.

"Do you have a minute?" Emma's smooth brow revealed nothing.

"Of course." Diana unlatched the gate beside the desk and held it open for Emma to precede her into the apartment. Had Ted put his slippers away? Yesterday's paper still lay on the coffee table.

Emma seated herself on the sofa and patted the fabric for Diana to sit down beside her. Diana perched on the edge.

"I wanted to come over before your busy day began." Emma folded her hands in her lap, as serene as ever. "I'm afraid we don't tell you often enough what a fine job you're doing."

Was Emma mocking her? "Mrs. Toos," she began. "I'm so sorry for what happened. It was a stupid thing for Ted to do. He realizes that, and it won't happen again."

Emma shook her head. "Stupid? Naïve, perhaps, but not stupid. I deem Ted's actions honorable. A lesser man would have been taken in and then tried to hide the fact."

Diana frowned. "But it's so humiliating!"

"You would have handled it differently. Is that it?" Emma laid her hand on Diana's arm. "How do you know?"

"I'm a woman. I would have known better."

"I see. And what if they had been two men? It happens."

Diana fell silent. Of course, Emma was right, she didn't know.

Emma continued. "During your initial interview, you took exception when James said both you and Ted should be involved in running the hotel. He knows the importance of that from experience, as do I. When he shared the burden, it took much of the load off my shoulders."

Diana's eyes filled with tears. Another verse one of the women quoted came to mind. Something about 'bearing one another's burdens.' Was she shutting Ted out—wanting to be the one in charge, garnering success for herself?

Emma was all business again as she stood and smoothed down her skirt. "As James told Ted, he has connections in the police department.

A detective will come by sometime this morning to make sure the women leave."

"But Ted took their money."

"Have it ready when he comes. He'll return it to them. The rules are different for hotels."

"Life is a series of learning experiences," she continued. "We're very pleased with the fine job you are doing . . . and, by the way, please call me Emma."

The detective called mid-morning and asked if the two women were still there. Diana took the call at the front desk where she worked at her laptop in case they came down the stairs. She assumed they hadn't left, but she told the detective she would check for sure and call back. He gave her the number and she took the laptop back in the apartment and went looking for Hattie.

She found her in thirty-one and told her to take extra towels to number twenty-one. "Be sure to knock first."

"Why extra towels? Who's there? The Queen of England?"

"Never mind," Diana told her. "I have my reasons."

"Makes more steps," Hattie grumbled. "Half an hour and I'd be down there anyways."

"Do it now." Diana's tone of voice left no room for argument.

She followed as Hattie huffed her way down to the second floor and jerked towels from the supply closet, causing several to fall to the floor. With a grunt, she bent to pick them up, bumping Diana aside with an ample hip when Diana stooped to help.

"I'll do it," she muttered.

Diana waited on the landing while Hattie disappeared down the hallway. Diana heard the knock and a muffled voice.

"The answer is no," Hattie came back to tell Diana. "They don't want no towels. Now I have to climb back upstairs for nothing."

"Thank you, Hattie."

Diana called the officer back and he said he would be there shortly. She waited in the lobby for him to buzz the front door.

The door to number five opened and Mrs. Talbot came out. "Good morning," she said when she saw Diana. "I must say your husband did a good job fixing my door."

"I'm glad," Diana responded.

"I'm leaving for my appointment now. My cab is here. Remember, I'm still waiting for that room to open on the second floor."

"Yes, I know."

A dusting of Denver's first snow settled on the patio window ledge. As Diana continued to wait, the radiators came to life.

At last the buzzer sounded and Diana hurried to answer it.

"Detective Moon," he told her.

She shook his hand. "Thank you for coming. Apartment twenty-one on the second floor. I can take you up—"

"Ma'am, let me handle it." His tone was firm. "Better for you to remain out of sight. I have a signed report from Mr. Toos. The women will leave and not bother you again."

"We're so grateful," Diana told him. "What about the money they paid?"

"Put the money in an envelope with a copy of the receipt. I'll have them count the bills and sign the report saying they received it."

He waited at the front desk while she pulled the money, printed the receipt, and put them in an envelope. Then he crossed the lobby and climbed the stairs.

Diana went back into the apartment and watched out the front window, hoping the women would walk in her direction when they left, or better yet, be pushed into a squad car—preferably in handcuffs. Were they as attractive as Ted described? What was his idea of attractive?

But the officer rang the desk bell, dropped off the key, and a copy of the report and that was that. He was as competent as Mr. Toos said he would be.

"They won't trouble you again," he assured.

Diana thanked him and took a deep breath and then she watched him leave.

She owed it to Ted to make amends— show her appreciation for the way he handled things with the Tooses and celebrate his new job in the manner he deserved. She punched in Cousin Fanny's number on her phone.

"Please congratulate Ted for me," Fanny said. "Well-deserved! It's tough to find a job in this economy, but Ted hung in there and didn't limit himself to his past experience. That was so smart. Now he can help others do the same. By all means—get yourself gussied up and go someplace real nice."

Diana smiled to herself as she replaced the phone. 'Gussied up'—an expression her grandmother would have used and, yes, Ted deserved it.

She thumbed through the Yellow Pages and found the number for The Broker Restaurant. A guest described it as intimate—housed in the downstairs vault of a former bank building.

It would be expensive, but Diana wanted to make it up to Ted for blaming him for something she might have done herself. Emma was right. She had no right to be so judgmental.

She made the reservation and then went to her closet and flipped through the garments hanging there; stopping at a sexy, low-cut gauzy dress. Two years ago, while shopping in the city one day, Ted had insisted she try it on. When she came out of the dressing room, he told her she looked fantastic and pleaded with her to buy it. She never felt at ease wearing it around people they knew, but tonight they would be among strangers.

She held the dress up on the hanger and turned around to view herself in the mirror over the fireplace. Yes, it would be perfect to wear some place nice—somewhere expensive.

In truth, she wanted the night out for herself as much as for Ted. Emma's visit had rattled her, not only the mild rebuke concerning her need to partner with Ted, but Emma's assurance they were doing a fine job.

She hung the dress back in the closet and walked back to the living room. Emma's words kept coming back to her. What did she mean by 'a fine job'? Yes, the occupancy rate was up, and she had accomplished some cosmetic changes— rearrangement of furniture and use of the matching china and silverware Ted sorted. But what mark of her own had she made so far?

When the desk bell rang, she hurried to see who was there.

"Is this a safe neighborhood?" Anita Byers, the elderly guest in thirty-two asked. "I saw a scary-looking bag lady wheeling her things in a Safeway cart and some other people on the street who don't exactly look respectable."

"It's a main thoroughfare," Diana told her. "Safe during the day, but I wouldn't advise anyone to be out alone at night. We're always happy to call a cab for you."

"No, I'm just walking to the corner drugstore—need the exercise. Thanks though. You're always very helpful."

As Diana watched Anita walk away, she considered that comment. Did she mean to be or was it just the manners her parents taught her? Mr. Toos had said during their interview to "consider it a calling." She had thought that quaint at the time. A calling required real commitment. Was she ready for that?

Interrupting her thoughts, the buzzer sounded at the front door. That would probably be Mr. and Mrs. Edward Whitney, people who had a reservation. Diana pushed the button to let them in.

They crossed the lobby and approached the desk. Doris Whitney appeared to be near Diana's age, her husband some years older.

"We're so glad to be back and to have number twenty-one, the suite we've always preferred." She was already removing her coat as Mr. Whitney filled in the registration form. "We've been staying at Hartwick House since our kids were little and Mr. and Mrs. Toos ran the place themselves. How is Emma?"

"She's fine," Diana said. "She was pleased to hear you were returning."

"Funny thing about Emma," Doris continued. "She said they had no children of their own, yet she took such an interest in ours. She always remembered their names and even would have cookies waiting for them."

Diana smiled to herself. She knew why, considering the prodigious size of Emma's old-fashioned Rolodex. Just last week when she took bills over to be paid, she mentioned a returning couple for whom she needed to search online for an address. She had accidentally deleted their email.

"No need," Emma had said as she reached for the wheel, spinning it until she stopped it with her thumb and pulled out a card to hand to Diana. Not only did it contain the name, address, and telephone number, but the names of the children and their ages.

"Reservations are so much more satisfying than drop-ins," Emma had told her. "I like a name to put with a face. Reminds me of meeting a distant relative for the first time at a family reunion. There's already a connection."

Edward Whitney started up the stairs with their suitcases, but Doris lingered. "I can picture just how she escorted us to our suite."

"Sounds like something Emma would do," Diana commented.

Doris continued. "'Come along, we have your room prepared,' Emma would say in that proper, old-fashioned way of speaking she has."

"Sounds just like her." Diana giggled.

Doris continued again. "A style all her own. On the way up, she always pointed out the view of the garden, reminded us of the hotel's history and—of course—picked up the kissing cupids and let them fall to announce our destination."

Her delighted laugh showed her reliving the moment. "But I mustn't keep you," she told Diana. "I'm sure we'll enjoy our stay, but if you see Emma, please give her my fondest regards."

"I will," Diana promised. "I'm sure she'll want to welcome you herself."

Doris Whitney gave a wave and disappeared up the staircase as Diana turned back to the apartment. *Style.* Did she have one?

She answered questions about the hotel and its history if asked, attempted to be helpful and pleasant while not intrusive. But how would guests remember her? Or would they remember her at all? Ted would now leave for work every morning while she remained to settle into the same routine of the day before and the day that would follow. How dull. What could she do to leave her own mark?

Ted had showed the courage to reinvent himself by using his knowledge and talents to launch a new career. Could she do the same?

Yes, she would wear the sexy dress. They would make a night of it at The Broker and drink a toast to new beginnings.

"Wow! I didn't know you kept that dress. You look great." Ted whistled long and low as Diana performed a slow dance out of the bedroom. She reached to give him a big kiss, right in front of Fanny, who was already there.

Ted had answered Fanny's knock promptly at seven.

"Ah, to be young," she exclaimed. "Go and enjoy a wonderful evening. Put Hartwick House right out of your minds."

"We will," Ted called back as he took Diana's arm to help her negotiate the steps in high heels. He opened the car door with a flourish. "Be seated, Madame."

Diana giggled. They hadn't had a real date in ages. Ted circled the car and got in. While he maneuvered the traffic, Diana sat back and relaxed as the lights of the city flashed by them.

When they arrived at the restaurant, Ted utilized the valet parking. The maître d' confirmed their reservation. Diana took note of his bow tie and starched shirt. "Mr. and Mrs. Rutherford. Welcome to The Broker. Please follow me."

He led them down a dimly-lit hallway bordered by recessed cubicles, some already occupied by couples dining by candlelight. Diana's shoulders relaxed. She squeezed Ted's arm as the maître d' held a chair for her to be seated.

"Don't even look at the prices," Ted told her. "We might never do this again. But for tonight, the sky's the limit for my beautiful wife."

Diana's eyes filled with tears. "I'm so proud of you, darling," she told him. "The way you persevered and found something that suits you so well. I jumped all over you about those women and I'm so sorry."

Ted's eyes crinkled in the candlelight. "I'd like to think you were maybe just a wee bit jealous."

"Jealous? I didn't even get to see them and believe me—I tried!"

"They weren't that special. They're gone and good riddance." All tension fled as the waiter arrived and laid out their menus. Ted ordered prime rib and Diana ordered lobster.

"Excellent," their waiter said. "Is this an occasion for champagne?"

"Yes," Ted answered. "Please choose a bottle for us."

"Very good, sir."

"Oh, Ted," Diana protested after the waiter had departed. "It's so expensive."

"Not tonight. How often will I have a new job to celebrate with my beautiful wife?"

Diana laughed. "Not often, I hope . . . about the new job I mean."

Ted lifted his glass to hers. "To our future."

The hardship and tension of the past months faded as Ted told her more about the firm and the people with whom he would work. They also talked of Brad and Laurel and how well they appeared to be adjusting.

"I do have concern for my mom," Ted confessed. "She hated to see us move so far away."

Diana set her glass down. "Do you notice how forgetful she's become, even about things we've recently told her? She called last week and asked what town we live in now. Then she laughed and said, 'Oh, of course, I have it written down—Denver.' Very odd. I meant to tell you sooner."

"We need to stay on top of it. I think I'll make an appointment with Doctor Adams sometime when I can go with her. Having this specific example to express as a concern will help both Mom and Dr. Adams recognize the problem if one exists."

"As for my parents," Diana said as she sipped her champagne, "my mom still thinks we're completely nuts. When they drove over last week, all she could do was look around and say, 'I can't believe you're living here.' It bothered me then, but you know what? She'll have to get used to it. This is our life to live."

"Right on, Babe. Nothing's changed that matters. You're as beautiful as ever."

"And you're as handsome." Diana raised her glass. "To new beginnings."

CHAPTER 10

DIANA CHOSE NUMBER TWENTY-TWO ON purpose, gambling on it being one of Emma's favorites because it was the only suite with a king-sized bed and because its doorknocker was the Hartwick Coat of Arms.

She waited until Hattie arrived, then put a note at the desk and climbed the stairs with notebook in hand. At the end of the second-floor hallway, she paused in the doorway and surveyed the possibilities.

Twenty-two was a corner room. The bay window in the corner alcove overlooked both the side street and the main thoroughfare. The room wasn't exactly spacious, but the alcove gave it a cozy feel.

A canopy for the bed would be nice, with curtains to match. Maybe with a floral design. Cushy pillows for the window seat and some new prints for the walls. The carpet wasn't bad—plush, in a soft sage color. As scribbled notes filled the page, her excitement grew. She needed to get estimates and run them by Emma. Perhaps Hack could construct the canopy. That would cut the cost.

She pulled her cell phone out of her pocket and dialed his number. Yes, he could come right over. While she waited, she made some quick sketches. Through the open door she saw Hattie going into number twenty-four. How had she finished on the third floor so soon?

Going back downstairs, Diana waited in the lobby for Hack.

"What's up?" he asked when he arrived, a toothpick between his teeth.

Diana led him up to twenty-two and motioned for him to sit in the window seat. "I have some ideas," she said as she consulted her notes.

He appeared curious and removed the toothpick as he sat down.

Diana talked, and Hack listened. His bushy eyebrows arched, but he didn't interrupt. When she finished, he took his time surveying the room. Then he stood, took measurements with his steel tape measure, cocked his head, and stroked his mustache.

"Ain't done nothing like it before but can't see why not. Just a sturdy framework should do it, held up with mahogany posts at the corners. Could stain it all to match. I'll figure an estimate and get back to you."

"Great." Diana let out the breath she hadn't realized she was holding. She had thought Hack might laugh—think the idea ridiculous, but he appeared more intrigued than anything else.

"I've done plenty of repairs here over the years, but never looked at these rooms as anything but somewhere to spend a night. Not as homey and especially not glamorous, but I'm willing to give it a try. Might be fun."

Diana felt like hugging him. For some reason she felt confident he might be handy at whatever he set his mind to accomplish.

When they arrived back downstairs, Hattie waited in the lobby. "I signed out," she told Diana. "Wind kickin' up like it might rain and I have only this sweater, so I need to hurry to catch my bus. Oh, and by the way, we're out of dish soap."

On Saturday, Diana left Ted to mind the desk while she went to the fabric store on Clayton Street. Ready-mades would be pricey, but she had in mind what she wanted for the canopy, curtains, and window seat and found the perfect multi-colored floral chintz. She also bought foam rubber padding for the seat cushions and material for them as well.

"All right, Diana," she told herself. "You asked for it."

On Monday she set up her sewing machine in the bedroom alcove. The light was good and interruptions few. She made good progress throughout the week.

Hack arrived on Friday with a supply of wood and an electric saw. "Can't help the noise," he warned her.

"The adjoining room is vacant and the people across the hall are gone for the day," she told him. "I think it's a good time."

The project progressed. By late October, Diana felt ready to show Emma their handiwork.

She waited in the entryway. Shortly before noon, she had observed Emma getting off the bus across the street. It wasn't the first time. Where did Emma go on Wednesdays? James drove their black Buick, but Emma didn't drive. Oh well, none of her business.

"Updating the decor is long overdue," Emma had said when Diana had approached her with the project. "I'm delighted you want to take this on. It's essential that we regain our three-star rating. James and I were devastated when the rating was lowered."

Now Diana saw her approach the front steps. She hurried down the foyer stairs to open the door before Emma could insert her key.

"I'm sorry to be late," Emma said. "Our greengrocer arrived just as I was leaving."

The panel truck made a weekly stop at the mansion. *Fresh to You* was on both sides amongst a motif of fruits and vegetables. Diana had never heard of such a business, but then many things about James and Emma's lifestyle were new to her.

"No problem," Diana hurried to assure her. "I'm just anxious to see what you think."

She grew anxious as she escorted Emma up the stairs, worried that the owner of Hartwick House would think she had gone too far—overstepped her bounds. After all, Emma lived with things at Hartwick House the way they were for many years.

"Good gracious, Diana," Emma exclaimed as she entered the room. "I wouldn't know I was in the same apartment. It's utterly transformed and lovely, just lovely!"

Anchored by the sage carpet, the flowered bedspread and canopy matched the fabric on the window seat cushions where rose-colored pillows lay scattered. Hack had stained the bedposts a darker shade to match the headboard. The dresser and chest of drawers were stained the same. On one wall, a print of a young girl dressed in red, holding a white kitten, hung opposite an English hunting scene in shades of green and brown.

"I'm very impressed," Emma said. "And please tell Hack what a good job he did on the canopy. I would never have thought he had the experience to do something like that. I've underestimated him."

They made their way back down to the lobby. "What suite do you plan to do next?" Emma asked.

"Twenty-five, I think."

"I can hardly wait."

CHAPTER 11

FROM THE FIRST DAY DIANA entered number twenty-five, she longed to change it. One of the smaller suites, it was usually occupied by a single person or a couple staying only one night. Probably the bucking bronco doorknocker inspired the Western theme that was out of keeping with the high ceiling and Victorian moldings. A horseshoe was carved into the headboard of the double bed and dozens of green cacti sprouted on the cream-colored bedspread and matching curtains.

In its place, Diana pictured a cozy, old-fashioned décor to complement the rose carpet and the old-fashioned claw-foot bathtub in the black and white tiled bathroom. But how to get rid of the ugly horseshoe carved in the headboard?

She showed it to Hack, wondering if he could use wood filler and stain over it. He rocked back on his heels, hooking his thumbs in his belt loops while he studied it. Then he pulled at his chin and cocked his head. "Might be hard to make it smooth. Maybe the horseshoe could turn into something else."

"How?"

"Used to whittle as a hobby—not lately, but don't know that one forgets how. I could give it a try. If I make a mess of it, I'll just take out the board, put in a new one and stain it. Nothing lost."

Diana pondered. Then she smiled. "Oh yes, Hack, let's try it. I'll cut out a stenciled design. Come back tomorrow and see what you think."

The next day Hack sat cross-legged on the bed and settled himself facing the headboard. Diana had taped the stenciled design over the wood, swirls of flowers and leaves incorporated the horseshoe and went beyond. Hack muttered and complained about his awkward position on the bed as well as the texture of the wood, but as the chips flew, the shape of the horseshoe disappeared, and the new design took form. Then Hack sanded and stained the footboard and the surrounding headboard in a softer oaken hue while Diana worked to achieve the same effect on the dresser and desk.

"You know, you're really something," Hack said at one point, laying down his brush to open his can of Copenhagen and take a pinch between his fingers. Diana saw her reflection in the dresser mirror and swiped at the smudge of stain on her nose.

Hack hurried on. "What I mean is, when I first met you, I took you for the timid housewife type. But you've got real gumption. Real ideas for this place. I like workin' here now and the money don't hurt neither. My girl's mighty impressed."

"And who is your girl?" Diana ventured.

"Name's Fern."

"I'd like to meet her. Bring her to see what we've accomplished sometime."

"Might do that." He said it with enough emphasis that Diana believed he would.

"What's Fern do?" she asked.

"She's a waitress. Works odd hours."

"Of course, we'd have to check first to make sure the rooms aren't occupied, but I'd like to show her what we've accomplished and have her opinion."

Hack beamed. "Sure thing, boss."

Hack went on to paint the walls a soft green and Diana accessorized with pastel wall prints and accessories—a yellow lampshade, a blue desk blotter, and a violet cushion in the wicker chair.

The cactus prints vanished, replaced by a cream-colored bedspread and matching tie-back curtains. Diana had stepped back to admire the effect when Nina Gilmore appeared in the doorway.

"Hey," she exclaimed. "Thought I'd find you here. Stopped at the desk and read your sign."

"I'm sorry," Diana said. "Did you need something?"

Nina Gilmore walked with two canes. When she first arrived with her son to inquire about an apartment, she had turned to leave when Diana told her there wasn't an elevator. Her son, however, asked to see what was available and Diana took them up to twenty-three. It had the same floor plan as the redecorated twenty-two across the hall, but was on the back of the hotel, away from the traffic. Even though it hadn't been redecorated, Nina loved the room the minute they walked in. "It's so spacious, with such a nice view of the neighborhood. Besides, I don't get out much. I can order my groceries to be delivered and Curtis here runs errands for me when I need my medicine or something."

Curtis granted a grim nod. Nina went on to say she suffered from severe arthritis.

Now Nina answered Diana's question. "No, I was just bored. Managed the steps for something to do. Didn't think to look in here on my way down although the door was open a crack. My goodness, what a pretty room! I like mine better though, bigger and all, but most women would like this. Don't know about men though."

Diana agreed. "It is on the feminine side, but quite a few single women stay here. We'll just have to see." She thought of Mrs. Talbot. Maybe she would venture to try it on her the next time she returned.

"Well, don't start on my room," Nina warned. "I like it just the way it is.'

Good. Nina had enough other complaints, not only to her, but to anyone who would listen.

"How very clever!" Emma exclaimed when she arrived for her showing. "The hotel's original furnishings are all of good quality, but we are well aware many are outdated. You're performing wonders, Diana. What will you think of next? By the way," she added, "I've ordered new towels and bathmats—white Egyptian cotton with the 'HH' monogram in gold. Thanks to you, Diana, Hartwick House is making its mark."

Diana related the conversation to Ted over dinner. "It's amazing— as if Emma's seeing the hotel in a whole new light. It surprises me how open she is to my ideas."

"To your credit."

"Well, partly. We all grow accustomed to our surroundings. That's the fun of decorating—creating new and different environments for people." She stabbed a piece of asparagus as she talked and twirled it around on her fork.

"And don't forget Hack's part," she added. "I'll never forget the sight of him sitting there cross-legged, carving on that headboard. He managed a few choice words before he finished, but I know he's proud of the outcome." She laughed at the memory and put the asparagus in her mouth.

"Wish I'd been there. Could have taken his picture on my phone for posterity. By the way, speaking of phones, Brad called on my way home."

"Yes?"

"Said he's bringing a girl with him next week when he comes for Thanksgiving."

"A girl?" Diana's eyebrows shot up. "He's never mentioned a girl. I don't know if he's even dated anyone in his three years of college."

"He said they'll get here Wednesday night and leave Friday morning."

"What's her name?" Diana managed.

"I think he might have said, but we'll learn it when they get here."

"You men! I'm going to call him back." She started to get up, but Ted laid a hand on her arm.

"He'll say you're making a big deal of it. Might even change his mind about coming."

Diana sank back down. Well it *was* a big deal. She wouldn't make it one when they arrived, but Brad bringing a girl with him? Unbelievable.

At least she could call Laurel. But no, Laurel might run right to Brad and pester him for details—maybe even cause him to change his plans, too.

She surveyed their apartment, endeavoring to see it through a stranger's eyes. Small, yes, yet somehow welcoming. Over the months, it had begun to reflect their personalities—Ted's pipe rack on the lamp table beside his recliner, plush pillows on the couch, a new print purchased on a whim one day as they browsed at a street fair—vibrant splashes of color that drew the eye away from the horrid pine cones on the wallpaper opposite. Yes, when she walked in now, it was home. When had that happened?

Thank goodness she had purchased a fall centerpiece for the table and planned a traditional Thanksgiving dinner. First impressions mattered, and besides, it would be unfair to Brad and Laurel to think of doing otherwise. Family traditions remained important no matter where you were. The preparations lifted her spirits, even before Brad's phone call.

Late Wednesday morning, Diana watched Laurel park her bright orange VW Bug at the curb and swing a backpack from the back seat.

"You'd think professors would take pity over a holiday, but no . . ." Laurel plunked the backpack in the side hallway with her laptop beside it. She paused and surveyed the apartment, her eyes lighting on the table centerpiece. "Oh Mom. I'm so glad," she said, relief in her voice. "I worried you might not make much of the holidays this year. But I should have known better. You'd do it for us, if for no other reason."

Diana welcomed her hug and hung Laurel's quilted jacket in the hall closet. Then she doled out the first hint. "Your brother is bringing someone with him."

"Brad? My brother Brad? Doesn't sound like him. No, that's not fair. Brad has a kind heart under that stern exterior. Probably someone from work—maybe Mosul, an Egyptian guy here on a fellowship."

Diana followed her daughter to the kitchen where Laurel opened the refrigerator and stared at its contents. "It's a girl," Diana told her.

"A girl? No kidding?" Laurel shut the door and turned around to give Diana her full attention. "What's her name?"

"Your dad took the call." Diana frowned and shrugged her shoulders. "He didn't ask."

"Figures." She retraced her steps, Diana following, and dug in the backpack to retrieve her cell phone. "I'll call Brad right now and find out for myself."

"No, I think we should wait," Diana told her. "You know how Brad is if he thinks he's being cross-examined. We'll get the silent treatment."

"But Mom! A girl? The suspense will kill me," Laurel whined. She settled back on the couch, kicked off her shoes and perched her stocking feet on the edge of the coffee table. "Okay then," she sighed. "Distract me. Tell me the latest scoop on Hartwick House."

Should she tell Laurel about the hookers in twenty-one? It made a great story and Laurel would think it a hoot, but no, that wouldn't be fair to Ted. Instead, she took Laurel up to twenty-five where she basked in Laurel's praise.

"I remember that awful Western theme. What happened to the horseshoe on the headboard?"

"Hack's idea to get rid of it." Diana explained the whittling and how the design had transpired.

"From what I've heard of Hack, who would expect he'd conspire with you for something like that?"

Diana laughed. "So true. Anyway, this room is booked next week. Maybe we'll find out then what the verdict is."

"Is it a woman?"

"Yes, her name's Vangie Emerson. She sounds young."

"Then she'll love it."

As mother and daughter started back down the stairs, they met an older couple just starting up. "Hello, Mr. and Mrs. Schaller. This is my daughter, Laurel."

"Hello, Laurel." Mrs. Schaller held out her hand and Mr. Schaller doffed his cap. "We just love Hartwick House. Your mother makes us feel right at home. Much friendlier than staying in a big, impersonal hotel."

"I agree," Laurel answered. "It's nice to have met you."

When they reached the lobby, Diana turned to Laurel, feeling suddenly shy. "I'm thinking of offering something new," she began.

"Yes, Mom? Like what?" Laurel sat down behind the desk and played with the feathered pen.

"Just casual gatherings once a week here in the lobby, or maybe on the patio when the weather's nice—with coffee or tea, maybe cookies or cake."

"And?"

Diana leaned against the wall and plunged ahead. "Sometimes guests tell me they choose Hartwick House because of its central location, but also because of the charm it projects in the guidebook description. I thought I might share the history of Denver and how Hartwick House came to be."

Laurel put down the pen and paid close attention as Diana continued. "It would be up to them, of course. If they have the interest, that is, or if they just want to come and mingle with other guests."

Laurel nodded in vigorous agreement, her voice picking up speed. "Tie the history of the hotel to Denver's history—affirm their decision to choose Hartwick House in the first place."

"Exactly. I haven't thought it through yet. I'd welcome your suggestions."

Laurel stood and hugged her mother. "I'm so glad to see you take real interest, Mom. First the decorating and now the guests themselves. You know I'll help in any way I can, but it sounds as if you already have it covered."

Diana had shopping left to do and Laurel agreed to go with her. Cousin Fanny arrived mid-afternoon, her eyes lighting up as soon as she saw Laurel.

They launched into a discussion leading to the revelation that Fanny had not only graduated from the university but had gone back in later years as a housemother in one of the dorms.

"You must have been wonderful," Laurel exclaimed. "Not like crabby Mrs. Monroe—better known as Monster Monroe."

Fanny laughed, like the tinkle of a tiny bell. "You didn't know me then, my dear," she said. "People change."

"Not that much."

Fanny winked at Diana. "Ah, the innocence of youth. Have fun, you two. 'Fleet the time carelessly.' *As You Like It*, Act 1."

"Isn't she something?" Laurel exclaimed as the door shut behind them.

"Yes, she is," Diana agreed. She breathed a sigh of relief—as she always did once free of the place. Especially when she was leaving with Laurel.

Ted locked the car and took a tour around Laurel's VW parked ahead of his. It now sported a Colorado Buffaloes bumper sticker. As always, he was glad to see she had arrived safely.

He never gave much thought to holidays. In the furniture business, November was usually a slow month, allowing time for store inventory and bringing the books up-to-date for the tax man. Except for smaller items—accessories like pictures or pillows, people weren't prone to buying furniture for gifts. They waited for the after Christmas sales.

He had expected Diana to downplay Thanksgiving this year. But of course, Laurel was coming—sentimental Laurel who loved each and every holiday. And Brad—what a bombshell that was. He'd never brought a girl home before—unless maybe once or twice for the obligatory prom picture.

As he entered the apartment, he found Cousin Fanny in a heated back and forth with Hattie who stood with her hands on her ample hips. "Why you rent him a room?" Hattie demanded.

"Why not? He paid good money."

"Trouble. That's what he is. I'll have a mess on my hands."

Fanny used a sterner tone. "You shouldn't judge people by their appearance."

"Not a matter of judging. Matter of knowin."

"Just because he had long hair and some tattoos?"

"And beer. I seen them carry in three cartons of Coors beer plus a guitar and one of those loud music machines." She broke the pencil lead as she signed out and left with a loud huff. The door slammed behind her.

"What was that all about?" Ted asked Fanny.

Fanny stood on tiptoe to see in the hall mirror and secure the tiny black hat to the thin topknot at the back of her head. Ted winced as the long hatpin jabbed through the thin tuft of white hair.

"I hope I did the right thing," she told him. "After all, he paid cash. With so few guests registered over Thanksgiving, I thought Diana would be happy to rent the apartment. By the way, there are three of them. I told Randy that suite has only a king-sized bed, but he said they have a sleeping bag in their bus."

"Bus?" Ted remembered a beat-up black van out front plastered with various decals and slogans.

"He asked me where to park it. Told him to either find somewhere on a side street or plug the meter all night."

"His problem, I guess."

"Well, I'll run on. Happy Thanksgiving!"

"Just what we need," Diana moaned when Ted told her. "I love Fanny, but sometimes . . . " It wouldn't be the first time Fanny left her in a predicament—quoted the wrong rate or placed a guest in a room reserved for someone else. "You'll straighten it out," Fanny always told her with a wave of her hand over her shoulder.

Laurel went out to the hall to look at the register. "Randy Stone is his name," she reported. "I'm glad it's not Stoned," she giggled.

Brad and his girl burst through the door in the midst of a sleet storm. Diana had fretted about the roads all afternoon.

Brad stamped his feet on the rug. "Hi Mom. This is Charlotte. Charlotte Swanson."

Charlotte appeared fine with the brief introduction. Indeed she was a counterbalance to Brad, like sunshine to clouds.

Not quite as tall as their son, but at least five foot eleven, Charlotte's short blonde hair curled around the edges of a soft angora cap. Sapphire blue eyes and porcelain-like skin reminded Diana of a Nordic princess despite a fine smattering of freckles across her nose.

"I've been dying to meet you," Charlotte exclaimed, swiping the rug with the cowboy boots she wore with jeans. She smiled all around, took off her gloves, and stuffed them in the pockets of her navy stadium coat, then relinquished the coat to Brad. "And now I'm here at last."

"Welcome to Hartwick House," Diana said. When did she become Emma Toos herself? She hastened to add, "We're so very pleased you could come."

"Hi, Charlotte," Laurel called over her shoulder as she took Charlotte's coat from Brad's hands and headed to the hall closet. "We met in the library, remember? But this big lug held out—telling me you only shared study notes."

She turned and gave Brad an exaggerated frown.

"Well we did share notes," Charlotte told her. "Then a cup of coffee, and at last he asked me out. But since his first mention of Hartwick House, I've tried to worm more information from him. Finally, I had to come see it for myself." Her blue eyes darkened as she hastened to add, "And meet you, of course." Her blush caused the freckles to stand out on her skin. "I mean—"

"You mean you talk too much," Brad said, but the tease in his voice and the squeeze of the hand he put around her shoulders showed he didn't mean it.

Unbelievable. He's in love. Diana took this amazing creature by the arm and led her into the living room. "It's an hour before we eat. Do you mind peeling potatoes? Time is short. We'll have to talk fast."

"I'm a great potato-peeler," Charlotte answered as they headed to the kitchen. As they passed the dining room table, she picked up a corner of the tablecloth and examined the intricate cutwork. "What a beautiful tablecloth!"

"It's cutwork embroidery, an almost lost art," Diana told her. "My grandmother made it. I use it on special, intimate occasions."

"Intimate? At Hartwick House?" Laurel's burst of laughter expressed her glee. "Don't count on it. That's what I love about this place—it's so unpredictable."

Diana steered them into the kitchen. "Well maybe just this once, it'll be peaceful. The only guests are in number twenty-four—a couple from Ohio. And Nina Gilmore—she's paying by the month now, but she'll be at her son's for the weekend."

"Don't forget Randy Stone and friends," Laurel reminded her. "Cousin Fanny's doing."

Diana frowned. "Oh yes, them! They better not cause any trouble."

"Cousin Fanny?"

"Let me tell you." Laurel's colorful description of Fanny left out further mention of the new occupants in twenty-two.

Charlotte finished her raspberry sherbet and laid her spoon on the dessert plate. "Delicious," she proclaimed. "Thank you so much, Mrs. Rutherford. Let me help you clear the table and then I can't wait another minute for a tour of Hartwick House."

Diana smiled and pushed her chair back. "Please call me Diana," she said. "I'll clear the table while Brad and Laurel show you around. There's really not that much to see."

"That's what I keep telling her," Brad said.

"Not true," Laurel protested. "My loft for example and the rooms Mom has redecorated. Too bad you can't see what Mom's done with number twenty-two."

"Why is that?"

"It's occupied tonight by some rock band."

Charlotte giggled. "Just as I expected! Not your run-of-the-mill establishment."

Brad groaned. "Oh, that it were."

Hoisting Charlotte's suitcase and the duffel bag still parked at the entrance, he headed for the hallway, calling back over his shoulder, he said, "Hey, Mom! What room?"

"Number twenty-five for Charlotte."

"For both of us." Brad left no room for argument.

Diana had chosen twenty-five on purpose. A girl's room.

The three young people left, their voices fading across the lobby. Ted settled into his chair and picked up the *Denver Post*.

"Did you hear that?" Diana demanded.

"I did."

"We didn't raise Brad that way."

"They're adults. Say one word and Brad will probably leave."

"I know. It's just such a shock. Never one hint. It must be serious."

"Hope so," Ted said behind his paper. "She gets my vote."

"She's wonderful. And it's so like Brad. No preliminaries. Take it or leave it. I guess they could take separate rooms and then sneak down the hall. At least they're above board about it."

Thanksgiving morning dawned brisk and bright. Charlotte insisted on turning the bacon in the skillet while Diana scrambled the eggs and Laurel set the table. Brad stood at Charlotte's elbow as he sipped his coffee and teased his mother about their room.

"It was so sweet. I thought I was in Candyland."

"I didn't pick that room for you." There. She had said it.

"Pay him no attention," Charlotte told her. "I love it. Laurel told us how you're changing the hotel room by room. Makes me want to come back to see what you do next."

"Oh, I hope you will," Diana answered, meaning it with all her heart. She glanced at Brad to see if she had gone too far, but he kept the same indulgent grin on his face that he gave Charlotte so she must not have.

Ted retrieved the morning paper from the front steps and proclaimed the hallways quiet except for a faint strumming noise in twenty-two. "Must be Randy's guitar."

"We heard it last night when we went up to our room," Charlotte said.

Diana frowned. They sat down to eat, taking their time. Charlotte asked about Ted's job and that led to a discussion of the economy and what impact it might have on future job prospects.

Diana looked at her watch. "We'd better be making our appearance next door," she said. "James and Emma are expecting us. Leave the dishes. I'll put a note at the desk and tell Hattie—"

She got no further when Brad looked up from checking his iPad. "What's this?" he demanded.

Diana had dreaded this moment, knowing it would arrive. "The Tooses want to get to know you and Laurel better and of course they will be delighted to meet Charlotte."

"No way." Brad's eyebrows furrowed. "Get us out of it, Mom."

But Charlotte intervened. "Aren't the Tooses the owners of the hotel? I would love to meet them!" She literally danced on her toes. "And who's Hattie?"

Brad groaned. "Char . . . " he began.

Diana hurried on. "Hattie's the weekday maid," she said. "Not a very good one, not like Margie who works weekends, but I don't have a reason yet to get rid of her."

"I know what you mean," Charlotte responded. "I'm learning all about that in my employee relations class."

"Employee relations?"

"Yes, I'm working toward a degree in accounting, but I'm a business major."

For Diana, each new revelation added another layer of admiration. Charlotte tugged at Brad's arm, playfully prodding him toward the door. Brad displayed his reluctance but was on his feet.

"You're in for a treat," Laurel said. "True relics of another age."

"I can't wait," Charlotte answered as she tugged her cap down over her ears.

"It better be fast," Brad muttered.

They bundled up against the wintry weather. Ted took Diana's elbow as they followed a few steps behind on the icy sidewalk. "Brad will be lucky if we get out of there in an hour," he told her. "They'll take to Charlotte like bees to honey."

And indeed, they did. Even Henderson perked up his ears and nosed into Charlotte's hands when she knelt to take his face in them.

"We had a German Shepherd before . . . " Charlotte's voice broke and Brad placed his hand beneath her elbow to lift her up and embrace her shoulders with his arm.

"I've never seen him so at ease with a stranger," James remarked. "But, of course, a friend of Brad's isn't a stranger. We're delighted to meet you, my dear."

"Please sit down," Emma urged. "Tell us what you think of Hartwick House."

Consuela came in with a tray containing demitasse coffee cups and a crystal plate of pastries.

"This is Consuela," Emma told Charlotte. "She speaks little English."

Charlotte rattled off something in Spanish and Consuela smiled.

"Gracias," she replied.

"She likes you," Emma said as Consuela left the room. "She's very competent, but her smiles are rare."

"What did you say to her?" Brad asked.

"I told her the enameled comb in her hair is beautiful."

"Like you," Emma told her. "Brad's a fortunate young man. But then he's special himself."

"Yes, he is." Charlotte's look lingered long enough for Brad's neck to turn red at the collar.

They socialized until at last Diana used the excuse of a turkey in the oven to get them back to the hotel. The aroma stoked their appetites as Laurel and Charlotte helped her in the kitchen.

Ted carved the turkey and gave the blessing. They lingered at the table, eating the last crumbs of pumpkin pie with whipped cream and learning more about Charlotte.

Charlotte had also grown up on Colorado's western slope. Her parents both died of cancer, just a year apart.

"It's still hard to talk about it," she said. Brad laid his hand on hers. "I'm an only child. I was a junior in high school when my father died. His cancer was diagnosed just a month after my mother's funeral. Seemed like he almost welcomed it."

Diana's chest tightened, but Charlotte took a deep breath and continued. "My grandparents lived nearby, so I went to live with them for a year until I graduated from high school. They're wonderful, but they were in their seventies when it happened. It's been hard on all of us."

"They must miss you terribly," Diana commented. Her voice broke over the words.

"Oh, they do," Charlotte agreed, "but I took Brad to meet them and he made them laugh." She turned toward Brad, who used his thumb to dry the tear that coursed down her cheek.

Diana felt a twinge of jealousy. Them before us? But it was only right. Now it was their turn.

After the table was cleared, they moved to the couch and chairs and continued their conversation. Then, about eight o'clock, the amplified strum of a guitar reverberated overhead with heavy metal music behind it.

Charlotte looked up and then at Laurel. "Wow! Who's up there?"

"Registered as Randy Stone," Laurel told her.

Charlotte reached to grab her arm. "Let's go see!" And they were out the door.

Brad scowled at his parents. "Just for once, couldn't things be just a little bit normal around here?"

Ted lightly punched him on the arm. "Normal? What fun would that be? You can see that Charlotte loves every minute. To her, it's a big adventure!"

"Sure, everyone loves a circus when it belongs to someone else. But you're my parents. This is where you live."

"And you're ashamed of us?" Ted held his son's eyes until Brad lowered them.

At last it's in the open.

Brad took his time before he answered. "That's not it. I know you didn't have many options. You had to take what was available. But I had hoped this time might be different. I just want to make a good impression."

"So do we." Ted put his hand on Brad's shoulder. "Some things just happen in life. You can let them defeat you or meet them head-on. That's what we're trying to do here."

Diana hoped to find Ted's eyes with hers, to express her agreement, but just then Laurel and Charlotte burst through the door,

Laurel leading the way. "It's a guitar all right," she reported. "The place is rocking."

Charlotte's cheeks looked flushed. "The couple in a room down the hall came out to listen. Said they found it interesting."

"Mr. and Mrs. Schaller," Diana groaned.

Ted pushed on the arms to propel himself out of his chair. "I'll take care of this," he told them. "Stay here."

"I'm coming with you," Brad insisted, and they left.

In hushed tones, their eyes and ears attuned to the ceiling, the three women speculated on the scene above. The loud music continued until they heard the loud rap of the doorknocker. Then it dwindled to a few strums of the guitar and stopped.

"What do you suppose is happening?" Charlotte whispered.

"A lecture, I hope," Diana answered.

Laurel giggled and stretched out her legs to cross them at the ankles. "What a story for Cousin Fanny!"

Before long the men returned, Ted laughing and Brad with a broad grin of his own. Ted's hand rested on his son's shoulder.

"You should have seen them," Brad said. "Randy Stone is now Randy *Stoned*."

"The place reeks of weed," Brad told them, dropping to the couch beside Charlotte. "You could tell that standing out in the hall."

Diana groaned. "Marijuana? Of all rooms. Not twenty-two! Why did Fanny have to put them there? It's not as if there weren't other suites available."

"At least the music's stopped," Brad commented. "Dad was pretty firm. Besides, they look like they'll pass out some time soon."

Ted reached up to pat down his cowlick. "I didn't have the heart to throw them out on Thanksgiving. Besides, it might have taken the police to do it. They didn't look like they'd make it on their own. I must admit Bud plays a pretty good guitar, though. Made me a little jealous."

"What was Cousin Fanny thinking?" Laurel moaned. "You told me about the van parked out front."

"She was thinking 'rent the room'." Diana knew by now how Fanny thought—the pride she took in renting the first room she saw vacant on the roster. "I need to have a talk with her."

"But it's such a wonderful story!" Charlotte exclaimed. "The couple that came out of their room called it a serendipity, said it added to the ambiance."

Ambiance. Diana rolled the word on her tongue. "Of course—ambiance. This place is full of it."

Diana made coffee and finished setting the table for breakfast just as Brad and Charlotte came down with their bags.

"We're leaving now," Brad told her. "It snowed some after that sleet and the roads may be slick. Want to be sure I make it back in time for work."

"Oh dear." Diana's voice conveyed her disappointment. "I'm making French toast."

"Thanks anyway, Mom." He crossed the room to give her a peck on the cheek. "We'll grab something on the way. Where's Dad?"

"Right here." Ted came out of the bedroom dressed for work. "Come again soon, you two. We'll try hard to stir up some more excitement for you."

Charlotte giggled. "I love Hartwick House and you all made me feel so welcome. Thanks for everything. Tell Laurel I'll give her a call next week and we can make plans."

"She'll be sorry she didn't see you off," Diana told them.

"Let her sleep," Charlotte answered. 'It's such a cozy nook up there."

"It is, isn't it?" Diana remarked, pleased to hear Charlotte describe it that way. She took Ted's arm and followed the couple to the door. "I hope you'll come back again," she said to them.

Charlotte turned to wave as Brad opened the door of the 'Vette for her to get in. They watched Brad circle the car, slipping a little on the grass.

"She's lovely, isn't she?" Diana remarked as they waved them off. "I'm still shocked that they shared a room though."

"They're adults," Ted remarked as he put on his coat.

"Still . . ."

Ted left for work. Diana kept the lobby door open to watch for Randy Stone and company. She would take action if they didn't leave. Call Hack, the police, something. But she would make sure they left.

Near ten o'clock, Diana saw them amble down the stairs to the lobby. She watched the descent, anxious to have them gone so she could find out what they left behind.

The one she assumed to be Randy carried a guitar case while the bearded man behind him hefted the boom box and a duffel bag. The third hoisted a sleeping bag over his shoulder and leered at her as they passed.

"Nice place here, lady. Real fancy-like."

Diana gave a semblance of a smile but didn't answer. She sighed with relief when she heard the front door close.

Hattie stood at the supply closet. "I knew it." Her voice sounded grim. "Room will be a mess. Told Fanny that, but no one listens to me."

"I'll go up with you." Diana followed Hattie's ponderous progress to the second floor. The door to twenty-two stood wide open, a sickly-sweet odor wafting down the hallway. Hattie's frame blocked much of Diana's view, but her snort of disgust told Diana what to expect.

The flowered coverlet trailed on the floor, tangled with the rest of the bedding. A brown stain stared up from the carpet and empty beer bottles littered the window seat. Hattie exploded.

"You expect me to clean this up?" She threw her arms in the air. "Will take hours!"

"I'll start some cloves boiling on the stove," Diana told her. "That should overpower the odor."

Thinking how different things would be if Margie were there, she pried a window wide open despite the cold and the rattling radiator. "You start on the bathroom," she ordered, leaving no room for argument. "I'll help."

"How about *me* boiling the cloves?" Hattie whined.

Diana turned her back before she lost her temper. Fanny would hear about this. It was one thing to respect Fanny's age and availability, but another to overlook poor judgment. Not that Fanny would be inclined to take to heart any lecture Diana might give her. Instead, the incident would probably make a nice tidbit to entertain the other inhabitants of Arlington Arms.

Mid-morning, Laurel came down from her loft and found Diana putting new sheets on the bed.

Laurel wore a heavy cable-knit sweater and jeans, but she still crossed her arms to hug her shoulders. "It's freezing in here! Wish I'd been up to get a look at them before they left," she exclaimed. "You should have called me."

"They weren't anything special."

"Well, Hattie told me I'd find you here. Talk about a bad mood." She crossed the room to pull the window down. "By the way, Cousin Fanny called. Wanted to know how our Thanksgiving went and what we thought of Charlotte. I filled her in on Randy the Stoned and she relished every tidbit. I told her you weren't happy, and she said, 'Your mom will look back on it and see the humor. *Henry IV, Part One*— 'Argument for a week, laughter for a month, and a good jest forever.'"

"Easy for her to say." Diana shoved a pillow into its case.

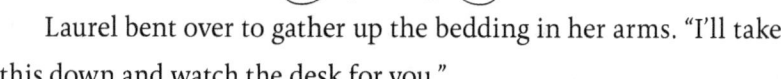

Laurel bent over to gather up the bedding in her arms. "I'll take this down and watch the desk for you."

"Thanks." Diana paused to give her daughter a hug.

Hattie continued to vacuum the second-floor hallway, pushing the upright back and forth in languid strokes. Laurel watched her waddle and wondered how anyone could move so slow.

When she saw Laurel, Hattie stopped and let the vacuum idle in place. "Hello, Miss Laurel. Aren't you nice to carry them sheets down? That room 'bout did me in."

"Yes, my mom's still at it."

"Room's good enough, but Miz Diana always finds something more to fix."

"That's why people come back," Laurel told her.

"And make more work again."

Laurel gave up and carried the bedding down to the laundry room. Then she stayed at the front desk to work on her English assignment and keep an eye on things. It was such a different experience for her that she wondered how her mom must have felt those first few weeks. She'd never given it any thought before.

Mrs. Schaller came down the stairs bundled up with a scarf and gloves. "Hi, Laurel," she called. "Are you in charge today?"

"Not really," Laurel told her. "Mom's upstairs."

"Well, I'm sure she loved having you here for Thanksgiving. I enjoyed meeting your friend and didn't we have a good laugh over the loud music?"

"Yes, we did." Mrs. Schaller struck Laurel as someone having good laughs over many things.

"Please tell your mom we'll be checking out before noon. I'm just running an errand first."

"Fine," Laurel told her with a smile. "No hurry."

The door opened to number one and a man in a robe and slippers poked his head out. "Excuse me. Is the manager here?"

"She's upstairs. I'm her daughter. May I help you with something?"

"It's a little cold in here. The radiators are rattling, but we don't feel much heat coming out."

"I'm sorry. Is it all right if I come in to check them?"

"Please do." He opened the door wide. "This is my wife, Alma."

His wife sat in the window alcove with a blanket wrapped over her robe. "Hello, dear. We plan to stay in today but would like it warmer."

"Of course." Laurel crossed the room and loosened the valve at the base of the radiator. The radiator started to rattle. "Should be more heat soon," she told them.

"Should have known," Mr. Butler told her. "My grandparents had radiators."

"Mine didn't, but I've watched my dad turn up the heat in their apartment." She felt pleased with herself.

"It's part of the charm," Mrs. Butler said. "Always some new experience when we stay here."

Hattie grumbled throughout the day and then left early before the towels were dry in the dryer. "Got a bad headache," she pleaded. "Twenty-two did me in."

"Margie would have stayed overtime if need be," Diana later told Laurel. "How am I ever going to get rid of that girl? She doesn't care in the least that anyone sees how lazy she is."

"Keep your eyes open, Mom," Laurel said. "Someday she'll go too far."

CHAPTER 12

EMMA WAITED AT THE NUMBER thirteen bus stop. Wrapped in dark-brown mink with a matching hat pulled down over her ears, she wore gloves as well as old-fashioned galoshes against the deep slush that swamped the gutters with melting snow.

The bus lumbered into view and Emma pulled herself up from the bench. Climbing the steps, she dropped her fare in the box and straddled the aisle as the bus lurched forward.

A young woman stood and motioned Emma to her seat. Emma thanked her. It was not unusual for someone of Emma's social standing to be riding a city bus. Designer clothing rubbed shoulders with threadbare jackets and tattered jeans, distanced only by the averted eyes of their wearers.

Emma knew city bus drivers dubbed this route "the loony run" because of the characters who rode it to the free health clinic or to deposit cans at the redemption center for coins to buy cheap wine somewhere or a burger at Wendy's. Some just wanted to sit in a warm place and ride to the end of the line and back. Across the aisle, an old man hummed to himself and conversed with an unseen companion. Emma paid him no heed. She resented the "loony run" label. For her, it discredited decades of respectability.

Emma's thoughts turned to Joshua, the person she was on her way to see. Joshua Jefferson Toos—her son, her only son . . . born to her and James twenty-seven years ago. *Joshua, my dear, sweet boy. What will you share with me today?*

It was such a blessing that Joshua was always so ready to tell her of incidents at work, his relationships with friends, his thoughts and feelings. Most of the credit went to his foster parents, Sandra and Riley Sheedy. They had raised him in their strong Christian faith and never judged her for abandoning him. But she had abandoned him. That she knew. She did so the minute she gave in to James, who convinced her that they should announce their baby's 'death' and allow the child welfare department to place their child with foster parents.

The doctor told them the baby wasn't right. They could have other children. She was still weak from the difficult birth, but she should have fought harder to keep him, even if it meant giving James an ultimatum. James had been so firm, so persuasive, but no more at fault than she.

Withdrawing from the social obligations she had once considered important, she gave herself over to running the hotel, working hard at making it her focus, striving to overcome her resentment and being a good wife. There had been no more children.

She pulled the bell cord and stepped off the bus to walk the half-block to the nondescript brick duplex. James never spoke of her Wednesday excursions nor tried to stop her. It remained a charade between them to pretend she never came here, never addressed a grown man as son.

Oh yes, she often fantasized about bringing Joshua home with her, confronting James with the truth of the man their son had become. But that time had passed long ago. James wasn't well. The shock would be terrible and perhaps Joshua would still fail to measure up. He knew

James only as Uncle James and never questioned her story. As long as she came every week, he appeared content.

The Sheedys had wanted to adopt Joshua, but they accepted the fact that Joshua could remain with them, just not as their son. Nevertheless, Emma knew they loved him as their own.

Besides, what would the truth accomplish? Better to leave well enough alone—let Joshua believe his father dead. The barrier had become too impenetrable—the subject between her and James too silent.

She turned up the sidewalk to the familiar dwelling, her spirits lifting as they always did in anticipation of seeing her son. Grasping the wrought-iron railing, she pulled herself up the four steep steps.

Sandra Sheedy answered the doorbell. Middle-aged and childless herself, Sandra's pleasant features glowed with the goodwill that reflected her inner peace and calm assurance.

"Mrs. Toos, come in!" The genuine friendliness that lit up her face always put Emma at ease. Turning, Sandra called, "Josh, your mother's here."

"I'm coming." His deep voice accompanied confident footsteps crossing the hardwood floor. Joshua entered the living room and hugged his mother. Though not a tall man, he was well-built, muscular. He wore khaki pants and a Denver Nuggets sweatshirt. Emma's blue eyes reflected back to her from a pleasant face that modeled James' square jaw and aristocratic nose. As always, Emma thought him handsome.

"Hi, Mom. I love you."

Emma welcomed his warm embrace. "I love you, too, Joshua."

Sandra slipped from the room to leave mother and son alone.

They sat side-by-side on the couch. "You're looking well, son," Emma told him. "Are you over the cold you had last week?"

"I am. Aunt Sandra gave me some medicine and lots of Vitamin C." He made a face. "Sometimes she acts like I'm two years old instead of twenty-seven."

"She cares about you, just as I do." Emma reached to squeeze his arm. "It makes me happy that you do as she says."

"Yes, like going to church and learning about God."

"That's right. Are you reading your new Bible?"

Emma had given Joshua a large-print New Testament for his recent birthday. He could read well, but Sandra told her the large print helped him focus more easily.

"I love it. The pictures are awesome—like Jesus and the disciples are really talking to me."

"I'm glad. Besides your job, what else have you done this week?"

Joshua worked at a nearby Safeway, stocking shelves and other odd jobs as assigned to him. Just last week he showed her the "10-year pin" he received as a loyal employee. Even today he wore it on his sweatshirt.

"You'll never guess, Mom." He bounced a little on the couch. "Alex took me to see the Nuggets play."

"He did? How nice." Alex, an assistant manager at Safeway, had taken a liking to Joshua and often included him on family's outings. "What did you like best about the game?"

"The winning, of course!" Joshua's blue eyes sparkled, and Emma knew he was teasing her because she knew so little about the game. Oh, if James could see him now—that sly grin that proved he was so much more normal than James believed.

But she didn't dwell long on past regrets because Joshua jumped up and grasped her arm to pull her to her feet. "I almost forgot. You haven't seen my new leg press. Come on."

The basement of the duplex housed a small laundry room and a large rec room taken over with Joshua's workout equipment. A couch, two armchairs, and a television remained in one corner.

Over the years, Emma had paid for bar bells, a rowing machine, a top-of-the-line treadmill, and now this new apparatus. Nellie, the law firm's long-time secretary, wrote out the checks, James signed them, and that was that.

Joshua hurried ahead of her down the steps. "I'm adding more plates every week," he told his mother. "My legs are getting really strong."

"Plates?"

"Yeah, they make it heavier, harder to push."

They arrived in the room and Emma saw the round discs that added weight to the sides of the heavy machine. They looked very imposing to her.

Joshua sat down on the reclining seat and put his feet up on the platform to demonstrate how he pushed his feet to move the plate. "It took three men from Sports Authority to carry it down here and set it up," he told her. "I'll run faster in the Special Olympics this year. Will you come to watch me?"

"You know I will. I wouldn't miss it."

It would be on a Saturday, but James never questioned her fib about "special sales downtown." The Sheedys picked her up at the bus stop and returned her there. After all, it was only once a year.

"I'll take a nap," James would tell her.

"I might have lunch at The Tearoom."

"Henderson will keep me company."

When she came home empty-handed, she would tell him, "I couldn't decide" or some other excuse. Sadly, that sufficed, and the charade continued.

After a time, Sandra called from the top of the stairs. "There's hot chocolate and cookies on the kitchen table."

"Thanks, Sandra. We're coming." *How much I owe this selfless woman. She's raised Joshua as she would her own son yet shared him with me.*

Later Joshua walked her to the bus stop. "See you next week, Mom," he said.

He gave her a hug and a kiss on the cheek and that was that. Boarding the bus, Emma never looked back. She didn't want to see him still standing there.

CHAPTER 13

THE WALLPAPER CAME AS A total surprise. Rolls and rolls of it via UPS.

Diana stood on a stepladder spraying cleaner on the chandelier and polishing each individual crystal when the doorbell rang. She climbed down to answer it.

"Ordered by Mrs. James Toos," the driver read from his clipboard when she opened the door. "Sign here, please."

Diana signed, and the driver made several trips to place packages on the floor inside the entrance. *Now what could this be?* She took out her cellphone and called next door before she opened one.

"I probably should have told you," Emma said, "but I wanted it to be a surprise. The men came to measure the day before Thanksgiving while Fanny was here, and you and Laurel were gone. Cousin Fanny mentioned you'd called her to cover for the day. I made the appointment for the time she would be there to let them in."

"You can return it if you want something different," Emma continued. "The decorator from Best Interiors selected it to coordinate with the hallway carpet. He recommended a soft beige paint for the wainscoting. Hack can do that. I have a sample of the shade."

"I can't wait to see it," Diana told her. She said good-bye, opened a box, and pulled out a roll to tear off the outside wrapping. What if she hated it? There was nothing she could do. Emma said she could return it, but of course she wouldn't.

No need to have worried. A subtle watered silk in a light sage green to match the leaves on the roses that patterned the hall carpet. The horrid pink wallpaper with vivid green vines would be gone at last.

"It's perfect!" Diana reported back to Emma.

"I can't imagine why I didn't do it sooner," Emma replied. "Not until I saw what you're doing with the suites themselves did I realize how shabby the hallways looked in comparison. It will be the first thing my reception guests notice when they step in the front door."

Emma's annual holiday reception was a fixture on the calendar of her invited guests. James called it Emma's Annual Do. This year the occasion would be on the second Tuesday of December and would include a tour of Hartwick House. Thirty guests were invited, and Emma told Diana she expected all to attend.

"I'm so proud of you and what you have accomplished here," Emma told Diana. "I want my friends to view the results and meet the person responsible."

Two men from Best Interiors arrived the following Monday and worked all week to wallpaper the lobby, the staircase, and the two upper hallways. What a difference! No more war of the roses. Just a pleasing background for the floral carpet.

Diana prayed it wouldn't storm. While ski areas high in the mountains welcomed heavy snowfall, Denver basked in fifty-degree sunshine. She needed to stay on top of every detail for the reception tour's success, but the weather wasn't in her control.

Any defect magnified itself—making her mindful of things she previously overlooked. She kept Hack busy fixing dripping faucets, touching up paint on kitchen cupboards and woodwork, and caulking bathtubs.

Ted took a personal leave day to travel over the mountains and take his mom to her scheduled doctor's appointment. He was gone overnight, and Diana missed him. Restless, she prowled the hotel, trying to envision it through the eyes of strangers.

As she was passing through the lobby, the hotel sign out front caught her attention. She hadn't noticed before that the painted signpost looked shabby. She put it on her mental list of items needing attention.

When Ted arrived home, he told her of the verdict they had feared. After many questions, Dr. Anderson gently confirmed the onset of his mother's dementia.

"I talked with our realtor about the sale of her house," Ted told Diana. "In the meantime, I'll research care facilities where she can be near us."

"I'm so sorry," Diana told him.

"Actually, it will be a relief to know she's nearby."

The next morning the front doorbell rang. When Diana saw the disheveled-looking man standing there, she stepped out on the stoop rather than let him in.

Probably in his late fifties, the man resembled the typical hard luck story—traveling on foot looking to find a dollar here, a dollar there. Not that he was dirty or especially unkempt, but his hair shagged over his ears and the sharp elbows and scrawny neck suggested a skimpy diet. He stood on one foot and then the other.

"I seen your sign," he said. He nodded his head sideways in the direction of the street, stuck his thumbs behind the straps of his bib overalls and rocked back on his heels. "Looks like it needs some touchin' up. I come cheap and would do a good job."

The sign, mounted on a black pole at the edge of the sidewalk, read HARTWICK HOUSE in black letters. They were definitely faded.

Diana knew better than to take on the responsibility of hiring him herself. Hack could do it, but time was running short before the reception and this man was available right now.

She walked to the side of the stoop in order to get a better look at the sign from that angle. Behind the gate opening to the garden, James was seated on the bench beneath the bare maple tree. He wore a gray wool jacket and cap and a plaid blanket lay over his knees. Holding a cup with both hands, he leaned over an open newspaper on the wrought-iron table in front of him.

Diana was surprised to see him. Emma had expressed her worry at the congestion in his chest, so why would he be sitting there? But how opportune.

"Wait here," she told the man as she lifted the latch on the gate.

The gate clanked shut and James looked up. "Hello, Diana. Emma thought this would do me good—that the sunshine would penetrate my bones. But it hasn't so far. I'm as cold as this coffee."

Diana couldn't believe her eyes. His knit cap and the heavy jacket over his three-piece suit were so different from his usual office attire that he reminded Diana of a sly little elf, especially with the twinkle in his eyes.

James was such a gentleman, always affirming of her efforts, but this was the first time she had been in his company alone without Emma.

He struggled to his feet as she hurried to his side. "No, don't get up," she said, "I came out of the front step and saw you here. I need your advice."

James sank back on the bench. "What's the problem?"

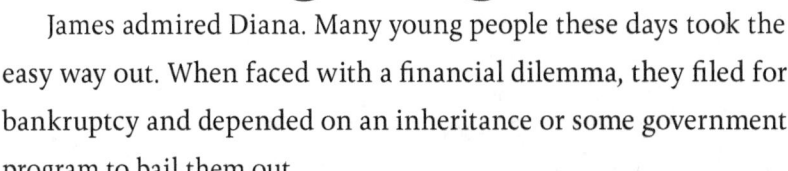

James admired Diana. Many young people these days took the easy way out. When faced with a financial dilemma, they filed for bankruptcy and depended on an inheritance or some government program to bail them out.

But she and Ted had gumption. They both worked hard, and Diana had accomplished wonders with the hotel. Still, all things considered, he liked Ted best. Straightforward. He liked that. Women were sometimes manipulative and couldn't always be trusted.

"You know the hotel sign out front?" Diana asked.

"What about it?"

"It's faded, and I know Emma wants everything just right for the reception. A man rang the bell just now. Says he can do a good job at a reasonable price. I wouldn't think it would take too much skill just to trace over the existing letters and he would probably do it for less than what Hack would charge."

"Bring him here. I'll talk with him."

When Diana returned with the man, James greeted him with his usual dignity. "Good morning. I understand you want to do some work for us. Are you a sign painter?"

"Sure thing. Been workin' my way 'cross town fixin' up signs for people. Seen yours could stand some work."

"What do you charge?" James inquired.

"Ten dollars an hour. Figure it'll take me two hours to do a careful job on yours. Have my own brush and paint, but I'd need a stepladder."

"Sounds reasonable." James stood, casting the blanket aside on the bench. "Mrs. Rutherford can show you where to find the ladder. I'll be out front when you return."

"Much obliged."

"Just be sure to do a good job. I'll be watching."

Diana preceded the man down the basement steps. She was relieved that James had done the hiring and would supervise. She had so much else to do that morning. "What about paint?" she asked.

"Right here." The man patted the pockets of his baggy bib overalls, well-spattered with various shades of paint. "Don't take much for touch-up work."

He shouldered the ladder and Diana followed him back up the stairs. Outside, he set up the ladder on the sidewalk and took a brush and several small jars of enamel out of the deep pockets. Selecting the black jar, he put the others back and climbed the ladder rungs to position himself on one side of the sign.

Satisfied that the work appeared underway, Diana hurried back inside to climb the stairs to twenty-four and remind Hattie to vacuum the hallway. She lingered there to make sure Hattie did as asked.

James watched the man position the ladder under the sign and begin the climb.

"Keep a steady hand," he warned in a stern voice.

"You bet, boss."

James had every intention of keeping a close eye on things, but just then Abe Feinstein hailed him from the open door of his shoe repair shop half a block away. Mr. Feinstein's two children lived in

Israel and James always felt obliged to inquire about them and look at the current photos of the grandchildren that Abe posted on the wall above his sewing machine.

Abe stood under the striped awning that hung above the door to his shop. "Good to see you, Mr. Toos," he said as James approached. "I see the No Vacancy sign turned on a good bit these days."

"Yes, we have new managers. Doing an excellent job. How is your family?"

"Gut! Gut! Come see the picture of the fish my grandson caught in the Sea of Galilee."

James watched the painter make the first stroke on the horizontal bar of the letter H. Then he followed Abe into the shop and leaned over the counter to peer at the photo. "Big fish and big grandson," he observed. "He's grown, hasn't he? You must miss seeing him."

"Of course, but we'll go next year. My son knows computers. Makes good money. He's sending us tickets."

"That's wonderful," James replied.

"Such a pity you and the missus don't have children. Such a comfort as we grow old."

James remained quiet for so long that Abe turned to look at him.

"You're right," James finally said. "We've missed out on that."

When Emma appeared in the doorway of twenty-four, Diana was thankful she had remembered to leave a note at the desk.

"Who is that man out front?" Emma demanded. The toe of one low-heeled pump tapped nonstop. Diana had never seen her so agitated.

"Why, he's a sign painter," Diana stammered, at a loss as to what might be wrong. "He rang the bell to ask about retouching the letters on the sign. I thought they'd look better for the reception, so when I saw Mr. Toos in the garden I asked his advice and he hired the man to do it."

Emma's scowl deepened, and Diana hastened to add, "I was about to go down and check on his work."

"Too late for that." Emma turned on her heel. "Besides, I came looking for James and didn't find him in the garden." She marched back down the hall, Diana right behind her. The vacuum cleaner motor died, and Diana knew Hattie would be spying out one of the front windows.

"I can't imagine what possessed James." Emma reached the stairs and turned to address Diana. "You shouldn't have bothered him with it. You know he isn't well. At the very least, you should have satisfied yourself of the man's competency before leaving."

Yes, of course. Diana prepared herself for the worst, but still could not believe what she saw when they reached the front entrance.

Her heart sank. A child could have done better. The letters wavered, the lower part of the sign was smudged, and drips of paint splattered the sidewalk.

"Come down from there at once!" Emma ordered, her cultured tone elevated to an imperious shrill.

The man held his brush in midair. "The owner of this place hired me. I take my orders from him."

Emma turned to Diana, her eyes dark with fury, and the chords in her neck rigid. Diana had the terrible thought that Emma might be about to have a stroke.

"I came to fetch James home to take his medicine when I saw this—this rank amateur destroying our property. And James nowhere to be found. "

Diana swallowed hard. She wanted to protest, tell Emma that James said he would be watching. "I'm so sorry," she said instead.

Just then James reappeared on the sidewalk a few doors down, looking shocked to find Emma standing at the foot of the ladder waving her arms at the painter. So, unlike her. But then he saw the sign.

"Stop!" he shouted as he shuffled toward them.

Emma turned and hurried to meet him. "I've already told him to stop, but he insists on hearing it from you."

James thrust back his thin shoulders and mustered authority into his voice as he approached the ladder. "I believe you deceived me, sir. I wager you've not painted many signs." He put a hand on his chest to slow his breathing. "Nevertheless, I take the blame. I should have checked you out more thoroughly. My mistake. I'll pay you ten dollars, an hour's wage, for my error in judgment." James took a bill from his wallet and extended a palsied hand. "Just stop what you're doing and come down immediately."

The man descended one rung at a time, took the money from James, and pocketed it. "Obliged," he muttered, scowling at Emma.

He left the ladder where it stood and jammed the brush and paint jar back into his pockets. "Some folks are hard to please," he muttered as he strolled off down the street.

"Why, I never," Emma declared.

James turned to Diana. "Find Hack. We can't leave the sign like that."

"I'm so sorry . . . " Diana began. "I should have . . . "

Emma interrupted. "We can trust Hack." She turned now, her point made clear. "Come, James. You must go home to rest and take your medicine."

"Don't hover, Emma." The old man refused her arm. "I hate it when you hover."

Diana watched them walk to the corner past Hartwick House and turn right toward the mansion. How could she have let them down like this? A movement at a second-story window caught her eye and she looked up to catch sight of Hattie, who ducked back and pulled the curtains shut.

Never mind. She must find Hack and set things right.

When Hack didn't answer his phone, Diana had his landlady's number as back-up.

A scratchy voice answered. "Better try The Lair," the landlady told her.

Diana had never set foot inside the tavern on the corner—or any tavern for that matter. The smell of beer and stale cigarettes wrinkled her nose. The bright sunshine outside made the interior a dark cave and Diana paused inside the door for her eyes to adjust.

A horseshoe-shaped bar dominated the room with four booths lining one wall. The female bartender looked up from the glass mug she was filling with an amber liquid under what Diana surmised to be a beer dispenser. "Looking for someone, dearie?"

"Hack Cummings." Diana surveyed the semicircle of men hunched over their drinks.

Hack swiveled on his stool. "Diana? Whatcha doin' here?"

"I need you right away, Hack. An emergency. I'll explain on the way back to the hotel."

The bartender frowned. "What shall I tell Fern?"

"Ruby, this here's my boss. Tell Fern anything you want. Tell her to go jump, for all I care." Hack extracted some change from his jeans pocket and threw it on the bar, then stood up and paused a moment to find his balance.

Diana knew Hack frequented the bar, but she'd never found it her business to look for him there. Now she worried she had another problem on her hands. She could only hope the sight of the sign would sober him up.

When they came within view of it, Hank struck his forehead with the palm of his hand. Then he stuck his thumbs in his belt loops and rocked back on his heels to survey the damage. "Who did that?"

"Hack . . . "

"I get it. Some jerk said he'd do it cheaper and it wound up like this. Well, now it'll cost ya. That's a major job you're lookin' at."

"I know. I'm sorry." Diana felt the heat rise in her cheeks. "Just get started, will you? It can't stay like that another minute."

"Yeah, I know. You don't want the Tooses to spot it."

Diana left this assumption alone. "Oh, please, Hack," she begged. "Just fix it."

"Find me a brush, some red and black paint, and a razor blade."

Diana rushed inside, first to the basement to find a brush and paint in the storeroom, then to the medicine cabinet in their apartment bathroom. Thank heavens Ted still used a regular razor.

Hack braced himself against the ladder and scraped at the paint smudges with the razor blade. He looked pale. Steadying the brush by clamping his wrist with his left hand, he filled in the letters and repaired the background. Diana held her breath through the final strokes of the brush.

At last Hack threw the brush to the ground, rubbed his eyes with his thumbs, then climbed back down the ladder. "Don't ever do that to me again or I'll quit for good. I do a job the first time or not at all."

"You don't know how much I appreciate this . . . " Diana began, but Hack wasn't finished.

"Wouldn't be so bad if I'd had any sleep last night. Fern and me had a fight."

"Oh, I'm sorry." Diana had met Fern the week before. She came with Hack when he stopped by to pick up his paycheck. Diana found her friendly and funny and liked her straight off.

"Well, I'm not sorry," Hack said. "Good riddance."

"Maybe you'll patch things up."

"Maybe." He folded the ladder to carry it back down to the basement. Sweat still beaded his brow even though the sun had begun its descent behind the mountains to the west. "By the way," he called over his shoulder. "Tell Ted I'll take Denver and give him Dallas and three."

Diana took a deep breath and went back inside the hotel. Hattie stood by the front desk, hands on hips. "I could'a told you, but who listens to me?"

Diana knew Hattie was fishing. "What could you have told me?" she asked, taking the bait.

"I know old Sam. He's always lookin' for some way to make a buck. Painter? Huh? Probably found those paints in a dumpster. Saw a new con to try. He's not dumb, just broke."

Diana sighed. She had no one to blame but herself for not turning the man away in the first place and waiting for Hack. "Well, Hack's fixed it."

"Miz Toos mighty mad. Can he fix that, too?" Hattie pushed the vacuum into number four and pulled the door shut behind her.

Diana put a note at the desk, then went next door, and waited for Emma to answer the bell. She dared not put this off. Her finger found its way to her hair, but she suppressed the nervous habit and returned her hand to her side.

"Please come in," Emma said, as gracious as ever, exhibiting none of her earlier annoyance. "You look tired, Diana. Consuela just baked some brownies. Sit here with James and I'll fetch some. They should still be warm."

James collected the pile of mail in his lap and placed it on the marble-topped table. Then he pushed on the arms of the chair to stand and greet Diana. "Hello, my dear. Always a pleasure."

Henderson slept at his feet and didn't lift his head from his paws though his ears twitched. Everything appeared as though nothing had happened, as though neither James nor Emma had left the house earlier.

"I can stay only a minute." Diana sat down on the edge of the sofa. She knew James wouldn't sit unless she did. "I just wanted you both to know that Hack repainted the sign and it looks like new."

"I'm sure it does." James sounded as matter-of-fact as if she were reporting the weather. "We never doubted your ability to handle the situation. Did we Emma?"

Emma had entered the room bearing a crystal plate piled with brownies. "Of course not."

She offered the plate and Diana took one of the brownies even though she thought she might choke on it.

Emma seated herself in the chair opposite James. "Tell us the latest news of your wonderful children," she said.

Greatly relieved, Diana settled back on the sofa and reported in general terms concerning Brad and Laurel's activities. Then she excused herself, saying she had left a note at the desk and didn't want to be gone too long.

James saw her to the door, though once again it took an obvious effort. Henderson stood also, and James placed his hand on the dog's head. "Thank you for coming," he said. "It wasn't necessary, but thoughtful."

As the door closed behind her, Diana heard his wrenching cough. In just a few months' time, she felt she had come to know James well and now she worried about him.

CHAPTER 14

THE FOLLOWING MONDAY, KATE DANSON called about the Bible study. The members took a break over Thanksgiving, but Kate reminded her they would be meeting again on Wednesday.

Diana was tempted to tell Kate she was too busy, but she liked Kate and didn't want to appear ungrateful for her hospitality. It wouldn't hurt her to go one more time. Besides, her friend Dorothy might ask, and she didn't have a good excuse, so she would go. As it got closer to Christmas and Emma's reception, she could beg off attending.

Kate Danson, a widow, lived alone now that her children were gone. Her narrow house, a two-story yellow clapboard with brown gingerbread trim, wedged between two substantial mansions similar to the Toos.' Diana found the pinewood floors, dark wood furniture, and cushy chairs charming.

As they arrived, the five women surrendered their coats and placed their Bibles on the round table before taking their seats. Thanksgiving became the immediate topic—who was present and how it went.

Diana remained quiet. As the newest member, she deferred to the others. Then Kate turned her way.

"Diana, you told me your children were home from college."

"Yes, they were." Diana told them of her surprise to learn Brad planned to bring a girl with him and how much they liked her.

"I had recently redecorated a suite that I knew would be perfect for her," she told them, "but then Brad told us they would share the same room. I was totally shocked."

No sooner had the words left her mouth than she felt the heat rise from her neck into her cheeks. What would these women think? What kind of person had a son 'living in sin' as her mother would say. She reached to clutch her Bible as if to somehow redeem herself.

Grace, an older woman who Diana found to be very sweet, but seldom said much, reached to lay her hand atop Diana's. "This new generation faces many snares that today's society puts in front of them. I'm sure each of us can relate in one way or the other." She turned to Kate. "If it's all right, I think we should begin with prayer for Brad and Charlotte. I'm sure they are fine young people who need God's guidance—as we all do."

Diana had expected censure, not acceptance and understanding. Tears stung her eyes as the women joined hands around the table and Grace prayed.

"Dear Lord, we bring before You Brad and Charlotte who, like so many young people today, find themselves subject to the pressures of the world. Draw them close to You, Lord, to guide them in their decisions and give them a future and a hope. Amen."

The Bible study commenced, and Diana entered the discussion, feeling at ease and accepted. As she put on her coat and thanked Kate, she remembered her earlier intention to beg off attending because of Christmas and the upcoming reception, but now she looked forward to coming again.

The next morning, Emma and Diana sat down at the table in the alcove to make final plans for the reception. Diana made it a point to keep Constant Comment tea on hand ever since learning from Fanny that it was Emma's favorite blend. She had laid the table with her grandmother's tablecloth and their good china. A plate of freshly-baked ginger cookies sat between them with a pen and pad of paper at Diana's side.

Emma told her thirty invitations had been mailed and all thirty women had accepted. "We always have a good response," she reported, "but I'm sure this year the tour of the hotel is a real draw. When we lived here at the hotel, some of the women stopped by for one reason or the other, but they always used the side entrance. The most they might see of the hotel was the lobby. Perhaps many were curious about it, even then. But now, with my praise of your efforts and the frequency of the No Vacancy sign . . . plus Cousin Fanny's praise to anyone who will listen, none so far have sent regrets."

They talked of the time for the tour to begin, the tour itself, and the comments Diana would make concerning future plans and the importance of Hartwick House as an historic landmark. "These women are all long-time Denver residents who appreciate the role of tradition," Emma continued. "I grew up in a parsonage where entertaining was a primary role."

"Your father was a minister?" Diana's tone gave away her surprise.

"Presbyterian—the old-fashioned John Calvin variety. The Tooses were Episcopalian. James and I are members of First Baptist, but neither of us attend although I maintain my daily Bible reading and time of prayer."

The ensuing silence grew awkward. "There's a weekly Bible study group I attend . . . " Diana paused, uncertain, and then forged ahead.

"The leader makes the Scriptures very meaningful. I never realized before that people in Bible times had many of the same problems we have today."

Emma nodded her head. "So true. There have been times I'm sure I wouldn't have made it without the comfort of God's word."

Diana assumed life to be easy for Emma—the luxurious mansion, a maid that saw to her needs, their prominent social standing. Of course, Emma probably experienced her share of hassles when she ran the hotel, but the Tooses had the money to make things easier.

For several moments, the women remained in their own thoughts. Only the hum of the refrigerator, the undercurrent of passing traffic, and the occasional clank of the radiator broke the silence.

"Not many people know this—" Emma replaced her teacup in the saucer and fingered the slim handle.

Diana sat very still, alert to the change in Emma's voice—the hesitation and higher pitch.

"We had a baby boy." Emma's tone grew taut. "Born on Christmas Eve. We named him Joshua."

Diana fought to find her voice. "I didn't know," she managed.

"He's no longer with us." Emma pushed back her chair and stood to pick up her coat from the nearby chair. "I shouldn't have bothered you with it."

"Oh no," Diana protested as she also stood. "I'm so sorry." The tightness in her chest brought tears to her eyes.

"It was a long time ago." Emma put one arm in the sleeve and Diana hurried to help her with the other. "It's late. I must get James his medicine." Her voice had resumed its customary correctness. "You've done a wonderful job, Diana. My friends will be greatly impressed."

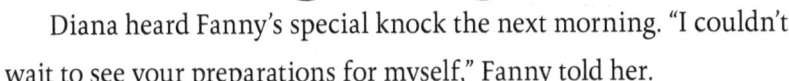

Diana heard Fanny's special knock the next morning. "I couldn't wait to see your preparations for myself," Fanny told her.

Diana took her on a tour of the decorated lobby and hallways. The tall Douglas fir, decorated with twinkling lights and red bows, as well as the pine boughs and red ribbon intertwined in the staircase railing looked festive indeed. Best of all, the restful background of the soft green wallpaper set everything off to its best advantage. Diana breathed a daily sigh of relief that the bouquets of roses were gone from the walls.

"Emma frets over this affair every year," Fanny told Diana. "With Mr. Toos feeling so poorly, it's a great help for you to share the burden."

Diana had dwelled on her brief conversation with Emma and now she replied without thinking. "Perhaps the holidays are hard for her and the reception helps her cope." She stopped, fearful of overstepping her bounds, but Fanny went way back with the Tooses. "Emma told me about their baby boy," she ventured. "Born on Christmas Eve."

"Joshua? I'm surprised she told you. Not many know—or remember."

"When did he die?" Diana asked, recalling the obvious pain in Emma's voice.

Fanny looked down, twisting the handkerchief in her lap. "He didn't, but he might as well have as far as James is concerned. According to Emma, James hasn't spoken Joshua's name in twenty-seven years."

"Why? What happened?"

"Joshua was a beautiful baby and James was ecstatic. They had waited so long for a child. James bundled him up and took him every-where they went to show him off to all their friends."

"Then what happened?" Diana asked.

"The child wasn't right. They put him away."

Diana couldn't believe it. "In an institution?"

"James is a proud man," Fanny continued. "Things were different then. Having a handicapped child still bore a stigma, especially in their social circles. He convinced Emma it best to make arrangements for Joshua, so they could have other children. It's ironic that no more came along."

"So, where is Joshua?"

"In a foster home. The same couple has raised him from infancy. When Emma ran the hotel, I came every Wednesday, so she could leave to visit him. James doesn't know that—or at least he pretends not to, according to Emma."

"Does Joshua know where James and Emma live?"

"I don't know what Emma has told him. I think he's satisfied that she comes every week. Emma says the Sheedys have raised Joshua as if he were their own child yet have never tried to take her place."

Fanny stood to leave. "I wouldn't have told you if Emma hadn't mentioned it first. Maybe it's just as well . . . helps explain her ways . . . why she's devoted her life to James and the hotel."

The desk bell ended the conversation. Diana answered it as Fanny left by the side door.

The day of the reception dawned bright and clear. To the west, the peaks of the mountain range made a jagged backdrop for the downtown office buildings.

Emma greeted her guests at the front door of the mansion. Nora Weeks, James' longtime secretary, waited to take their coats.

James felt well enough now to be back at his law office. To avoid distractions, Cloomer took Henderson for a long run, promising to use the back entrance and leave the dog in the enclosed back porch when he returned.

Hack had erected a tall artificial tree in the entry hall and Nora decorated it with ornaments Emma kept stored away in the attic. Nora knew all the guests by name and extended her own greeting as she took their coats in the foyer, hanging some on the wall pegs and piling others on the massive, high-backed armchairs that bracketed either side of the heirloom grandfather clock.

Several wore expensive outfits from Saks or Nordstroms and almost all were elderly with the exception of June Conover, wife of John Conover, James' law partner. Nora made sure each guest received a small, but expensive favor to tuck away in her purse—a Christmas snow globe containing a scene of a stone mansion that filled with snow when shaken.

Cousin Fanny stood in the doorway of the dining room. She also knew the women by name and greeted them warmly as she directed them toward the long table laden with candy, cookies, and a three-tiered cake. Consuela stood at one end to pour either punch or coffee.

The buzz of conversation concerning mutual friends and plans for the holidays was often interspersed with bursts of laughter. Consuela passed a tray offering more of the delicious pastries while Fanny re-filled cups as desired.

Emma allowed ample time to converse with each guest, relaxed and pleased with how the event unfolded. Only a few were close, personal friends. The rest were neighbors or wives of James' business associates, invited more out of duty than friendship. At last she called next door to alert Diana before tapping a spoon against a crystal plate and asking for silence.

"This year I have something different in store for you," she announced. The last bits of conversation faded away. "As many of you know, we have new managers at Hartwick House—Ted and Diana Rutherford. Diana has done wonders redecorating the hotel and I want to invite you to see it." An eager murmur spread amongst the guests. "If you'll please retrieve your coats and follow me . . ."

And the tour began.

Diana waited in the lobby for Emma's call. She wore heels and her tailored navy dress with a floral scarf draped at the neckline. Now she wondered if heels had been a smart choice for climbing the stairs and talking at the same time. She checked the keys on her wrist and clutched her cellphone. Emma said two o'clock.

At last the call came and Diana stepped out onto the stoop. It was cold, but she wanted to greet the women as they approached. She saw Emma turn the corner with her guests following.

As they drew near, Diana heard a woman remark on how pretty she was. "I never thought the job would attract someone like her."

Diana fought back the hated blush.

She shook hands with each guest, asked their names, and welcomed them to Hartwick House. Then she invited them in and led the way through the foyer and up to the lobby. The Christmas fir reached the ceiling, its sparkling lights reflecting in the crystals of the chandelier, the scent of pine permeating the air.

The soft green wallpaper formed a perfect backdrop as Diana paused to introduce herself and tell them briefly about her background.

As she moved to lead the way up the stairs, she directed their attention out the window to the garden. Poinsettias bloomed in the window box and the lower branches of the oak trees were festooned with tiny lights.

Diana described the flowers that would edge the paths in summer: ajuga, coleus, zinnias, and alpine strawberries. She had Mario to thank for her tutorial.

"Ooh, that sounds lovely," one woman remarked. "I must stop by to see it." Others murmured in agreement.

They followed her to the second floor where Diana pointed out the unique doorknockers and the newly-decorated apartments. She had Vangie Emerson's permission, but she knocked before entering twenty-five, knowing Vangie would be at work, but wanting to make sure. Vangie always left the room in order and indeed it was.

"We have a young woman staying here by the month until she moves into a place of her own," she told the women. A brimmed hat perched atop the dresser. A laptop rested on the desk and books stacked on the bedside table gave the room a homey, lived-in look.

"Charming," one woman whispered to another among the many compliments made. "I never dreamed it would be this nice." Standing to one side, Emma beamed with pride.

At that moment Nina Gilmore came out of twenty-three. Diana held her breath. What might Nina complain about in front of this group? She hurried to introduce her. "Mrs. Gilmore has made Hartwick House her home," she told them.

"And a lovely one it is," Nina told the women. "At first I complained about the absence of an elevator, but the stairs are good exercise for me and often enable me to meet the other guests."

Diana hoped her shock didn't show. More often than not, Nina took a dim view of things and had a complaint to voice, but today she appeared to enjoy her resident role.

On the third floor where the ceiling of the hallway slanted down, one woman said it reminded her of her own attic and others agreed. Diana hesitated and then ventured to unlock the door of Laurel's hideaway. The tiny room reflected her daughter's personality with peach-colored drapes framing the dormer window and the view of the mountains beyond. A flowered bedspread and braided rug brought "oohs" and "aahs" as well as laughter when they looked up and saw a Colorado Buffalo poster taped to the ceiling.

Emma followed at the rear and then turned to lead the group back downstairs where they gathered once more around the tree. There she gave them a brief history of Hartwick House and its historic importance.

"The hotel was built as an apartment house by my husband's parents," she told them. "His mother's maiden name was Hartwick—thus Hartwick House. When James inherited it, we changed it to an apartment hotel and it found its niche as such. Diana already has ideas to update the rest of the suites, so I hope you will return next year to view the results."

Diana watched with new compassion as she realized the secret pain Emma bore and the love she poured into Hartwick House, perhaps to compensate. She felt an almost fierce desire for these women to express their appreciation, not for her sake, but for Emma's.

And they did.

"It's lovely!"

"I never dreamed it was this nice inside."

"No wonder people stay here."

They thanked Diana for the tour and Emma became the recipient of many hugs.

The door closed behind the last guest and Emma turned to Diana. "I don't know how you did it," she exclaimed. "You even kept Hattie out of sight. Everything was perfect, right down to Nina Gilmore's testimonial. As James would say, 'Well done.'"

On impulse, Diana gave Emma a hug of her own. "Thank you," she said.

"No, thank *you*," Emma replied with tears in her eyes. "I've already discussed it with James. There'll be a nice Christmas bonus in your paycheck this month."

CHAPTER 15

DIANA HEARD THE FRONT DOOR buzzer—nine o'clock on the dot. Must be Margie. You could set your watch by her.

Margie shrugged out of her coat and reached into the closet for a hanger. She tugged off her knit cap and tucked it in the sleeve.

"I see your sweet daughter's back," she told Diana. "Saw that little car of hers parked at the curb and thought, Laurel's home."

"I do hope she considers this home," Diana answered. "Four months we've been here and sometimes it feels like home, other times not."

Margie patted down the clean gingham apron—one of several she owned—and smoothed back her hair with both hands, tucking any stray ends into the tight bun at the back of her neck. "Sure is dark out for this time of day—storm brewin,' I fear."

"So they say," Diana answered, reluctant to confirm it, hopeful the weather report would prove wrong. She followed Margie into the lobby and walked to the foot of the stairs to peer out the window at the western sky. Threatening gray clouds billowed over the mountain range.

Vangie Emerson appeared on the second-floor landing and began bumping a large duffle bag down the steps behind her. "Hi, Mrs. R! Hi, Margie. Taking my bag to work with me so I can take a cab straight to the airport when I get off. My flight doesn't leave 'til seven, but in case it storms, I don't want to take any chances on missing my flight and not making it home for Christmas."

Vangie was renting twenty-five by the month. As Laurel predicted, she loved the girlish room. "Until I find the right job and the perfect apartment, I want to stay right here," she told Diana. "Will that be a problem?"

"Absolutely not." Diana liked it when Vangie came home after her shift at the restaurant and called out 'I'm home' when Diana left the apartment door open or came in the lobby for some reason. Even though Vangie was several years older than Laurel, the two of them had become fast friends.

"Laurel stopped by to say hey last night. Know you're glad she made it ahead of the storm—if there is one. Suppose she's still sacked out this morning."

Diana pressed against the wall, so the bag could bump past her. "Actually no. She's in our apartment taking a shower."

"I envy her being here already. My mom's already called twice," Vangie said. "Bad enough to have a daughter with a master's degree cooking in a Mexican restaurant. Perish the thought she might be snowed in while the rest of the clan gathers in the sunny south."

"Just wait 'til you're a mom someday," Diana replied.

"Can't even imagine." Vangie progressed across the lobby and down the steps to the entryway. "Anyway, have a 'Very Merry Christmas' as the song goes. It looks like it'll be a white one, which won't be the case for me. I'll be back by the first to pay my rent, so don't give my room away."

"It's yours," Diana answered, leaning over the railing to watch Vangie leave.

Vangie stopped with her hand on the crash bar. "By the way, Margie. I left an eggplant in the fridge. Maybe you'd like to have it. 'Bye."

With a *whoosh*, the front door closed behind her.

Margie went right to work, and Diana returned to the apartment. Picking up a Swiffer to dust the furniture, Diana pondered the word home. Last week Vangie signed a contract to lease a place of her own—a loft in lower downtown. Yet she used home to identify where family was found.

Diana relaxed, satisfied with pies cooling on the counter, candy made and stored, and a honey-baked ham thawing out to bake later. Laurel had arrived late afternoon the day before and after dinner she helped her parents trim their small tree. A traditionalist like herself, Laurel wanted everything just so.

From her childhood, Christmas portrayed a closely-held family affair. Oh yes, the family went to church on Christmas Eve, sang the familiar carols and witnessed the nativity scene. Santa appeared in shopping malls and holiday lights and displays added to the festive spirit, but for Diana, the spirit of Christmas embodied family traditions, making the season special and reassuring in that no matter how much circumstances change, some things remain the same. Her parents planned to arrive late afternoon as well as Brad and Charlotte. Sadly, Mom Rutherford wouldn't be with them, but they would call and visit her sometime on Christmas Day.

After a thorough search, Ted had located a nice care facility only a few blocks from the hotel. Only a few days after her home sold and he brought her back and moved her in, she fell and broke her hip. She remained in the hospital where she received good care but would be missed.

Diana swished the duster over the fireplace mantel in the bedroom.

"Morning, Mom." Laurel startled Diana from her reverie. She wore a cozy terrycloth robe, her freshly-shampooed locks wrapped in a towel.

"It's really coming down," she observed as she peeked out the sheer curtain towards the street. "Looks like a fairyland."

'Yes, well I'd just as soon see more pavement myself," Diana answered from the kitchen. "At least until Brad and Charlotte and your grandparents arrive."

"Don't stew, Mom. Brad's a good driver. They'll get here—no problem. I'll go up and get dressed and then be down to help."

At Diana's insistence, Margie left early. "It's Christmas Eve," Diana told her. "Put down five o'clock and go on home."

"But it's only four o'clock. I could put the supply closet to rights."

"It's snowing harder now. You should be home with your husband and son."

"Yes, but—"

"No buts. Hattie got that closet in a mess, not you."

"Yes, Miss Diana. Only one bed to change—Miss Emerson's, so the day passed by. Those pilots didn't want nothin' and neither did Mrs. Gilmore. And the Raddisons in twenty-one said not to bother. I did mop the front entry tiles and fold the towels."

"Thanks, Margie. You run along and have a wonderful Christmas." Diana handed her the gifts wrapped and ready on the coffee table. "A little something for you and for Sam."

"You're always so thoughtful, Miss Diana." Tears glistened in her eyes. She shrugged into her coat, pulling the knit cap out of the sleeve and adjusting it to fit her head. "Oh, by the way. I left that eggplant in Miss Emerson's refrigerator. I wouldn't know how to cook one."

The few remaining guests shared plans of their own, including Nina Gilmore. Her son planned to come after her, so she could spend

Christmas with his family in the foothills. Once Brad and Charlotte and her parents arrived, the storm wouldn't matter. If anything, it would insulate them in their own warm cocoon.

"It will feel good to be out in the fresh air," Ted told Diana as he put on a warm jacket, boots, and a warm cap with earflaps to shovel the sidewalks. He donned fur-lined gloves, retrieved the scoop shovel from the basement and left to start scooping the snow from the front sidewalk, establishing a rhythm—scoop and throw, scoop and throw.

Brad stayed in good shape and he should do the same. He pictured Brad and Charlotte driving up any minute and seeing him hard at work. Diana stewed about them being on the road, but he didn't. If anyone had a level head and a steady hand, Brad did.

Diana worried too much. He turned the corner to continue shoveling past their side entrance and the Toos mansion. She always wanted the perfect setting, the perfect food, the perfect family Christmas. How likely was that at Hartwick House?

Take Thanksgiving with Randy Stone and friends for example. Charlotte proved herself a good sport, but now Diana zeroed in on an idyllic family Christmas. Well, she deserved it, accomplishing much in the four and a half months since the day they moved in. By this time next year, they would be in their own home. He was sure of it.

He continued past the Toos mansion, then up the sidewalk to their front steps. It would have to do 'til morning.

Back in the lobby, he inhaled the scent of pine wafting from the lit Christmas tree. A bough of holly topped the hall mirror and candy canes stood in a bow-bedecked glass on the front desk. Diana did have a touch.

"Hi, Dad," Laurel called from the kitchen. "Brad just called. They're minutes away. Says the windshield wipers barely keep up."

Ted took off his boots, tucked them under the desk, and walked into the apartment in his stocking feet. His pretty daughter greeted him dressed in red plaid, her long hair in soft curls pulled back with a festive red ribbon.

"Smells as good as you look," he told her.

"Thanks to Mom," she replied, standing on tiptoe to kiss his cheek. "She's baking more cookies."

Wet wisps of hair strayed from under the rust-colored hat framing Charlotte's face. A turquoise knit scarf matched her eyes and circled the neck of her white wool coat. Snowflakes clung to the long lashes and Diana decided she looked like a vision straight out of *The Snow Queen*.

"Merry Christmas everyone!" Charlotte stamped her boots while Ted waited to take her coat. She looked back at him with a huge smile as she turned to shrug out of it. "Brad told me to come on in while he finds a place to park. Hope he doesn't have to walk a long way back. It's getting fierce out there."

"I know," Ted agreed. "I shoveled the walk and it's almost filled back in already."

"Well, we made it. That's the main thing. Last week when we drove to Granby, the temperature was in the fifties—skiers wearing shorts on the slopes. That's Colorado for you."

Laurel hugged her, and Diana took her turn. "Brad can put your suitcases in number one," she said. "Right off the lobby."

Charlotte hesitated for just a fraction of a moment. "Fine," she answered.

"It's a large suite," Diana hastened to add. "Well insulated from the traffic noise. You'll be comfortable there."

"Oh, I'm sure it's lovely," Charlotte hastened to reply. "It's just that I don't need a big room. Twenty-five was perfect when we were here at Thanksgiving."

"I'm sorry. Twenty-five's occupied this time. Besides, you'll have more room in number one."

A blast of cold air heralded Brad's arrival. "Brrr. It's cold out here." He plunked their suitcases in the hallway and bent over to take off his boots.

"Any trouble on the turnpike?" Ted asked.

"Some stalled cars and not much visibility, but the 'Vette took it in stride."

Diana hugged him hard, pleased when he hugged her back. "I was just telling Charlotte," she told him, "you'll be in number one this time."

"*She'll* be in number one. I'll take the Murphy."

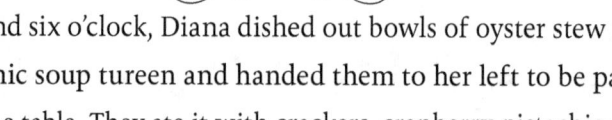

Around six o'clock, Diana dished out bowls of oyster stew from the ceramic soup tureen and handed them to her left to be passed around the table. They ate it with crackers, cranberry-pistachio salad, homemade soda bread, and a light Chablis. Pecan pie with whipped cream, Brad's favorite, followed for dessert.

"This is delicious. May I have the recipe?" Charlotte asked. "If it's Brad's favorite, I should learn how to make it."

"Of course." Diana exchanged looks with Ted as Laurel punched her brother on the shoulder. Diana stood to clear the table and Charlotte jumped up to help.

Then the telephone rang. Diana answered, surprised to hear her mother's voice. "According to the highway patrol," she told Diana, "I-70 is icy and snow packed. We're so disappointed, but it's an hour's drive on a good day. We've decided not to risk driving it tomorrow."

"Oh, Mom, not on Christmas! It won't be the same without you here." Diana blinked to hold back the tears. "Your own apartment's all ready for you. I even put those bath salts you like in the bathroom."

"I know, dear. I feel the same way. We so looked forward to being there, but things don't always work out the way we plan. Give everyone a big hug for us. We love you all." Her voice broke. "Merry Christmas."

Diana put the phone down and looked out the window at the falling snow. She fought to steady her own voice as she relayed the news. When she saw the disappointment on Laurel's face, she pulled back her shoulders and soldiered on. "It's our tradition to open our gifts to each other on Christmas Eve," she told Charlotte, "then wake up Christmas morning to see what Santa brought."

"Sounds perfect," Charlotte replied. "So, Santa finds Hartwick House?"

"There's a chimney on the roof and several fireplaces. What else does he need?" She loved Charlotte's response to things. Their family traditions would unfold just as always even though her parents couldn't be there.

Table cleared and dishes in the dishwasher, they gathered around the small tree to open gifts. Ted and Brad gathered up the wrappings and stuffed them in a black trash bag while Diana put popcorn in the microwave and Laurel started a disc of Christmas music. Close to nine o'clock, the desk bell rang.

"Now who could that be?" Diana said aloud as she headed toward the lobby.

When she opened the door, there stood Vangie Emerson—duffle bag at her feet, water dripping from her dark hair onto the shoulders of her gray, quilted coat. "DIA shut down. All flights cancelled."

"Oh no." Diana put her hand on Vangie's arm.

Vangie spoke in a tired, flat voice. "I caught the last shuttle."

She pulled off her gloves and placed them under one arm while she rubbed her hands together. "The driver dropped me two blocks away. Believe me; I felt lucky to get that close. Cars stuck all over the place—some just abandoned." She hurried on as if she didn't dare stop. "I need my room back because I won't be going home after all."

Her voice broke on *home* and tears flowed down her cheeks. Diana circled the desk to take the young woman in her arms. "You poor dear. You look frozen. Did you call your parents?"

"My mom cried."

Diana found herself close to tears. "Why don't you come in and I'll make you some hot chocolate and something to eat."

Vangie tilted her chin up and pulled her shoulders back. "Thanks, Mrs. R., but I just wanted you to know I'm back. I need a hot bath and my soft bed. Plus, I promised to call my mother again. Been putting it off."

Diana pictured Vangie's anxious mother and imagined how she must feel waiting for that call.

"Don't worry about me. I'll be fine." Vangie turned away, her shoulders slumped again. Diana watched as the duffle bag bumped back up the stairs.

The snowfall ended sometime during the night. They didn't stay up late, the mood subdued after Diana's anguished report of Vangie's return.

Diana woke to eerie silence. It took her several moments to figure out what made the difference—the usual hum of traffic obliterated. The digital clock at her bedside read 7:30.

She stole out of bed and went to the window to part the drapes. The light at the intersection blinked green, yellow, and red, but no vehicles of any kind started or stopped. Snow piled everywhere, the parked cars on the side street were almost buried with only their roofs exposed, like humpback whales.

"Ted! It quit snowing, but nothing's moving. Come look. It's unreal."

Ted grunted, but his eyes remained closed.

Then Diana remembered her last thought before going to sleep— when Ted already was, of course. She crossed to the bed and shook his shoulder. "What's up with Brad?"

"Why?" Ted didn't move, and his eyes were still closed.

"Why is he sleeping in the Murphy bed?"

Ted threw back the covers and swung his feet to the floor. "Don't know and don't care. Everything appears cool with them, so let's leave things alone. Why is it so quiet?"

CHAPTER 16

EVEN LAUREL WAS UP, AS if the silence became its own alarm. Ted and Diana exchanged looks when Brad kissed Charlotte good morning and asked if she slept well.

Three felt stockings propped atop the fireplace mantel in the bedroom bulged with candy, nuts, and small gifts—a tradition to continue. Diana hurried to make their bed, then invited Brad, Laurel, and Charlotte in to claim their presents from Santa. They sat on the bed and the floor, making it a fun, cozy time. So what that this was a whiter Christmas than they had bargained for? Diana basked in the closeness of family.

Brad folded the bed back into the wall and they sat at the table eating bacon and waffles with blueberries when a knock sounded at the side entrance. Ted answered it with Laurel at his elbow, as curious as ever.

The middle-aged man wore a ragged lightweight jacket with neither hat nor gloves. His cheeks were red and chapped, like dried apples. "Need your walks shoveled?" he asked.

"Sure thing," Ted told him. "How much?"

"Whatever it's worth to you, sir."

"Step inside and I'll bring you a shovel."

"Merry Christmas," Laurel smiled. "Wait here. I'll be right back." She crossed the room to the hall closet and returned with a cap and gloves belonging to her father. "Here," she told the man. "Wear these."

"Much obliged, miss." The man shifted from one foot to the other and ducked his head. When Ted returned, he took the shovel and left to start on the top step and work his way down.

Diana almost stopped her daughter from the generous act, but of course it was the right thing to do. What made Laurel so quick to respond while she tended to be cautious, always inclined to question herself and her actions?

The front buzzer sounded, and she knew it would be Margie. She had intended to call and tell her not to come. The registered guests would understand. Now here she was. Diana went out to greet her.

"Margie! I'm so sorry. I meant to call and tell you to stay home today."

"No problem, Miss Diana. It's right fresh out, and besides, Sam here just itched to make some snowballs. He pulled me all the way on his sled—right down the middle of Humboldt Street. We hid the sled behind the fence in the garden. Hope that's all right."

"Heavens yes," Diana replied. "Sounds like fun. Merry Christmas, Sam!" Diana formed a mental picture of big Sam pulling his diminutive mother on the sled.

"Merry Christmas," he answered. A big smile spread across his broad face.

"What do you tell the nice lady 'bout your present?" Margie prompted.

"Thank you, Ma'am. It's a fun game for sure."

"I'm glad you like it."

Charlotte came out from number one and Diana introduced her. "Pleased to meet you," Margie said, her brown eyes crinkling at the corners. "I wasn't working when you came at Thanksgiving. If you don't mind my saying so, you're mighty pretty."

"Yes, pretty," Sam agreed.

Charlotte gave him a cheeky grin and came right back at him. "Thank you. And you're handsome."

Sam ducked his head. Laughing, his mother took his elbow and steered him toward the supply closet.

Charlotte turned to Diana. "If you have a minute," she said, "I'd like to explain our sleeping arrangements." "Oh no . . . " Diana started. Why did Charlotte feel she owed an explanation?

But Charlotte continued. "You know how Brad is—a man of few words sometimes. But he doesn't want you to get the wrong impression and neither do I. Anyhow . . . "

Her words continued in a rush. "We went on a retreat sponsored by CRU—used to be Campus Crusade. It sounded like a fun weekend, so we thought, why not? Thing is—it caused us to reassess our relationship, evaluate our feelings for each other and what our values are. I'm not putting it well, but if we do decide to get married, we want to get off to the right start."

Diana felt weak in the knees. This lovely girl and their beloved son. "I think that's wonderful," she told Charlotte. "Thanks for sharing it with me."

"You're welcome." Charlotte smiled, and Diana saw her shoulders relax. She turned and went on into the apartment, a spring in her step.

Diana lined up the registration book on the desktop and straightened the pen in its holder, needing a moment to restore her composure. She felt deeply touched that Charlotte confided in her, but now something else nagged at her. She made up her mind.

"Laurel?" she called through the open door.

"Yes, Mom?" Laurel's appearance brought a smile to her mother's face—the green plaid pants and the brown buffalo motif on her gold sweatshirt.

"We can't leave Vangie upstairs all alone on Christmas Day." Diana meant the words more as she voiced them. "Why don't you go up and ask her to join us?"

"Oh, Mom, that's so great of you." Laurel scooted across the lobby and up the stairs before Diana entertained any second thoughts.

Laurel arrived at the top of the stairs when the lights went out. Reaching twenty-five, she lifted the doorknocker and let it fall.

"Hi, Vangie," she said when a puffy-eyed girl answered the knock. "Merry Christmas!"

Vangie peered into the hallway. "Why is it so dark?"

"The lights just went out."

"Some Christmas."

"That's why I'm here. You can't stay here in your room all day. We want you to come down and have Christmas dinner with us."

"Oh no. I couldn't intrude on your family celebration."

"But you wouldn't be intruding. It will be fun. The more, the merrier."

In the dim light from the windows, Laurel saw a spark return to Vangie's eyes and the shoulders of her flannel pajamas pulled back. "Okay then, I will," she said, sounding more like the Vangie Laurel knew. "But I must bring something. Maybe some chips and dip? Would that be all right?"

"That would be great. I don't think Mom planned for appetizers and it may be awhile before we eat with the lights out and all."

"Just as well. I need to see what I can do with this hair without a hair dryer."

"If I had your classic features, I'd just twist it up on top."

On down the hallway, a door opened, and the dim figure of Nina Gilmore appeared in her blue quilted robe. As she came closer, her face looked drawn as if she hadn't slept.

"Hi, Mrs. Gilmore," Laurel greeted her. "I didn't know you were still here."

"My son can't come down from the mountains to pick me up," Nina answered. "He has a four-wheel drive, but he called last night and said the roads are too bad. Makes a good excuse."

Laurel's soft heart spoke for her: "Plan on having Christmas dinner with us. I'm sure there'll be plenty for everyone."

"Well . . ." Nina looked down at her feet. Laurel could tell she was tempted. "I do have a pie and a green bean casserole that I intended to take to my son's. Don't know how we'd heat the casserole, but maybe the power will come back on."

"I'm sure it will."

"I'll send the pie with you, but someone will have to help with the casserole. I need both hands to manage the stairs."

"Just call when you're ready and I'll come up for it," Laurel told her.

"Then wait while I get the pie." Nina turned, moving visibly faster now.

Laurel turned and winked at Vangie, who winked back before closing her door.

Oh well, Diana thought when Laurel reported back. What's one more person at this point? Besides, Nina's casserole and pie would fit right in. The ham went in the oven twenty minutes before the power went off. Now she left it there in hopes the heat would continue to bake it.

In the meantime, she salvaged package ribbons from the wastebasket and Charlotte helped her tie back the drapes to let in all the light possible. She also lit fat candles and placed them on the end tables. She had meant them to be merely decorative, but now they needed the light. The sky was still gloomy as if it might snow again.

Charlotte giggled, sounding like Laurel. "Maybe it was meant to be. It's more festive and intimate this way. I can take lessons from you, Diana, on how to be flexible."

Flexible? Me? If you only knew. Just then the phone rang, and Diana hurried to answer it.

"Diana? It's Emma. Merry Christmas!"

Oh dear, the Tooses. We should have called them first. "Merry Christmas," she replied. How lame was that?

"Thank you, my dear. I hope you're staying warm. I had doubts about this electric furnace when we installed it last summer. Our plumber, Dennis Slovensky, insisted it would be more efficient to close off the fireplaces and get rid of our woodpile."

Diana recognized the name Slovensky, the plumbing and heating firm listed in Emma's Rolodex. Emma wrote down the name in case they ever had need of a plumber at Hartwick House.

"Oh dear," Diana replied. "You have no heat?"

"And no stove nor microwave. Consuela has the day off, but she left a roast and a potato casserole for us to reheat, so we hope the electricity comes back on. In the meantime, we'll stay in bed to keep warm."

Diana knew what they must do. "Emma," she said, her voice exerting an authority she didn't know she could muster. "Ted and Brad will come over to get you. You're celebrating Christmas with us."

Silence. Had she overstepped her bounds? She was ready to apologize when Emma spoke: "Are you sure? How very thoughtful."

"Just call when you're ready to come," Diana told her.

"James will be so pleased. Thank you, Diana. God bless you."

Nothing was as she had planned, yet Diana experienced a calm she wouldn't have thought possible. She had no idea how things would turn out, but somehow that made the day more interesting—like she was young again, only more daring.

"We'll need to turn the table in the other direction," she told Laurel and Charlotte. "Run it the length of the room and put the two extra leaves in." She felt in control—efficient. She could handle this.

As Diana spread out the tablecloth, Ted and Brad returned from making a round of the hotel. "The Addisons in twenty-one made reservations at a restaurant down the street," Ted reported. "They say they will enjoy the invigorating walk. The Tunisian pilots in twenty-two, however, said their hosts for the day are snowed in and won't be able to come after them. They looked so forlorn that I invited them to eat with us. Sorry, Diana. They'll be down soon."

Diana surprised herself with her answer. "Oh well, the more the merrier."

"They're pretty neat guys," Brad added.

Charlotte squeezed his arm. "Good-looking, too," she teased. "I talked with them in the lobby last night on the way to my room."

"Watch it," Brad replied, "or I'll rescind their invitation."

"No, you won't."

The knock on the side door signaled the return of the man who shoveled the walks. Ted invited him to step inside while he fetched a twenty-dollar bill from the cash box and left a note for the expense. "Looks like a good job," he told the man, peering past him.

"Thanks." The man pulled off the cap and gloves and gave them back to Ted. "These helped."

"Keep them," Ted replied. "I have others."

The man swallowed hard. "Thanks. Merry Christmas."

"And Merry Christmas to you."

"The Tooses have no heat and their fireplaces don't work," Diana told Ted when he returned from taking the shovel to the basement. "Emma said they would just stay in bed to keep warm. I said no, you and Brad would come after them and bring them over here."

Ted looked at his wife as if he didn't know her. Her cheeks were flushed, and her eyes sparkled. Perhaps she had a fever. He moved to her side while the young people continued their chatter.

"Are you all right?" he asked her.

"I'm fine, Ted. I really am. Nothing's turned out as I planned it, but maybe better. We'll see."

Ted squeezed her hand. "I'm proud of you," he said. "Really proud."

"Thanks, sweetheart. I appreciate that. However, the ham won't go far enough. Emma mentioned a roast Consuela had prepared. I'm sure it will be fine with Emma if you bring it back when you go after them. By the way, I take it radiators require electricity to keep the gas turned on."

"Right." Ted reached to touch the radiator nearest him. "If the power stays off, it will get cold in here soon. However . . . " He paused and pondered. "The storeroom in the basement has a big pile of wood in the corner—backup for the fireplaces. We have a fireplace in our bedroom and another in number one. We could use them for heat and for cooking—pioneer-style."

Laurel clapped her hands, rising onto her tiptoes. "Yes!" she exclaimed. "This is going to be so much fun."

CHAPTER 17

TED AND BRAD CARRIED ARMLOADS of wood up from the basement, placing them on the fireplace grates over wadded up newspaper to help start the fire. Soon the logs crackled with flame.

How strange. Diana had never thought of the fireplaces as anything but ornamental.

Vangie arrived bearing a bowl of bean dip and a sack of tortilla chips, her curls tied back with a red ribbon to match the red velour shirt she wore over black velvet slacks. "Slim pickins I'm afraid, but I'm pretty handy in the kitchen," she told Diana. "Put me to work."

The phone rang, and Nina Gilliam announced she was ready to come down. As promised, Laurel left to carry the green bean casserole and help Nina navigate the steps. Coming through the lobby, their voices mingled with the Middle Eastern accents of the two pilots.

Brad introduced them—Assad and Mosab. Assad was tall and distinguished-looking. Black curly hair framed his long face and a bushy mustache curved over his wide mouth. He was also the more solemn.

"We should have brought food," he proclaimed. "It's not the custom of our country to arrive empty-handed. Especially with so much beauty surrounding us."

Vangie's rich laugh countered his flattery. "I cook for a living, so I had less excuse. Besides makings for bean dip, all I had in the fridge was an eggplant."

"An eggplant? Really?" Mosab was short and dark, on the heavy side, but with a smile that drew all eyes his way. "If I had it, I would make an eggplant salad." His eyebrows wiggled up and down as he looked to Diana. "But I'd need a tomato and a green pepper . . . and maybe some greens?"

"I have those," Diana told him.

"Eggplant salad? Never heard of it," Charlotte said. "What do you do with the eggplant?"

Mosab's answer drifted back from the kitchen where Diana was leaning into the refrigerator to dig through the vegetable drawer. "Steam it over boiling water. Put in some tuna and some feta cheese— we have those upstairs. It'll be good—I promise."

A regular smorgasbord, Diana thought as she pulled out the items he needed. At this point, food was the basic requirement even though both the guest list and the menu were becoming more exotic by the minute.

"I've travelled quite a lot," Nina Gilmore said. "But never to Tunisia."

Assad answered in a solemn tone and made a courtly bow. "You must come. Tunisians are most hospitable people—like Mr. and Mrs. Rutherford."

"Hear, hear!" Charlotte agreed as she pulled out a chair from the table for Nina.

Ted and Brad made another trip to the basement. Brad helped Ted move the couch to find room for the card table and four chairs they found stacked in the storeroom.

Then Ted took time to call his mom. "Don't worry," Mrs. Rutherford told him. "They're taking good care of me here and I wouldn't want you to venture out in this weather. I'm so glad Brad and Laurel arrived safely and I'm looking forward to seeing them soon."

Relieved, Ted put on his coat and followed Brad out the door to retrieve James and Emma. Brad made three trips: first to bring back the roast and a casserole of potatoes that Consuela had prepared, then another to help his father escort James, each taking an arm.

Emma had bundled James into his black overcoat. A wool muffler wrapped his face below his eyes and the flaps on his cap were turned down to cover his ears.

On the third trip, Emma took Brad's arm, tucking it close against her side and clutching it with her other gloved hand to navigate the icy sidewalk. She wore her long coat with the beaver collar, fur hat, and fur-topped galoshes. "It's nice to have such a handsome escort," she said.

The elderly pair appeared slightly disoriented by the diverse crowd greeting their arrival, but they soon became their gracious selves as introductions were made. "Isn't this wonderful?" Emma exclaimed. "Leave it to Ted and Diana to have their wits about them in an emergency."

James nodded in agreement. "People of character," he added.

Wrapped in foil, the honey ham and the bean and potato casseroles made festive crackling sounds as they heated on the fireplace grates. Mosab's eggplant simmered in a pan on the grate in number one. He had also retrieved two tall bottles of red wine, clutching the necks of the bottles in one hand while he balanced the eggplant, tuna, and cheese in his other arm.

By late afternoon the food was assembled on the kitchen counter. Diana stood at the kitchen door. "Please pick up a plate and help yourselves," she told everyone.

Conversation and laughter filled the rooms so that when everyone was finally seated, Ted rapped his knife against his plate to get attention. Diana caught his eye to indicate she was pleased he remembered.

"Father God," he began. "Thank You for food and friends and for Your Son, Jesus, whose birthday we celebrate today. Amen."

Before bowing her head, Diana saw Charlotte and Brad join hands on top of the table. She lifted her head in time to see them squeeze hands and exchange smiles that had their own special meaning. She realized she had never changed into the dress she had planned to wear, but it didn't matter. The informal mood made her slacks and blouse more appropriate.

Conversation flowed around the table. The Tooses, seated with Nina and Laurel, began by discussing the weather, but soon their talk turned to Denver in general and why they each liked living in Colorado.

The pilots laughed uproariously at stories Vangie told about patrons of the Mexican restaurant. Ted asked questions about Tunisia and so it went.

Diana remembered Margie and Sam. She should have fixed plates for them.

"I'll be right back," she said as she excused herself, but sometime in the confusion Margie had already checked out, noting 12:37 as the time. So like her to be exact. By now she and Sam would be home to celebrate their own Christmas.

At that moment the lights came on and everyone shouted "Hurray" in unison. Moments later the radiators started to clang.

"Just in time for the dishwasher!" Diana exclaimed.

The bell rang at the lobby desk and Ted left the table to find Mr. and Mrs. Addison from twenty-one, their noses red from walking in the cold.

"Hi there," he called through the open door. "Come on in and join the crowd."

The middle-aged couple looked a little dazed. "We ate down the street at a Japanese restaurant," they said. "No lights, but the people were nice. Two other couples were there, and the chef cooked our food on hibachi grills. Quite an experience. We just now came back, saw the door open and couldn't resist finding out what's going on."

"The heat, for one thing!" Ted answered. "And the lights. We're celebrating. Come have a glass of wine and join the party."

And party it was. Diana's cherry pie and Nina's lemon meringue, plus cookies and candy Diana had stockpiled, were exclaimed over and devoured. Vangie, Laurel, and the pilots left the table to sit cross-legged on the pulled-down Murphy bed and play cards. Brad and Charlotte bundled up to "take a walk" as Brad put it.

Ted answered a knock on the side door. The same man, wearing the hat and gloves Ted gave him, asked if they wanted the walk shoveled again. "Deep out there," he said.

"Come around to the front,' Ted told him. "I'll hand you the shovel."

Diana appeared at Ted's side. "Have you eaten yet?" she asked the man.

"Yes'm. Breakfast at the shelter."

"When you finish, I'll have a plate fixed for you."

"Thank you, ma'am." His hunched shoulders pulled back. A smile crinkled his eyes and caused his chapped cheeks to form white parenthesis around his mouth.

The desk phone rang, and Diana answered it.

"Hartwick House? This is the sheriff's department. We're attempting to place stranded motorists in area hotels. Have a young couple with a baby. They can't pay, so you would be reimbursed by the county. Can you take them in?"

Diana knew the compensation would be about one-third the usual rate, but Emma had told her that Hartwick House honored such requests. "Yes, we have a room," she answered.

"Good. Name's Hawkins."

"Bring them on over. How soon?"

"Twenty minutes?"

"We'll expect them. Tell them to press the buzzer at the front entrance. I'll come out to let them in."

"Thank you, ma'am."

When Ted came back into the lobby from fetching the shovel, Diana relayed the message. "We'll need extra blankets and that crib in the basement. Be sure to wipe it down first. There's Lysol spray in the laundry room. They'll be tired and cold and probably hungry."

"Not much food left."

"I know."

Diana held the door open for the young couple. The black and white car with 'Sheriff' lettered on the side drove away, its tire chains biting into the icy ruts.

The young father carried their one suitcase. He had the gaunt face of a hard-working, perhaps undernourished individual. Beyond the dark circles, his eyes held an expression of obvious relief. He wore a light windbreaker over a cotton shirt and khaki pants.

The mother looked incredibly young, wearing faded jeans and a worn jeans jacket over a thin sweater. But the baby the young mother hugged close in its carrier was bundled snug in a zipped cocoon of pristine white plush.

"I'm Diana Rutherford, the manager. We've been expecting you."

The couple gazed at their surroundings as Diana led them back to the desk to sign the register.

"I'm glad you're safely here," Diana said. "Can I see?"

The young mother eagerly obliged, folding back the fabric to reveal the tiny face—silent and sober, but wide awake. "My mom sent this wrap for him before he was born," she said. "She didn't know the sex, so she picked white as safe. We live in Kansas and she lives in Cheyenne—where we were headed when the blizzard hit, and we slid off the road and landed in a snow bank."

"Icy," the young man offered.

"Thanks be to God a highway patrolman came along or we'd be there still."

The baby's brow scrunched up as if he had shared this worry, yet the innocence and vulnerability of all newborns prompted Diana to say, "How sweet. You must be very proud."

"Oh, we are! Can hardly wait for my mom to see him. Got so scared when I thought we just might freeze to death out there."

"Well, you're safe now," Diana said. "Your room is on the third floor, which is a climb. Hope you don't mind."

"Mind? This place looks like heaven. A place to lay our heads is all we need."

They heard the basement door shut and Ted came around the corner, the folded crib hoisted under his left arm. He extended his other hand. "Evening, folks. Ted Rutherford."

"Name's Hawkins. A crib! Would be fine if he just slept with us, but that's thoughtful."

"Have you eaten?" Diana asked.

"We ate before we started out this morning. Had some snacks along to tide us over."

"Don't you worry," Diana assured them. "We'll fix you something and bring it up right away. Won't be the Christmas dinner your mom might have served you but may taste good if you're hungry."

"By the way . . . " She addressed the young mother. "Not that it's any of my business, but have you called your mom?"

The man cleared his throat before answering. "We don't have a cell phone."

"Well, we do," Ted replied. "I'll bring it up with the food."

"Name's Bud." He cleared his throat. "This is Mary. We're very thankful."

Ted and Diana left them in thirty-two, the small suite with the dormers under the roof. They "oohed" and "ahhed" over the surroundings and the heat now pouring out of the radiators.

"I just knew her name would be Mary, as in mother and child," Diana whispered as she and Ted retreated down the hallway. "And do you know, Ted? I almost told the sheriff no—that we couldn't take them in, being selfish and not wanting anything to detract from a perfect day. But what could be more perfect than room at the inn?"

Ted squeezed her shoulder. "Who else but you would think of that? You're pretty special yourself, sweetheart. Talk about rising to an occasion!"

At the foot of the stairs, they looked toward the entrance and the street beyond. A few vehicles passed in the newly-plowed lanes. The old stone hitching post and the wrought iron hotel sign were both topped with tall white finials.

A heavy-set woman of indeterminate age pushed a grocery cart loaded with trash bags along the newly-shoveled sidewalk. Her coat trailed the ground, a plaid rag tied around her head. She looked their way, her lips curved in a toothless grin. "Merry Christmas," she mouthed.

"Merry Christmas!" they called back in unison.

CHAPTER 18

A BAD COLD KEPT TED home from work. The misery in his head and the boredom of having nothing to do were only part of the problem. He'd felt restless and discombobulated ever since Brad and Charlotte left a week ago. Now he reached for another tissue and asked himself, "What's wrong with me?"

It had been a joy to see his son happy and relaxed. But it wasn't just because of his relationship with Charlotte—great as that was. No, Brad had changed. He was more mature, more grounded somehow.

The day after Christmas, he had helped Brad load their luggage into the car. As they waited for Charlotte, Brad floored him with the last question he would ever expect his son to ask.

"Dad," Brad began, his tone calm, yet serious. "Have you considered your future—where you'll go when you die?"

Ted could not have been more startled if Brad had confessed to being on drugs. "What kind of question is that?" he answered.

Just then Charlotte came out the door, calling back her final goodbyes. Brad opened the car door. "Think about it, Dad," he said. "That's what Char and I are doing. We study the Gospels together . . . read them as letters written to us."

Charlotte hugged Ted, thanked him again, and they were off. He stood at the curb watching the car wend its way down the snow-packed street, wondering if he had heard Brad right, but knowing he had.

"Where will you go when you die?"

It wasn't as if he were a bad person. He had never hurt anyone on purpose, been dishonest or cheated on his wife. Yes, he'd made mistakes, but didn't everyone?

Besides, if God kept a tally, no one would make it to heaven. The Ten Commandments were a good standard to live by, but no one obeyed all of them every minute of every day. All you could do was your best. His dad had often said, "God helps those who help themselves."

At last the Tooses were getting around to redecorating the apartment and Diana was in her element. She deserved it, but he might as well be at work with all the noise going on in the apartment. Maybe he should get out of her hair—go down to the basement and check on the gas again, though the radiators appeared to be working fine.

Before he reached the lobby, a splash of cold water hit the top of his head. He looked up at the hallway ceiling and the next drop caught him on the nose. A dark stain spread over one of the ceiling tiles.

"Diana! The ceiling's leaking."

She was at his side. "Must be coming from twenty-two."

"I'll check." He grabbed the keys and was off at a trot, his head throbbing. "Might be a toilet running over," he called back.

Diana scooted a wastebasket under the drip and followed him. On the second floor, he met her in the hallway. "There's a leak from that ceiling also. Better call a plumber. What's the name of the one that installed James and Emma's furnace?"

"Slovensky." Diana returned downstairs and found the number on her laptop.

"Mr. Slovensky's out right now," the woman told Ted when he called. "I'll send Scotty."

The wastebasket held a good two inches of water before the front bell rang. Ted blew his nose hard as he opened the door to a stout, bearded man wearing faded blue jeans, a red plaid flannel shirt, and an orange and blue Denver Bronco's cap. A beat-up tool belt slung low on his hips. The pickup at the curb read *Slovensky's Plumbing and Heating* on the door.

"Name's Scotty. You must be the new guy Cloomer told me about." He didn't elaborate, and Ted didn't ask.

"Ted Rutherford. We have water dripping through the ceiling in our apartment and another leak in the ceiling of the apartment above it. Must be coming from the third floor."

"Doesn't mean anything." Scotty stroked the short brown beard streaked with gray. "Pipes don't always run straight down. Have to trace 'em. Got a ladder?"

"I'll get it." Ted unlocked the basement door. "Be right back."

"Thank you."

Ted carried the ladder to the second floor with Scotty following. Thankfully, the occupants of twenty-two were out. Ted positioned the ladder under the water stain that now produced a slim, but steady stream.

Scotty climbed the ladder. Then he pulled a hammer from its loop and knocked a hole in the ceiling in one swift motion. Chunks of sodden tile and insulation fell to the floor.

"Hey! Was that necessary?" Ted demanded.

"Want it fixed or not? No time to mess around." Scotty jammed the hammer back in its loop and used both hands to claw the hole wider. "Leak ain't here. Will have take a look upstairs. Need the key."

"I'll go with you." Ted's voice trailed off in a series of coughs.

Scotty carried the ladder this time, banging it twice against the wallpaper on the staircase. Ted caught hold of the back end to guide it. "Careful there," he warned.

"Water won't wait.'"

Ted didn't argue. At thirty-two, he knocked and then used his master key. No obvious leak, but Scotty set up the ladder in the bathroom and chopped another hole.

"Rats! Pipe turns again. Would sure help if I knew how these stinking pipes run."

Of course! Why hadn't he thought of it sooner? "I found the original blueprints in the basement," Ted told him. "Don't do another thing until I come back with them."

"You're the boss." Scotty sat down on the top step of the ladder and pulled a cigar from his shirt pocket.

Ted glared. "No cigar. This room is occupied. The guests could return at any minute."

"Then better make it snappy, Bub."

"Ted's the name." He was out the door and down the stairs two at a time. His headache pounded in his ears. What a nightmare.

The paper cylinders stood in the box where he had found them. Juggling them in his arms, Ted hurried back up to the second floor where he heard a mixture of angry shouts coming from the floor above him.

"Hack?" he called. Hack was putting up new wallpaper in thirty-one.

"Up here! This clown says he's a plumber."

"What's he doing? He was supposed to wait."

Ted reached the third-floor hallway as Hack came storming out of thirty-two, his face livid. "I heard this idiot banging around," he told

Ted, stepping aside for Ted to enter the apartment. "Came to investigate. See for yourself."

Scotty was down on his knees with head and shoulders tucked inside the cabinet beneath the kitchen sink. A pool of water and debris surrounded him.

Ted dropped the blueprints on the kitchen table. "I told you to wait!"

"As I said before, water won't wait. Just doing my job and saving you money. Time's ticking on your bill, you know." He pointed to the pipe. "Problem's right here. I'll have it fixed pronto."

Ted had nothing left to say. He turned back to Hack. "We have guests in twenty-two. There's a big hole in the bathroom ceiling. Can you stop what you're doing and patch it?"

"Stupid idiot," Hack muttered. "I'll do what I can."

Ted addressed Scotty's back beneath the sink. "Mr. Slovensky will hear about this."

Scotty's shoulders shrugged as he reached for a wrench. "You'll get the bill in the mail."

Ted returned to the apartment and grabbed the phone.

"There must be some misunderstanding," Emil Slovensky said, his deep voice calm and soothing. "Our employees are well trained. Has the leak stopped?"

Ted looked up at the ceiling where water no longer dripped. "Well, yes, but—"

"You see?"

"But he caused extensive damage."

"Sometimes inevitable. I believe James Toos pays the bills for Hartwick House. Have him call me if he has any questions."

"I'll do that." Ted slammed the handset into its receiver and turned to Diana. "Can you believe it?"

"What did he say?"

"Just brushed me off. Told me to have James call him if he has any questions."

"Then let Mr. Toos handle it," Diana said.

"James may want Mr. Slovensky to see the damage for himself while Scotty is still here," Ted agreed. Grabbing his jacket, he headed out the side entrance.

Emma answered the door. "I hate to bother James," she said. "We just returned from the doctor and he's resting."

"Emma?" The voice was weak, yet firm. "Tell Ted to come in."

As he stepped inside, Ted began to rethink the urgency of his errand, but James had already thrown back the knitted afghan and was using both hands to push himself to his feet. Shocked at how pale and weak the elderly gentleman appeared, Ted stated the facts without embellishment. As he finished, he pulled a handkerchief from his hip pocket and blew his nose. "I have a cold," he told James by way of apology.

"I can see that. You should be home in bed. Don't worry about the damage. What's done is done. Hack can repair it. As for Slovensky, I handle all their legal work. Things even out over time." He chuckled, the delicate skin around his eyes crinkling like dry creek beds. "As I've told you before, don't take things too serious over there. Both good and bad happen over the years, but good wins out over the long run."

Both mollified and embarrassed that he had made such a big deal of it, Ted thanked James and trudged back home. This was their life now—a series of hassles interspersed now and then with more enjoyable family events.

Right now, all he wanted was a hot shower and a clean bed. Tomorrow he'd discuss future plans with Diana.

CHAPTER 19

DIANA WATCHED THE HEAVY DRAPES fall to the floor in a cloud of dust. Soon after, the pine cone wallpaper tore off in long, satisfying strips. The room appeared to grow bigger and brighter by the minute.

Emma had called the day after Christmas, soon after Brad and Charlotte drove away. "I can't tell you how grateful we were to be included," she said. "Even Henderson was pleased. I wish you could have seen him chewing on the hambone you sent home with us."

"James and I had a long talk about how fortunate we are to have you and Ted in charge of the hotel," she continued. "You've done such a wonderful job updating the apartments. Now it's your turn. This morning I called Best Interiors and asked them to bring over sample books for you to select whatever you want, with their advice if you so desire. We'll do wallpaper and draperies first and carpeting after that. Price is no object."

Diana was overwhelmed. "I don't know what to say. Thank you so much."

"Don't mention it, dear. It's long overdue."

"Most people don't have an eye for the challenge that high ceilings and awkward floor plans present," the decorator told Diana as he concurred with the choices she had made. "They don't consider light, height, and the structural architecture itself. Take the dining alcove, for example. It needs to have a focus of its own and still be integrated into the rest of the room. What you've selected will achieve that."

Diana knew her choices were made easier because of the samples put before her, but the compliment pleased her. When the new drapes and wallpaper were in place and the new carpet installed, the apartment would be much improved.

When the workmen left for lunch, they took the discarded drapes and wallpaper with them, leaving the roller shades in place until the new window treatments were hung. Then the dirty, cracked shades would go as well. Good riddance.

Ted reported his conversation with James about the plumber, declined lunch, and went to bed.

"Rest well," Diana told him. Perhaps she should check on Hattie and see how Hack was coming with the ceiling repair. She had finished the novel Nina Gilmore loaned her. Might as well return it.

Scotty was long gone, and Hattie had much to say about the mess he left behind. Hack was in a similar mood as he patched over the hole in the ceiling of twenty-two. Diana was relieved to get away and arrived at Nina's door instead.

"Coming," Nina called, and the door soon opened. "Oh, it's you, Diana. What a nice surprise."

Diana was surprised by Nina's appearance. Unless she was going out, Nina wore her robe all day with no makeup, her hair limp and skin sallow. Today she had on slacks and a nice blouse and her blonde hair had been washed and curled. Diana even detected the scent of body lotion as she entered the room.

"It's so quiet on the hall since the pilots left," Nina commented as she motioned Diana to a chair. "They used to stop by now and then to play cards. I've been meaning to ask. What do you know about the distinguished-looking man with the mustache in twenty-four?"

"Mr. Churchhouse?" Diana perched on the arm of a chair. She didn't intend to stay long. "I believe he's from someplace back East."

"He told me that much when I met him in the hall yesterday. New York, though he's traveled all over the world, it seems. We compared notes after I mentioned a National Geographic program I watched on India. Is he staying long?"

"He paid for a week, but he told me he might stay longer."

Nina's face registered that as good news. Then she hurried to change the subject. "How's Laurel?"

Laurel had endeared herself to Nina when she insisted Nina join them at Christmas. "I wish my son was that considerate," Nina had said.

A frequent refrain. Yes, Nina was lonely, but Diana couldn't help but think her negative attitude created some of her problems.

"Laurel will be home again in a couple of weeks," Diana told her. Using the word *home* startled her, but wasn't it now? She held out the book. "Thanks for loaning me this. I enjoyed it."

"Can't you stay and visit awhile?"

"I wish I could, but I need to be downstairs when the workmen return."

"Ah, yes. I'm dying to see the apartment when it's finished." She sighed. "I appreciate you taking the time to stop by. You're usually too busy."

Guilt followed Diana down the hall. As she passed twenty-four, she pictured its occupant. Wallace Churchhouse was a polite man who spoke with precise, clipped syllables and walked with a stiff gait, reminding her of a short Henry Higgins. He had stopped by the desk the night before.

"I wanted you to know," he had said, "I'm hoping to stay on a few days, but my week will be up Thursday and I may not have additional funds until Monday when I'm expecting a royalty check in the mail."

"You're a writer?"

"A professor actually, but yes, I've published. Anyway, I'm embarrassed to be in this position, but could you be so kind as to wait until Monday for me to pay for another week? I know it's presumptuous to ask, but as you can see, I'm in something of a predicament."

Diana hesitated. Emma's policy was payment in advance, but she had allowed exceptions before, like the time Vangie Emerson lost her paycheck. "All right," she agreed. "If you're sure you'll have the money on Monday, I'll put you down for another week."

"Thank you, Mrs. Rutherford. That's most generous."

"Please call me Diana."

"It will be my privilege. Diana is one of my favorite names."

Yes, Wallace Churchhouse was an interesting man. No wonder Nina asked about him.

Hack disappeared. He didn't answer Ted's phone calls nor respond to messages. Ted didn't find him at The Lair either. Ruby kept her eyes cast down as she swiped the wide surface of the circular bar with a cloth towel.

"Ain't my business where Hack is," she told him, though Ted suspected she knew more than she let on.

"We can't rent thirty-one the way he left it," Diana complained when Ted returned with the news. "The wallpaper is only halfway done."

Ted heaved a deep sigh. Being Saturday, he needed to take the car to be washed. After that, he wanted to join a friend from work who played drums and wanted Ted to join a jam session in his basement.

"I'll try to track him down," he told Diana. "If I knew Fern's number, I'd call her, but I don't and if Ruby does, she probably wouldn't give it to me."

Hack's address led him to a small brick house only a few blocks over. A shoveled sidewalk and open drapes were good signs. Ted knocked.

Hack looked terrible. Dark semi-circles beneath his eyes, a scraggly mustache and flushed complexion hinted of someone on a recent binge.

"'Lo, Ted."

"We've been trying to call you."

"Sorry. Not answering the phone. Not listenin' to messages either."

"You okay?"

"Yeah." He paused and then raised his eyes to Ted's for the first time. "Had a fight with Fern again. She wants me to quit drinking and I can't. Besides, who's she to tell me what to do?"

"Maybe she cares about you. I thought you two got along well."

"Yeah? Well, not so much anymore."

"Sorry to hear that." Ted cleared his throat. "Listen, Hack. Diana needs you to finish in thirty-one."

"Yeah. I'll be around on Monday." The door closed, and Ted left.

Hack arrived mid-morning, his mustache trimmed, but still not the Hack Diana expected. *None of my business.*

He filled out his time sheet and left to climb the stairs to thirty-one. He didn't even comment on the changes in the apartment. Not like him at all.

When she went up before noon, she found him gathering his tools.

"Looks great," she told him.

"Yeah. Sorry it took so long."

"And I'm sorry you're going through a bad time." Instead of just going through the motions, Diana realized she meant it.

Hack looked down, not straightforward like usual. "Just as well to find out now as later," he muttered.

"Find out?"

"About Fern. She can't mind her own business."

"If she cares for you, maybe it *is* her business."

Hack clapped the stepladder shut, hoisted it under one arm, and stooped to pick up his tool kit with the other hand. "Let me know when you need me."

End of subject. Diana followed him down the hallway. "Don't forget to sign your time sheet," she reminded. "It's good to have you back."

A grunt came out as his only reply. Hack hit the second-floor landing before Diana made it halfway down.

Finished, the workmen gathered their things, shook Diana's hand and left with a job well done. Diana took a deep breath and surveyed the apartment. The peach-colored drapes complemented the wallpaper on the far wall and in the dining alcove. Peach stripes alternated with vertical rows of delicate green vines against a pale green background. The pale green on the other walls would blend nicely with the jade carpet to be laid next week.

"Must be nice," Hattie grunted when she signed out for the day and Diana let it go at that.

A bottle of wine chilled in the fridge and the table held candles ready to light. They would drink a toast to their cozy new surroundings. Then Ted could go off to join the group at another of their jam sessions, and she would be happy for him.

CHAPTER 20

THE WIND BLEW BITTER COLD, but Emma hardly noticed as she climbed the front steps of the duplex and rang the bell. With James still feeling poorly, she had almost stayed home, but she would cut the time short instead.

Joshua took her coat and hung it in the closet. "Is Uncle James feeling better?" he asked.

After all these years, Emma still experienced a jolt when Joshua referred to his own father as "uncle." Once again, she asked herself if it would have been kinder to tell him the truth from the time he was old enough to understand. Perhaps that would have lessened the other lies—that James was his uncle, that he wasn't well, and it took all her strength to care for him and run the hotel as well.

She had never told Joshua when they left the hotel to move next door and, in all the years, Joshua had never tried to find her there. Sometimes she wondered about that, but he appeared content with her weekly visits and, of course much credit went to the unselfish devotion of the Sheedys, truly remarkable people. Joshua's life revolved around work and home and her weekly visits.

Of course, the Sheedys had their telephone number, but she could trust them to tell Joshua no more than she did. Often she wondered what Alma and Riley must think of her, but their love for Joshua took precedence. They would never do anything to hurt him.

Today, Joshua had something new to tell her. "I made a new friend, Mother. His name's Sam. You must know his mother. She works at Hartwick House."

Emma felt her body tense. She paused before replying, but Joshua continued.

"They shop at Safeway and one day Sam saw me lift a heavy box and told me I had strong muscles. I told him I work out in my basement and guess what? He lives only two blocks from here. So, I invited him over to see my equipment and now he comes twice a week so we can work out together."

"Does his mother bring him?"

"Oh no, he just walks here. I like having a new friend. The Bible says, 'A friend loves at all times.' That's how it is with Sam and me."

Emma let her breath. "That's wonderful. I'm glad you have a new friend, Son."

"Do you have friends, Mother?"

It was the most personal question he had ever asked her. She must not let him down. "Yes, Joshua," she answered. "I've told you about Cousin Fanny. She's my friend and I have others as well." She busied herself with putting on her coat and preparing to leave. "If you're walking with me to the bus stop, you'd better get your coat. It's cold out."

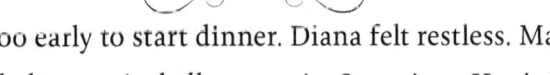

It was too early to start dinner. Diana felt restless. Maybe she should check the upstairs hallways again. Sometimes Hattie left a rag here, a glass there.

She climbed the stairs and made the rounds of the hallways, then headed back down to the lobby. As usual, she stopped to view the garden and was surprised to find the sky so dark, casting shadows on the carpet though it was only four o'clock. Sensors had triggered the street lights. She shivered, crossing her arms to hug herself even though the radiators clanked out the necessary warmth.

She trailed her hand on the railing and circled the banister post to cross the lobby. That's when she saw him in the entrance, his back to her as he looked back toward the street. No one she recognized, so he must have walked in behind a guest—or maybe caught the door when someone left. He stood very still.

"May I help you?" Her own voice startled her, as it did him. He jerked away from the door and turned toward her, his brown eyes large. "Sorry," she apologized.

The man smiled, and Diana could see how handsome he was. He wore navy slacks, a white knit shirt, and gold suede jacket and a squashed cap with a bill—more English than American.

"Actually, yes," he answered. "I debated whether to eat first, but it looks like snow, so I think I need to get settled. This looks like a nice place."

It was then she saw the blinking red light reflected off the window. Probably some disturbance at the liquor store down the block. There was often trouble there.

The man came up the steps to the lobby. "Do you have a room I could see?"

"We have a vacant suite on the third floor—no elevator if you don't mind the climb."

"Not at all."

Diana led the way, aware of his soft tread behind her. She hadn't thought him a big man, but his shadow loomed large on the wall. Most of the apartments were rented, but the place was quiet. She imagined that he stared at the back of her neck and the skin prickled there so that she had to concentrate to keep her hands at her sides.

On the third floor, she handed him the key to number thirty-two. "It's at the end of the hall," she told him. "I'll wait here for you."

"Fine," he answered. She watched as he fit the key in the lock and went inside. Shortly he returned. "Very nice. How much?"

"Sixty." The rate was fifty-five, but for some reason she had upped it.

"Okay. More than I'd hoped, but I need the central location. I'll take it."

This time she stepped aside for him to precede her down the steps. How silly. He seemed perfectly respectable. *It's just the cloudy day and the utter stillness.* As they crossed the lobby, she noticed that the red light no longer flashed outside on the street.

Arriving at the desk, she placed the pen on the registration form. "If you'll fill this out, I'll write your receipt. Cash or credit?" All business now, she turned away to unlock the apartment door and retrieve the cash box.

She had it in hand when she heard the gate by the counter swing on its hinges and turned back to see why. The blood drained from her face when that which she had never dreamt to behold appeared inches from her nose. Then her cheek slammed hard into the barrel of the black revolver.

"Give me all the money." He was perspiring, his face pale and void of expression. "I'm desperate," he told her. "Don't try anything."

Diana set the box on the counter, amazed to find her hands steady. "Please put the gun away," she said, her voice almost a whisper. How could her voice remain so steady when she shook so inside? "We have guests on this floor."

The man lowered the gun and shoved the hand that held it inside his open jacket. "Okay but make it fast. Show me the money. I want it all."

Not seeing the gun helped. She worked the combination, opened the box, and scooped up the bills followed by quarters, dimes, and even nickels. As she did so, his left hand deposited them into the pockets of his jacket. Then he turned and fled, the floorboards groaning under his running feet. At the end of the lobby, he turned toward the front door. She heard the crash bar slam against it and knew he was gone.

Only then did she start to shake all over. With difficulty, she punched 911 and listened as the dispatcher told her an officer would be there shortly. And he was. Diana heard the siren whine to a stop out front and hurried to the door to open it.

"We were down the block at the liquor store," the officer told her. "Sounds like the same guy who tried to hold it up. Got scared off there— probably ducked in here to get out of sight."

"Of course . . . the flashing red light!"

"Nothing new in this neighborhood." The stocky policeman took down the description Diana gave and flipped the fat notebook shut, forcing it back into his hip pocket. "My men are searching the grounds, but most likely they won't find him. Still want you to come down to the station and look at mug shots. Will be helpful if we know he has a record."

"I doubt if he has." Diana was calm again now. She found what had just happened hard to believe. "He seemed newly desperate, like he'd never done something like this before."

"Plenty like that these days. Too many people out of work. Anyway, you did the right thing. Never argue with a gun." He touched the brim of his hat and turned to leave just as Ted burst in the side door.

"What happened? I got off work early. Why are policemen searching the bushes outside?"

"Your name, Sir?"

"Ted Rutherford—this is my wife." He turned to Diana. "What's going on? Are you all right?"

"Your wife's a brave lady. The place got robbed, but I'll let her fill you in. Come down to the station tomorrow, Ma'am—35th and Tennyson. Anytime."

Ted started to follow the policeman out, but Diana pulled on his coat sleeve. "I am all right, Ted. I really am. I know it sounds crazy, but I couldn't help but feel sorry for him. I am positive he's not a hardened criminal."

"And that excuses him for what he did?" His voice rose in pitch, incredulous.

"No, of course not. I'm just saying these are desperate times and he was a desperate man."

"That's the problem, Diana. You rationalize everything—make excuses for anything that happens. And whenever I bring up the subject of leaving, you say 'Not yet.' When is 'yet'?" Ted peeled off his topcoat and hurled it toward the couch.

Diana felt heat in her neck. "And if we did leave, then what? We can't afford to buy a house yet. Where would we go?"

"We could rent an apartment. At least we'd have a saner lifestyle." Ted was pacing now—like a caged lion.

"Maybe I like life not being so predictable. We're providing a real service here. Just the other day—"

"Oh brother!" Ted drew the word out in disgust. "Spare me. How can you be so naïve? One thing after the next happens and you remain as gullible as ever."

"Bright side? That's not fair. You make me sound like a child. Yes, I get discouraged at times—like anyone does. But this is real life here and real people, Ted—good and bad—"

"Real people also live in normal neighborhoods," Ted interrupted. "People that mow their lawns, pay their bills. We've been in this place over six months. I have a good job and we've put some money in savings. I should have put my foot down weeks ago and given the Tooses our notice."

"That wouldn't be fair. They depend on us. James isn't well, and Emma isn't as strong as she would like you to think. Besides, look at all they've done for us."

Ted barely gave his new surroundings a glance. "It's the old 'carrot and stick' ploy," he said. "Emma gives you a free hand to fix things up, but then says you can't get rid of Hattie. She butters you up for making a good impression at her little reception, so you'll forget all the extra work it required. Don't be so naïve!"

"I don't call what I've accomplished *naïve*. Obviously, I've found rewards in achievements you can't—or won't—recognize nor understand."

"I'll admit you've done a great job here, Diana. But it's time to move on. I'm telling the Tooses tomorrow that we're leaving March fifteenth. That's the sixty day notice we agreed to." He turned on his heel and headed toward the bedroom, stripping off his tie as he did so.

"And if I decide to stay?" Diana's cheeks were hot. She held her breath, wanting to take the words back, yet not doing so.

The wall clock ticked off the seconds. "I can't believe you'd do that," Ted replied.

CHAPTER 21

TED APOLOGIZED OVER OATMEAL SPRINKLED with blueberries. "I'm sorry I flew off the handle. It's just that I felt so helpless—like I should have been here instead of you. Or better still, never have brought us here in the first place."

"I talked you into this job, remember? But I still say a robbery can happen anywhere."

"More likely here and you know it. But I must say, you were far more level-headed than I would have been."

"As I told you, I felt a strange sense of peace—as if I wasn't in any real danger."

"Well I'm sorry I flew off the handle like I did," Ted told her. "You deserve a barrel of credit for what you've accomplished here and any decision to leave must be made by us both. I'm going to tell James we'll stay on a month to month basis. But one day soon we're moving on, Diana. We need a real home, a place where our children and someday our grandchildren can visit, with a yard and neighbors."

Diana circled the table and placed a kiss on top of his head. "Thanks, sweetheart. And concerning Brad's remark, maybe it's time we found a church to attend."

Ted nodded, but his thoughts strayed away to his work day and what he needed to accomplish. First things first.

Kate Danson called mid-morning. "Are you all right?" she asked. "I felt this urgent need to pray for you yesterday afternoon."

"I'm fine." Diana almost left it at that, but then felt compelled to pour out the story. How could Kate's concern be only coincidence?

"The Bible tells us to pray for one another," Kate replied. "I'm so thankful God protected you. We also need to pray for that poor young man."

"Oh yes, of course. I'll bring it up at Bible study next week."

"That would be good," Kate replied, her voice gentle, affirming. "But you and I don't have to wait. We can pray here on the phone right now."

As she bowed her head, Diana's cheeks burned hot. She knew Kate wasn't being rude. It's just that she felt so ignorant of things she should know.

Before she said good-bye, Kate asked how their apartment looked. At Bible study that week Diana had shared with the group concerning the transformation taking place.

"Stop by and see it," Diana invited as she heard Hack's rap on the side door.

"I will," Kate replied.

Hack appeared in a better mood as he surveyed the changes. "Glad to see the Tooses show some appreciation. Fixing up your place is the least they could do, in my opinion."

Diana wanted to ask about Fern but instead she gave him a brief account of the holdup.

"I'm not surprised," he said. "When the Tooses ran the place, Henderson scared off the riffraff. Adds another example of how lucky they are to have you guys. Most folks would *vamoose pronto*."

She didn't tell him about Ted's initial reaction. "I'm leaving to look at photos down at the police station," she told him. "Fanny is coming to watch the desk."

"Mug shots? Waste of time."

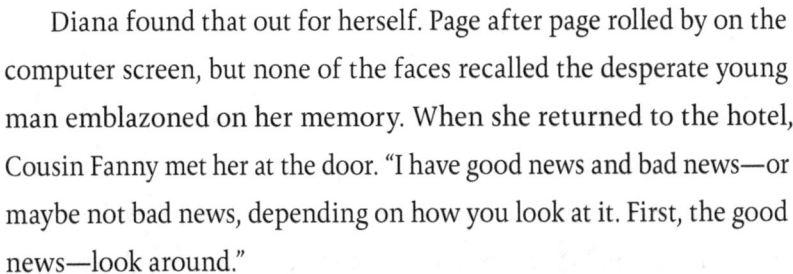

Diana found that out for herself. Page after page rolled by on the computer screen, but none of the faces recalled the desperate young man emblazoned on her memory. When she returned to the hotel, Cousin Fanny met her at the door. "I have good news and bad news—or maybe not bad news, depending on how you look at it. First, the good news—look around."

On their knees, the carpet layers worked to stretch and tack down a lush expanse of jade green carpet. "It's going to be lovely, isn't it?" Diana exclaimed but then she hurried on to ask, "And the bad news?"

"Soon after you left, Hattie called. She thinks it's shingles, which I doubt, but she's going to the clinic to find out. Says she broke out with a rash, but that could be anything. Anyway, I took the liberty of calling Standby, but they're already out of temporary help. I'm sorry, Diana."

Diana sighed. That meant maid duty for her. "Could you stay a while longer, Fanny? Watch the desk?"

"You know I will. I've nothing else to do."

Diana trudged to the supply closet, sorted out towels she would need, and piled them in the crook of her left arm. She grabbed a black trash bag, hoisted the cleaning caddy, and trudged up the stairs to start at the top and work her way down.

The guests in thirty-one only wanted towels. She visited for a few minutes with the young couple, learning that both came to town for job interviews. She wished them well, emptied their wastebaskets, and dragged the bag behind her down to the second floor. Just in time to see Nina Gilmore open her door for Wallace Churchhouse and close it behind him. *Interesting.* Possibly Nina wouldn't want room service today.

Just then Vangie Emerson burst out of number twenty-five and almost collided with her. "I'm so sorry, Mrs. R. I worked the night shift at the restaurant and then overslept. Today's my closing on the townhouse and I can't be late."

"Go for it, Vangie. But you know we'll miss you when you leave."

"Don't worry. I'll pop back in often. You're like family to me now."

"We'll count on it," Diana told her." She knew Vangie left her room neat, but she would vacuum and dust, clean the kitchen and bathroom and collect the trash. She wanted Vangie's happy memories of Hartwick House to linger and pull her back. As she closed the door, she heard Nina's high-pitched laughter at the end of the hall. How nice to hear it

The carpet layers left, and Diana ate the tasty lunch Fanny conjured up.

"The carpet's lovely, isn't it?" Diana commented.

"Won't Laurel love it?" Fanny finished her salad and helped herself to a slice of Diana's red velvet cake. "By the way, what's she been up to?"

"Well, she's dating someone named David. A pre-law student."

"That's interesting. And Brad and Charlotte?"

"Fine, I guess. You know Brad. We're lucky to get the bare essentials. But I got a nice note from Charlotte the other day. I only hope Brad knows what a jewel she is."

Then the phone rang.

"Diana?" Hattie's voice carried its usual whine. "Turns out I'm right. It's shingles—bad! Could be out for weeks. Can't sleep, can't eat. Hurts somethin' terrible, Boss."

"I'm sure it does." Diana tried hard to sound sympathetic. "Did the doctor give you something for the pain?"

"Yep, but it ain't helpin' none. Do you think I can apply for disability?"

"I wouldn't know. I'll call Standby and find someone to help out 'til you return. I hope the medicine works and you're feeling better soon."

"Doubt it. Can't sleep, can't eat . . . I'm downright miserable . . ."

What kind of replacement will Standby send? Couldn't be worse than Hattie.

Margie worked overtime on the weekend. She bemoaned the hardship Hattie's sickness imposed on Diana and vowed to help in any way she could.

"I've stocked the closets with clean linens," she reported as she signed out late Sunday afternoon. "Changed all the beds, even if they weren't due. Wanted everything ship-shape for the new help to start fresh tomorrow morning. I'll be prayin' they send the right person, Mrs. R."

"Bless you, Margie." Yes, Margie would think of praying when she hadn't.

"I'll be prayin' for Hattie, too," Margie added. "Shingles can be mighty painful, I hear."

Another need I've overlooked, thinking only of myself. It's as if I've blamed Hattie for getting shingles in the first place. How did one get a handle on prayer without being a hypocrite concerning one's motives? Would she ever get it right?

CHAPTER 22

PROMPTLY AT NINE O'CLOCK, THE front door buzzer alerted Diana to the new maid's arrival. "I'm Cassie from Standby," the young woman said.

With green eyes and a long blonde ponytail from which ringlets strayed at the temples, Laurel would call her a knock-out.

"I can come here for as long as you need me," she said.

Diana found herself drawn to Cassie's wide smile. Talk about answered prayer, or at least what appeared to be. "Welcome. I'm Diana Rutherford, the hotel manager. Please come on in and sit down and I'll explain what the job entails."

Cassie followed her into the apartment and perched on the edge of the couch as she surveyed the room. "What a surprise!" she exclaimed. "Coming from the bus stop, the building looked really old. I didn't think it would be this nice." She stopped and put her hand over her mouth. "Oh dear. I didn't mean . . . I talk too much."

Diana laughed. "I think you'll find it a pleasant environment. Margie, our weekend maid, worked extra hard this weekend so you could get off to a good start. She changed all the beds, so you would have time today to acquaint yourself with the job and not feel hurried. Have you done this type of work before?"

"Not in a nice place like this. Only for hot-sheet hotels."

"Hot sheet?"

"Yeah, you know—couples check in and leave and you have to go back and change the bed before someone else checks in later."

How naïve I remain.

"Well, you won't find that here." She smiled to herself, remembering Ted's call girls. "We'll fill in your time sheet. Then I'll help you get started."

Three short raps signaled Fanny's arrival, planned so Diana could get the new girl off to a good start that morning. "Emma's paying me," Fanny said. "Says it's the hotel's responsibility, not yours."

Diana introduced her to Cassie.

"You're a young'un," Fanny remarked, direct as always.

"Twenty-one," Cassie told her. She stood, tugging her sweater down over her ample chest and shifting her hips in the tight jeans. "Just moved here from a boring little town in South Dakota. Bound to be more action here."

"Action?" Fanny's eyebrows shot into an inverted V.

"You know. Excitement. Fun." Cassie giggled, a cute dimple appearing in her cheek.

"After work, you mean."

"Oh yes, after work. I'm all business on the job."

"Good." Fanny winked at Diana and turned away to hang up her coat.

By the time Diana returned to eat the lunch Fanny had prepared, the workmen had replaced the baseboards. The lush expanse of carpet took away her tiredness.

Fanny shared her news: "Emma popped over. Told me about the robbery and how terrible they felt. Said Ted had every right to be upset—lesser people would leave forthwith."

If she only knew.

"Also," Fanny continued, drawing out the drama. "She told the carpet layers to leave the side entry hall bare as they've decided to put hardwood laminate there as well as in the kitchen. How about that?"

Diana opened her mouth to express her delight, but just then the desk bell rang. She turned to see Wallace Churchhouse standing at the desk.

"I'm so sorry, my dear," he began. "I'm afraid I have only half the amount I promised. By the end of the third printing, I guess readership dwindles." He sighed, looking down as if unable to meet her eyes. Then he straightened his shoulders and brought new strength to his words. "However, I'm interviewing for a job for which I'm amply qualified . . . in the English department at the university."

Diana waited, unsure how to respond.

"Perhaps I should explain further. My wife, mother of my two sons, left me after twenty-seven years of what I believed to be a happy marriage. Totally shocked and devastated, I resigned my teaching position—impulsively, I admit, feeling compelled to leave New York and its painful reminders."

It sounded rehearsed and Diana wondered if he'd told the same thing to Nina.

"I let my wife have everything," he continued. "I still love her, you see, and, after all, she must make a new start."

Diana knew the stress of launching a new beginning. It touched her that Wallace Churchhouse, a gentleman so reticent and unassuming, would take her into his confidence, yet she felt uneasy about extending him credit. She counted the bills he laid out and prepared a receipt. "Are you sure you'll have the rest in only a few days?"

"Oh, most assuredly. I won't rest until I can pay you in full."

When Diana returned to the apartment, Fanny raised her eyebrows, but for once refrained from comment. "I'll see myself out," she said.

Cassie worked out fine. She ate lunch down the street at The Lair, but Diana never detected anything on her breath and she always returned on time.

At the end of the week, Hattie reported her continued woe. Diana felt guilty, admitting to herself she wasn't in a hurry for Hattie to return. Things were going along so well.

The buzzer sounded at the front door and Diana went to answer it.

"I'm Ruby. From the bar down the street. Believe we met that time you came to fetch Hack."

"Yes?"

"I need to reserve a room for one of our customers. Name's Branson."

"And where is Mr. Branson?"

"Havin' a beer at The Lair." Ruby frowned as if it were none of Diana's business. "Any a problem with that? He don't want to bother you with comin' in late, that's all." She held up a Visa card for Diana to view. "Sent me over to pay and get a key."

Diana held the door for the middle-aged woman to pass in front of her. "Just seems odd that Mr. Branson didn't come himself," she observed.

"Now see here, lady." Ruby turned, placing her fists at the sides of her ample waist. "Toby ain't a bit odd. He's a real gentleman. 'Case you think he's some drunk off the street, you're wrong. In fact, it so happens he's a big shot. The only time you'd know it, though, is when he's buyin' rounds for everyone. He just hankers after gettin' away onc't in awhile . . . where he can be his own self."

Ruby marched ahead to the desk and slapped the card down on it. "Not that you can understand that," she sneered, "bein' so 'hifalutin' and all. Do you have a room or don't cha?"

Diana picked up the card and looked at the name—Albert R. Branson. "I'll have to call for authorization," she said.

"So do it. I can't be gone all day."

The card cleared. "All right," Diana told her. "I'll give you the key, but Mr. Branson will have to stop by the desk to register."

"I'll tell him. May be mornin' though. He might be late getting over here tonight." Ruby snatched the key and the credit card and dropped them in the pocket of her apron. She crossed the lobby and started down the steps to the front door before she craned her head around the corner and called back. "Almost forgot. Is this here room on the first floor?"

"Yes, it is, as a matter of fact. Number five. Why?"

"Good. He 'specially wants the first floor." Diana heard the front door close and Ruby was gone.

Diana found Hack in number twenty-one repairing a towel rack. As she approached, she heard the conversation through the open door. "Yeah," Hack said. "Something's always busted around here. Last week some jerk took a rung from a kitchen chair to prop open a window in thirty-two."

"You're kidding! Well, I guess you can fix anything. I could tell that right off."

"Oh yeah? How's that?"

"Those muscles and the confident look about you."

Diana entered the room and Cassie jumped up from the chair. "Mrs. Rutherford! I'm just now finished in here . . . heading up to the third floor."

"Good."

Cassie made a quick exit and Diana turned to Hack. "Looks solid. Will it hold?"

"You bet."

"I've a question for you."

"Fire away."

"Do you know a person named Albert Branson?"

"Who?"

"Albert Branson. According to Ruby, he's a customer at The Lair. She came over to book him a room for the night."

"You mean Toby. Toby Branson. So good old Tobe's back. Been awhile."

"Has he stayed here before?" Diana asked

"Yeah, Cloomer put him up a couple of times. He's a big shot rancher over on the Western Slope. Has a wife and family. Drives a Mercedes and boasts lots of important connections. Says now and then he has a hankerin' to have a good time with ordinary folk, so he comes to Denver and ties one on. Wanted a room on the first floor, right?"

"How did you know?"

"That's a must with him. By closing' time, he can't navigate stairs. But don't worry. He won't give you trouble. Just comes and goes, smooth as can be."

Hack gathered his tools and Diana followed him out of the room. "How are things with you and Fern?" she asked.

"Need to ask her. Better, I guess. Serving Mexican food at The Lair tonight, so she'll be there. Should be a blast now that Toby's back buyin' drinks for the house."

On Saturday morning, Diana had errands to run. Before leaving, she put a note under the door of number five asking Mr. Branson to please stop by the desk. Upon returning, she asked Ted if he had stopped by.

"No, but the bartender called. Mr. Branson's staying another night. Same room."

Diana checked the computer. "I have someone else . . . arriving this afternoon."

"Can you rearrange it?"

"Probably."

Just then Margie came out of number five. "Whoever's staying in this apartment is neat as a pin. Makes the bed. Used one towel . . . razor and toothbrush lined up just so on the sink."

"Nevertheless," Diana said. "I'm going to The Lair . . . take this mysterious Mr. Branson the registration form and get his signature. It's illegal for him to stay here without registering."

"I'll go," Ted replied. He took the form from Diana's hand and headed out the door before she could say another word. "I want to meet this character."

CHAPTER 23

ONCE INSIDE, TED MADE STRAIGHT for Ruby. "Is Albert Branson here?" he asked her.

"Toby?" She waved her hand toward a table in the corner where several men clustered around a poker game—some playing their cards, others watching. The robust man sitting against the wall had to be who he was looking for. Like Ted's own father, the weathered skin and muscular build fit that of a rancher—a wealthy one. He wore an expensive suede jacket and snakeskin cowboy boots crossed at the ankles and propped on a chair next to him. Mugs and a half-full pitcher of beer sat on the table.

The men looked up from their cards as Ted approached. Toby was the one to speak.

"Hello, stranger. Want to join in?" Toby's deep voice and lazy way of speaking conveyed his self-confidence.

"No thanks," Ted answered, extending his hand. He judged Toby to be about fifty. "I'm Ted Rutherford. My wife manages the hotel. She needs you to sign this registration form."

Toby stood to shake Ted's hand. "Toby Branson. Nice to meet you." Then he turned to his tablemates. "How about that?" he drawled. "This poor guy had to go to all the trouble to come here just to get my signature." He raised a hand to signal Ruby. "I owe him a drink, don't you think?"

Heat rose in Ted's neck. He felt like a teenage errand boy. "No thanks." He laid the form down on the table, kicking himself for not bringing a pen. "Just fill this out please and I'll be on my way."

"Just an oversight." Toby reached inside his jacket to remove an expensive-looking pen. "Cloomer always took care of it and I assumed . . . "

"Cloomer's not in charge anymore."

"I can see that." Toby took the form and scribbled on it, then handed it back to Ted. "There you are, my fine friend. No hard feelings?"

"None."

"Good. Sorry for the trouble."

"No trouble. Thanks."

Toby sat back down, and the game resumed. Ted walked toward the door, feeling the stares that followed him. This is what he meant by their position here. Always some dumb quirk to deal with.

Toby called after him. "Didn't catch your name."

"Ted. Ted Rutherford."

"I'm checking out Monday morning, Ted, but I need to reserve the same room again for next weekend. I'm not usually back in town so soon, but this time I have some unfinished business."

Ted saw the men at the table exchange quick glances, then return to their cards.

"I'll tell my wife. She's the one who runs the hotel."

"Thanks," Toby called after him. Ted kept walking.

Ted strode back down the street and climbed the steps two at a time. At last he entered the apartment and laid the signed form in front of Diana.

"Thanks," Diana said without looking up from the computer. "Before he leaves, I'll make sure he knows he must register himself next time."

"Oh, there'll be a next time," Ted told her. "Next Friday—same room."

Diana flipped the screen to the registration schedule. "Can't do. That room was promised to Mrs. Turner weeks ago. She comes every year to see her tax man."

The next morning Diana watched for Toby Branson to leave his room. He came out a little after eight. She hadn't expected him to be so distinguished-looking.

"I hope everything was satisfactory?" she asked.

"Oh yes. Very pleasant. In fact, I plan to be back next Friday . . . the same room, if possible. Maybe your husband told you . . . or maybe not."

"I'm sorry," Diana said. "He did tell me, but number five is reserved for another party. The only room I have available is on the second floor—one of our deluxe suites that I'm sure you'd find very comfortable."

He appeared to be considering for a long moment before shrugging the shoulders of his leather jacket and hoisting his suitcase. "That'll be fine," he told her.

"Oh, and Mr. Branson . . . " Diana called after him. "I must insist you register yourself next time."

He turned and bowed, sweeping back his honey-colored cowboy hat in courtly fashion before replacing it on his head.

Margie came down the hall and went into number five to collect the towels. Then she burst back out of the room Toby vacated while Diana still stood at the desk.

"Look it here!" she exclaimed, holding up a fifty-dollar bill. "Course, most of it belongs to Cassie, but I never seen the likes."

Diana was impressed as well. "I'll make change and put Cassie's share in her pay envelope. She'll be as surprised as you are."

But when she came on Monday, Cassie simply smiled and pocketed the tip. "Knew Tobe was a big spender."

Hack came up the steps to the lobby just then, having entered the front door with the key Diana had recently given him. "Came for my paycheck," he said. "Then I'm goin' back home to bed."

"Are you sick, Hack?"

"Sick and tired, you might say. Fed up to here." He used his index finger to make a slash across his throat.

"What's wrong?"

"Ask Fern." Hack stuffed the pay envelope into his shirt pocket. "She's got all the answers. She and Toby."

"You're talking about Albert Branson and Fern?"

"That's right. Two-timing lovebirds."

"I happen to know Fern is fond of you," Diana protested, having chatted with Fern when she came by after work and waited for Hack.

"Nah . . . all that money's turned her head." He turned to go. "There's other fish in the sea."

Right then Cassie came out of number five with an armful of towels and sheets. "Why so down in the mouth, big boy? A handsome dude like you ought to be fixin' to paint the town again."

Hack stroked his chin and fixed her with his eyes. She held his gaze. "Want to help me do that?" he drawled.

"Thought you'd never ask." They walked away together, Hack's face turned toward hers.

Diana shook her head. Hack must be forty-five to Cassie's twenty-one.

The phone rang, and Diana went back inside to answer it. "I'm a mite better," Hattie twanged, "but still poorly. You cain't imagine how much I hurt."

Diana forced herself to summon sympathy. "I'm sure shingles can be very painful."

"Who's workin' in my place?"

"Her name's Cassie, from Standby."

"Same one every day?"

"So far."

"I *am* comin' back, you know."

"Yes, I know," Diana answered, "but get well first." She hung up the phone with a sigh. Though fickle and flirtatious, Cassie was so much better.

On Friday, Laurel burst in late afternoon. "I'm dying to see," she said before flinging her arms in the air and drawing in her breath. "What a transformation! Remember the day we arrived here and found all those pansies?"

Diana managed a smile. It had taken her months to erase that image from her mind.

"It's so spacious now—so inviting," Laurel went on. "Mr. and Mrs. Toos must think the world of you and Dad or they wouldn't have gone to all this expense."

"Well, maybe," Diana replied. "It's your father's opinion they know they need to update to get decent replacements when we leave."

"What?" Laurel's brown eyes grew even larger. "Are you thinking of leaving?"

"Nothing immediate, but probably someday." Diana hurried to change the subject. "Now what about David?"

Laurel's eyes sparkled. "As a matter of fact . . . " She paused, as if for dramatic effect. "He's driving up from Boulder tomorrow—wants to stop by to meet you and Dad. And see Hartwick House, of course. He's heard me go on and on about it, so he wants to see if it's real or just a figment of my imagination."

Diana laughed. "Text him and tell him to come for lunch."

Laurel clapped her hands. "Will do."

The desk bell rang, and Diana left to greet Toby Branson, handing him the pen to sign the register and turning to get the key. "Number twenty-two," she told him.

Laurel strolled out of the apartment and extended her hand. "You must be Mr. Branson," she said. "Laurel Rutherford. I grew up on the western slope."

The suede hat tipped. "My pleasure, Miss Rutherford. Anyone raised in God's country is at the top of my list."

"Welcome to Hartwick House," Laurel answered, enjoying the role she borrowed from Emma.

Ted heard the exchange as he returned from work and entered the side door. "Don't be taken in," he told Laurel when she came back in the apartment. "He's a gambler and a drunk. I don't trust him."

"Oh, Dad. He can't be that bad." She hurried to change the subject. "I also hope to meet Wallace Churchhouse, Nina Gilmore's friend. I hope he's the real deal."

"What do you mean?" Diana looked up from where she was updating Cassie's hours on the computer.

"I don't know. You said Nina glows when he's around and I don't want her to get hurt."

"They're just friends," Diana replied, her eyes back on the screen. "She's lonesome and he's going through some tough times himself."

"Yeah, you're probably right, Mom," Laurel agreed, but she still sounded wary and Diana admitted to herself that she harbored her own concerns.

Laurel read in bed late into the night, snug in her tiny room under the eaves. The lights of the city twinkled far beyond her gabled window. All remained quiet until she heard a woman's voice at the far end of the hallway.

"Toby, are you sure this is the right floor? Let me see your key."

Laurel got out of bed, turned off the light, and carefully turned the knob to open her door just a crack. Down the hall, Toby Branson's arm draped over Fern's shoulders. Hack's girlfriend! Fern staggered a bit to keep her balance as she took the key from Toby's hand.

"It's twenty-two, not thirty-two. We're on the wrong floor."

Laurel closed her door, ever so careful. How could it be? Fern and Toby Branson? The thought made her sad. Poor Hack.

Near noon the next day, Margie reported to Diana. "Can't get in number twenty-two. Man says to leave him alone."

"It's all right, Margie. Mr. Branson is staying over."

"Mom," Laurel interjected. "Last night I heard—" But just then a knock sounded at the side entrance and Diana hurried to open the door and welcome David.

Boys had flocked around Laurel for years, but Laurel had never taken any of them seriously—until now. Laurel had mentioned him being a star basketball player in high school, but Diana was still surprised to find him so tall. Laurel came only to his shoulder.

He tipped Laurel's chin back with his index finger and leaned over to kiss her fully on the lips. "Hi, Babe. So, this is Hartwick House. From your many descriptions, I would have recognized it anywhere. And this must be your mom. Hi, I'm David . . . David Miles."

"I gathered that," Diana smiled. "I'm very glad to meet you, David." He wasn't as handsome as some others Laurel had dated, but the wide smile and dark eyes looking straight back into hers formed an instant bond. Diana felt as if she had known him a long time.

"Come on in," she said. "Laurel's dad ran an errand, but he'll be back any minute." She noticed how Laurel kept her eyes fastened on David's face.

When Ted returned, the two men exchanged hearty handshakes and over lunch talked of David's interest in the study of law. Ted told him of James Toos and the respect he had earned as a Denver attorney. "He's semi-retired," Ted said. "In his late seventies and in poor health. Has his office in his home now and his long-time secretary—Nora by name—comes every day to open the mail and help him remain in contact with his clients."

"Ah yes, James and Emma Toos. Laurel told me all about them."

"Fairly, I hope. They're fine people."

"She makes them sound a bit eccentric, but I know how much she admires them."

"Do your parents still live in Greely?" Diana asked.

"My mother is an English professor at the University of Northern Colorado. My father was a police officer. He was killed during a drug bust when I was ten."

"How terrible!" Diana gasped. "I'm so sorry."

Laurel reached to squeeze David's hand. Diana remembered doing the same when Ted's father died in the plane crash. They're in love. Really in love.

On Monday, Cassie didn't show. She also didn't answer her phone after many rings and Standby hadn't heard from her. Totally exasperated, Diana told the agency to send anyone they had available by that late hour of the morning.

She found Toby Branson's key on the desk. Maybe Ruby could shed some light on Cassie's whereabouts. She didn't know who else to ask.

Inside The Lair, she found Ruby swiping the counter with a wet towel, making large, circular motions. Ruby didn't look up, forcing Diana to go over to her. "Whatcha want, lady," Ruby asked.

Diana avoided looking at the men seated at the bar. Did they ever leave? Did Ruby? "Have you seen Cassie?" she asked. "She hasn't shown up for work and she doesn't answer her phone. I'm worried that she might be sick or something."

Ruby snorted and slid Diana a look of disgust. "Sick? That girl ain't got a feeble bone in her body—scheming brat, that's what she is."

"Excuse me?"

"You heard me. Set her eye on Hack from the beginning, but I never thought he'd cheat on Fern. Show's what I know!"

"Cheat on Fern?"

"You heard me." Ruby flung the towel into the sink behind her and braced her arms on the counter, fingers grasping it under the edge as she leaned toward Diana. "Toby tied one on and Fern helped him get back over to his room. Just doin' a good deed, that's all. Had some trouble, I guess—took a while. Toby was pretty far gone. Anyways, Hack comes in lookin' for Fern and Cassie, the sneak, tells him where Fern and Toby went—hinting at what never happened. Never seen Hack so mad! Grabbed Cassie by the arm and they took off together. Fern's broken-hearted and that's all I know." She let loose of the counter and turned her back in dismissal. "Said too much already."

Diana wondered why she cared. All she needed was a maid. But no, it was more than that. As she trudged back to the hotel, she felt sick at heart for Fern.

A middle-aged woman arrived near noon, proved sufficient, but Diana had to keep tabs to show her what needed to be done and where to find things. When the hotel phone rang late afternoon, it was Hack.

"Hack, where are you?" Diana demanded. Not that he was supposed to report to her, but he was linked in her mind with Cassie.

"Kansas."

"Kansas!" she nearly shouted.

"We drove this far before stoppin' last night."

Diana could tell he'd been drinking by the slur in his words. Her voice rose in pitch. "We?" she demanded.

"Cassie and me. She wants me to tell you she's sorry and hopes to come back to work after our honeymoon, if you ain't too mad."

Diana fairly shouted. "Honeymoon?"

"We're getting married. Cassie's never been East. Wants to honeymoon in Chicago—see Lake Michigan and all."

"Married?" Diana knew she sounded like a parrot, but she couldn't help it.

"It'll take all my savings, but as Cassie says, 'You only live once.' I'll be needin' my job when I get back, though."

"But Fern—"

"Fern who?" he asked, his voice soured with sarcasm. "Sorry to spring this on you, but Cassie and me decided kind of spur of the moment. And Cassie's right. Life's too short to waste on someone who's two-timin' you."

"Hack!"

"We'll be livin' at her place. Gave up mine. Gotta go." The phone went dead, and Diana slowly put it down.

When she heard the bell at the front desk, Diana somehow knew it would be Fern. It was about the time she got off work and Diana had been halfway expecting her.

"Hello, Diana." Instead of her usual bubbly self, Fern spoke barely above a whisper. She wore no makeup and her arms hung straight down at her sides, making her small and somehow vulnerable.

"Come in, Fern," Diana said, doing her best to sound upbeat. "Did you just get off work?"

"Yeah." Fern followed Diana inside the apartment. "Your place looks nice."

"Thanks. Please sit down." Diana motioned to a chair and sat in one opposite. Fern was definitely not herself. Diana didn't know what to say. The silence lengthened.

Fern braced her arms on the chair. At last the words burst forth. "Thought you might have heard from Hack."

Diana was tempted to lie but couldn't. "Yes, I did. He's with Cassie."

Fern drew a deep, shaky breath. "It's all my fault." She slumped down in the chair and put her face in her hands. "Toby Branson meant nothing to me. I wanted to make Hack jealous, but Ruby warned me. Said Hack's proud and it would only drive him away—make him drink more instead of turnin' over a new leaf like I want him to."

"Hanging around The Lair didn't exactly help either of you," Diana said, keeping her tone gentle.

"I know, I know. Things got all mixed up. I flirted with Toby, helped him back to his room, but that's all. Honest."

Diana believed her. She didn't tell Fern that Hack and Cassie were getting married nor that Hack had given up his place.

"I believe you, Fern," she said and then there was nothing left to say.

"Glad to see you appreciate my services, Mrs. R. I'm still sickly, but I'll do my best."

Diana gritted her teeth. She couldn't take another day of starting a new person from scratch. At least Hattie knew the routine and where to find the supplies.

Hattie took her time filling out her time sheet. Then she pulled up her sweater to show off the remaining rash on rolls of flesh spanning her upper belly. "You have no idea how much it hurts."

Diana steeled herself to acknowledge the unwelcome sight with a sympathetic murmur. "Perhaps being back at work will distract you from the pain," she offered.

Hattie huffed. "Don't think so, but I'm here. By the way, why did Cassie leave so sudden? Hear Hack's gone, too. My landlord knows Ruby, the bartender at The Lair."

"Oh, I see." Diana refused to comment further. Even in a city the size of Denver, the gossip pipeline thrived.

"Anyways," Hattie said as Diana let the silence linger, "I'm back now, Boss, so you can take your ease. You sure spiffed up your place while I was gone."

"Mr. and Mrs. Toos did it for us, Hattie."

"Well, la-te-da. I was surprised how the old lady let you change the rooms, but at least they bring in money. Never thought she'd spend it in here where guests don't see it."

At the end of her patience, Diana picked up the time sheet. "It's time to go to work," she said.

"Yes, Ma'am!" Hattie grabbed the paper and took off in another huff.

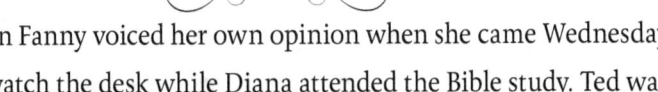

Cousin Fanny voiced her own opinion when she came Wednesday night to watch the desk while Diana attended the Bible study. Ted was attending a work-related seminar and wouldn't be home until later.

"I thought Hack had more sense than that," Fanny said. "Guess 'Rebellion lay in his way, and he found it.' *Henry IV*, you know."

Diana usually found Fanny's quotes amusing, but not this time. Maybe because this one had the ring of truth. "I know he cared for Fern," she told Fanny. "That's what's so sad. Cassie's too young, too flighty. I'm afraid Hack will live to regret it."

The desk bell rang, and Diana saw Nina Gilmore through the open door to the lobby. "Hi, Fanny," Nina called. "Haven't seen you for a while."

Fanny asked about Nina's various ailments, so Nina was always glad to see her. "I just stopped by to let Diana know I surprised Wallace with tickets for the symphony this evening," she told them. "The taxi will be here shortly. And, by the way, I'll be spending Easter with my son and family. He's actually coming to get me. I invited Wallace to join us, but he declined. Said he was already too far in my debt. I'm sorry he feels that way."

"Well, enjoy your evening," Diana told her. "It will be good for both of you."

Fanny looked after her as Nina left. "I hope Wallace Churchhouse is all she thinks he is. He didn't get that teaching job, did he?"

"No," Diana answered. "Turned out to be too far from the bus line and he doesn't have transportation. He let his wife keep both their cars."

"While his bill continues past due, right?"

Diana regretted having said anything to Fanny. She had her own concerns about Wallace, but they weren't Fanny's business. "He tries," she answered, turning away in hopes of ending the conversation. "He's always so grateful for my patience."

"I'm sure he is. Just remember *Hamlet*, Act I: 'Neither a borrower nor a lender be.'"

Diana felt the flush in her face. "Wallace Churchhouse is not a borrower and I'm not a lender."

"Whatever you say." Fanny changed the subject. "I'm worried about Emma. She looks exhausted—says James' cough has settled in his chest and keeps them both up at night."

"I know. She needs me to stay with him on Wednesday. Can you come then?"

"Oh dear. I have plans to go to the art museum with a friend that morning. I should have remembered it's Emma's day to see Joshua and heaven knows she needs to get out. Time with Joshua always lifts her spirits. Wouldn't you think James would see that, especially now that he's homebound? But no, Nora calls or comes to the house with papers for him to sign. It's business as usual."

"Don't worry, Fanny. Nina told me she'd be glad to watch the desk on occasion. She can answer the phone and take messages and I'll be right next door if she needs me."

Fanny pursed her lips but said nothing.

Diana put on her coat. "I won't be late," she said. "Ted shouldn't be either. So, one of us will drive you home."

Fanny lifted the footrest. "Run along. I'll be fine."

James lay on the sofa under a plaid afghan, his frame so thin it hardly caused a ripple. A book lay across his chest as though weighing him down. He made no attempt to get up when Diana entered the room which wasn't like him.

"Hello, Diana," he said, his voice hoarse. "All this fuss. I would have been fine here alone, but I always enjoy your company."

"And I, yours," Diana answered.

Emma smoothed on leather gloves and collected her purse from the coffee table. "Consuela fixed us a late brunch," she told Diana. "So, lunch can wait until I return—probably around two o'clock. Is Fanny at the desk?"

"No, she had other plans. Nina Gilmore is there. She'll take messages or call over here if she needs me for anything else. I believe you met Nina at Christmas."

Emma hesitated for a moment and then pulled on her gloves and turned to leave. "Yes, I remember her, but you know we're always willing to pay for qualified help."

Diana heard the disapproval in Emma's voice. She hadn't been pleased herself when Nina and Wallace had arrived together.

"I knew you wouldn't mind," Nina had told her. "Wallace is teaching me how to play backgammon. My son gave me the game a year ago, but I never opened the box. Since Wallace, I have a whole realm of new interests."

But Diana did mind. "Please call if you need me," she answered, her voice crisp. "I can be back here in a flash. The number is there on the desk."

Nina waved her hand in dismissal. "Don't worry about a thing. I've lived here so long now I could practically run the place myself."

When Diana narrowed her eyes, Nina backpedalled. "What I meant to say is that I take full responsibility to do my best."

"Fine." Diana left, remembering Fanny and her pursed lips.

Now James addressed her as though Emma had already left. His face held a frown, like a petulant child. "Foolish for Emma to go out on a cold day like this."

Emma ignored the interruption. "His medicine is on the table," she told Diana. "He'll need to take the white pills at noon with the soda crackers in the plastic bag. They prevent the pills from upsetting his stomach."

"She treats me like a child." With a sigh of resignation, James tipped the book back up and appeared to give it his total attention.

"I see you brought your own book," Emma observed. "Happy reading, you two. I'll be off now."

Diana heard the key turn on the other side of the old-fashioned lock. The mansion quieted except for the steady ticking of the grandfather clock in the entry hall. Henderson must be shut away on the back porch. She wondered if he pouted like his master.

James lowered the book back down to his chest. "Now that she's gone, we can talk. Tell me about Laurel's young man."

Why you old fox, startled by the renewed vigor in his voice. She gathered her thoughts.

"David is funny and intelligent," she began. "With obvious strength of character. His father died when he was ten, so he's been the man of the family. Has two younger sisters."

"Ambitious, too. Ted tells me he's specializing in estate law."

"That's right. He already has a business degree and is in his last year of law school. Makes him several years older than Laurel, but it doesn't appear to matter to them. In fact, he seems to be a stabilizing influence on her. Laurel can be a bit flighty at times. And I do believe they're in love."

James had closed his eyes and didn't answer though a smile flickered on his lips. Diana opened her book and settled back in her chair, slipping off her shoes and crossing her ankles on the needlepoint footstool.

Precisely at noon, she roused James to take his pills with a glass of water and two crackers. Several times she had paused in her reading to monitor the slight rise and fall of the book on his chest.

"I'm rereading some of the old classics in our library," he said as he nibbled on a cracker. "Might as well put this dratted sick spell to use. This one's *Great Expectations*. Have you read Dickens?"

"In high school."

"What was your favorite?"

"*Tale of Two Cities*."

"Ah, yes. The virtues of friendship and loyalty. Bonds of Christian love. My one love is Emma. As you know, we have no children. You're very fortunate to have Brad and Laurel."

"Yes, we are. All children are a blessing from God—without exception." She meant the last two words to have implied meaning, but she had said them with more emphasis than intended.

James turned his head to look at her, but Diana concentrated on her book. She hadn't meant to sound so judgmental.

"Emma reads the Bible," James said. "I've tried, but I lose interest." He turned back to his book without waiting for her answer and Diana drew an inward sigh of relief.

Emma returned shortly before the clock struck two. She waved in Diana's direction and walked directly to the couch where she stooped to plant a firm kiss on her husband's cheek. "And how did you two get along?" she asked him.

"Fine. Didn't miss you at all."

Amazing. Emma's home and nothing else matters. Life goes on— their mutual denial the bridge to harmony. Diana gathered her things; then—on impulse—leaned over and brushed her lips across the top of James Toos' shiny, bald head. "Goodbye, Mr. Toos. I enjoyed our visit."

He managed a weak smile. "Me, too."

Emma hovered, straightening the afghan, plumping the pillow under his head. "Thank you for coming, Diana. If you don't mind, I'll let you see yourself out. It's time for James to take his medicine again."

CHAPTER 24

ON FRIDAY, TED MADE HIS nightly rounds, eying the front entrance, as he had ever since the robbery. What surely looked like Hack's truck was parked at the curb.

Descending the lobby steps, Ted pressed his face to the glass for a closer look. Hack's head rested on the steering wheel, his arms encircling it.

Ted hit the crash bar, then bounded down the cement steps, and pounded on the window of the cab before jerking open the unlocked door. "Hack!" he demanded.

When Hack raised his head and turned toward him, Ted realized he'd been asleep, not drunk as Ted had feared. Under the street light, he saw the dark pouches under Hack's eyes and the drooping corners of his untrimmed mustache.

"What's wrong, buddy?" Ted asked. "What are you doing here? Where's Cassie?"

Hack's face contorted in a peculiar mix of anger and exhaustion. "Gone. Took me for a good time. Spent all my money and now she's gone." He struggled to sit up a little straighter. "Good thing," he continued. "I never loved her—not like Fern." His voice broke. "Too late for that now."

"But you told Diana you were getting married."

"Naw. Just booze talk. That's all it was. She wanted a fling and I wanted to forget Fern. Now I'm down to my last dime. Couldn't think of where else to go." He cleared his throat. "Sorry, buddy. Bad idea. I really messed up this time."

Whatever had transpired, Hack was dead sober now. "Come inside," Ted told him. "We'll figure something out."

Hack stumbled out of the truck and followed Ted into Hartwick House, apparently too whipped to do otherwise. His eyes remained on the floor while Ted gave Diana a brief explanation.

"What about Laurel's room on the third floor?" Ted asked. "Could Hack bunk there 'til we sort things out?"

Ted's earnest plea squeezed Diana's heart. Sometimes she forgot how truly goodhearted her husband was. When Ted first came in with Hack, she was angry, thinking Hack brought his troubles on himself. But Ted cared about him—really cared—and that caused her to look at things in a different light.

When Fern injured Hack's pride, Cassie just happened to be there to bolster his ego, take advantage of his hurt. Things happen when people are vulnerable and feel betrayed.

"You'd have to come down and use our front bathroom, Hack."

His eyes met hers for the first time. "I wouldn't mind. I'll keep it clean. Do anything you need doing around the place."

"I know you will. Bring your things in while I fix you something to eat."

"I'll go with you," Ted told him. "We need to find a place on the side street to park your truck."

"Cassie's landlady let me get my things. They're in the back of my truck."

"We'll store them in the basement," Ted told him.

Tears welled in Hack's eyes and Diana turned away to spare him any more embarrassment. Big, tough Hack Cummings. What awful hurt people cause one another.

The next morning Diana intercepted Hack as he slipped out of the bathroom, fully dressed and heading for the door. "Hack," she said, "You're eating with us this week. No arguments. Breakfast is ready."

"Aw, Diana. I can't impose—"

"It's not imposing," she interrupted. "You're our friend—in a tight spot. You'd do the same."

"I'll do any work you have—inside and outside. Except for heights. I'm scared of heights."

"Yes, I remember." Diana smiled, recalling Hack at the top of the ladder repairing the hotel sign. "Mrs. Toos told me last week to go ahead and order new kitchen cupboards for thirty-one."

Hack ran a hand through his wiry hair. His eyes failed to meet hers. "And I ran out on you."

"The boxes were delivered yesterday and are piled at the end of the third-floor hallway," Diana told him.

"I'll get to work right after breakfast. I'll also put out feelers for odd jobs in the neighborhood that I can do when I'm finished here, so I can be on my own again as soon as possible."

Ted kept the conversation going during breakfast—discussing the Denver Nugget's season and the upcoming football draft. Before he left for work, Hack helped Diana carry the dishes to the kitchen.

"Hack?" she asked. "It's none of my business, but Fern will want to know you're back. She's devastated. Says there was nothing between her and Toby Branson."

"Maybe, maybe not, but I'm not ready to see her yet." He looked hard at Diana, assessing her readiness to comply. She nodded.

As Hack was leaving, Ted answered the ringing phone. "You're married?" he almost shouted.

Diana flew out of the kitchen. Ted raised one hand to hold her off and mouthed "Brad." She ran to the bedroom to put the phone on speaker.

"What did you just say, Brad?" she demanded.

"We were married yesterday by the pastor who led the retreat we attended last fall. I hope you aren't too disappointed, but Charlotte knew her grandparents would insist on a church wedding with a reception and all and they simply can't afford it. So, we went this route instead. Are you guys okay with that?"

"I admit it's a shock," Ted answered, "but Charlotte is a wonderful young woman and we wish you both all the happiness in the world."

Diana fought to hold back tears and level her voice. "Shock isn't the word for it, Son." Her voice broke and she hoped Brad hadn't noticed. She'd missed her son's wedding. "I wish we could have been there, but we love Charlotte and will be thrilled to welcome her as our daughter-in-law."

"Thanks for understanding." Diana heard the obvious relief in his voice. "It means a lot to me. By the way, Laurel stood up with us as well as my friend Tom from work. So, she already knows."

Laurel was there? Diana fought back outrage once again. Did Charlotte's grandparents get the news before them? Her thoughts were petty, but she couldn't help it.

"I have some other news as well." Diana heard him take a deep breath. "The pastor led us in a prayer to receive Christ as our Lord and Savior. We promise to make Him Lord of our life together."

"Of course, you will." Diana didn't know what else to say. Hadn't she faithfully taken her children to Sunday school and church? Of course, they knew about God and Jesus. Why would Brad make it sound like something new? "Please tell Charlotte we hope to see both of you soon."

"Here—tell her yourself."

Tears came into both Diana's voice and Charlotte's as they shared their honest feelings. Diana knew Charlotte would have preferred a church wedding, but her concern for her grandparents took precedence and Diana told Charlotte she admired her for that.

"Where will you live?" Ted asked at his end.

"We'll stay at Brad's apartment until after he graduates this spring and finds a fulltime job, or maybe until I graduate in August. We'll be cramped, but what's the difference?"

A pause followed, then "Mom? Can I call you that?"

"Please!"

"Laurel also committed her life to Christ."

"That's good," Diana replied after a pause. She searched for a way to change the subject. "Again, welcome to our family."

She wanted to ask if Charlotte's grandparents already knew, but she stopped herself. What difference did it make? "We so look forward to seeing you both at Easter," she added, knowing it sounded lame.

"Dad? Are you there? Can I call you that?" Charlotte asked.

"Of course, you can call me Dad," Ted said. "I'd love it. I just can't take in this prayer thing you're talking about. Maybe Brad can explain it at Easter."

"Of course." Excitement rose in her voice. "I know Brad will consider that a privilege."

It took several days for Hack to stain and install the new cabinets and another couple of days to put on the Formica countertop. He worked long hours without a word of complaint.

Hattie was a different story. She used every opportunity to exploit the fact she was back, as if her return granted Diana a huge favor.

One day as Diana prepared to leave for the post office, Hattie stopped her. "The supplies in the caddies were all mixed up," she complained. "I straightened them out."

"Whatever works best for you," Diana told her as she sidled toward the door.

"I'm still hurtin', you know, but I'm doing my best to keep going."

"That's good," Diana said.

Hattie held out the armful of sheets she carried. "What's with the 'D' and 'S' on these sheets?"

"Cassie used a marker to label them double or single," Diana told her.

"Why? I just measure them out from my nose."

Diana wanted to tell her the sheets got wrinkled when she pulled out the wrong one and stuffed it back on the shelf. With difficulty, she held her tongue. Laurel kept assuring her Hattie's day was coming. When was Hattie's day?

Hack appeared on the stairs, tool kit in hand. "The job's finished," he told her. "Looks good, if I do say so myself. By the way, I got me some other work. Abe Feinstein needs a new counter."

"That's great, Hack." Diana had taken shoes to Abe's shop for repair and mentioned Hack. "He called your boss," Hack continued. "I guess the old man gave me the go-ahead 'cause Abe said anyone James Toos puts in a good word for is good enough for him."

Fern stopped Diana as she came out of the post office. "Is Hack staying at the hotel?" she asked. The tightness in her voice revealed her need to know. "I heard he was."

Diana hesitated, but what reason did she have to keep it from her? "Yes, he is," she answered.

"I went and talked with his landlady—knew he moved out. It was just a hunch when I saw his truck parked in the alley behind the hotel." Tears flooded her eyes. "Oh, Diana," she continued. "I don't know what happened, but I know I hurt him bad. I love him. I really do." Her shoulders shook, and she put both hands over her eyes and sobbed out loud. A woman passing on the sidewalk turned and stared.

Diana put her arms around Fern's shoulders and hugged her tight. "He's staying up on the third floor—in the little room where Laurel stays when she's home. Hardly room for him to turn around, but he never complains. If you want to stop by tonight, you can go up and knock on his door. It's up to him if he wants to talk."

"Oh, thank you, thank you, Diana! All I want is a chance."

Ted called it matchmaking, but he had a twinkle in his eye and no complaint when Diana let Fern in that evening and told her where to find Hack.

"I don't think she'll stay the night," he told Diana. "There's not enough room."

Much later, as they lay reading in bed, a soft knock sounded on the door of the short hallway that led back to their bedroom. Ted got up to open it, but when Diana heard Hack's voice, she grabbed her robe and stood behind him in the doorway. Fern stood behind Hack, clinging to his arm.

"I'm returning the key," Hack told them. "Fern and I made up and I'm moving in with her." His suitcase rested on the floor beside him. "Be back in the morning to get the rest of my stuff out of the basement." He paused and cleared his throat. "Can't say enough to thank the two of you. Nicest thing anyone's ever done for me."

Ted ventured out in his pajamas to clap him on the shoulder. "You're a good man, Hack. Glad we could help you out."

"Well, I've learned a thing or two. It's important for people to be able to trust each other—like you and Diana trusted me. Booze threw a monkey wrench in that, so Fern and me are stayin' out of The Lair from now on."

"Good thinking," Ted agreed.

"One more thing." Hack looked to Fern and she nodded, bright spots in her cheeks. "We might even get married."

Diana pushed past Ted and embraced Fern in a fierce hug. "That's wonderful news!"

"Whoa. I said *might*," Hack scolded, but his eyes crinkled at the corners. Then he added, "But if we do go through with it, will you two stand up with us?"

"*Wow!*" Ted's loud exclamation brought a pajama-clad man out from number five. "So sorry," Ted told him, soliciting raised eyebrows and a grumpy nod before the door closed again.

Fern giggled, and tears choked Diana's reply. "We'd be deeply honored," she said.

CHAPTER 25

TINY CROCUS AND GRAPE HYACINTH plants poked through melting snow in the garden and Diana saw a robin hop down the front steps. Spring had arrived just in time to celebrate.

The small reception they planned for Brad and Charlotte would include her parents, her sister and family, Ted's mom, Charlotte's grandparents, and, of course, Laurel and David. They had also invited James and Emma.

Diana had picked a small bouquet for the table, but she remained quiet as they ate their breakfast. Finally, she laid down her napkin and spoke. "Ted, there's something I need to tell you."

Ted raised his eyebrows at her serious tone.

"I made a phone call to the personnel department at that school where Wallace Churchhouse said he applied for a job. Denver Academy? They have no record of his application and they keep all applications on file for a year."

"That was a smart thing to do, Diana."

"Well I needed to remind myself this is a business and I must run it like one. I've been way too lax. Emma said at the beginning it was better to cut one's losses and send bad risks on their way than to compound the situation."

"What do you intend to do?"

"Give him an ultimatum—a deadline to pay up."

"Good thinking."

What about Nina? Had he tricked her as well?

She stood a long moment in front of his door. Then she picked up the doorknocker and rapped it twice.

"Good morning, Diana." Dressed for the day, Wallace Churchhouse looked as neat and precise as ever. "What a nice surprise. Won't you come in?"

"No thank you, Wallace. I just came to ask you something." Diana forged ahead before she lost her nerve. "Did you actually apply for that teaching job?"

"Why do you ask?" He stood very still, his eyes meeting hers.

"The school has no record of it and they keep all applications for a year."

Wallace looked down. "I'm so sorry. I felt too ashamed to tell you the truth. You see, my credentials aren't up-to-date and I have no certificate to teach in Colorado. When I realized I wouldn't qualify for the position, I didn't apply."

Then he raised his eyes as renewed vigor came into to his voice. "But I do have good news. My broker is selling some stock I own. Today, in fact. The money should bring my bill up-to-date, even ahead a week or two."

Diana wanted to believe him, but she forged ahead. "I'm afraid I'll need a certified check by five o'clock this afternoon or I'll be forced to report the delinquent amount to the hotel owners."

"Of course. I'll get right on it—have the money wired to my bank."

"Thank you, Wallace." Diana started to leave, then turned and added, "We've faced financial ruin ourselves. I do understand how difficult it can be."

"Of course, you do. Most people don't."

The day dragged by. She listened for Wallace to come to the desk, but he didn't. Hattie left, and Diana began to think about dinner. The clock inched toward five o'clock. Ted would be home soon.

At last Diana straightened her shoulders and climbed the stairs again. This time her knock went unanswered. She put her master key in the lock and opened the door.

At first everything looked the same. The bed was made and through the open door of the bathroom she saw a used hand towel draped neatly over the towel rack. But something was different. When she had looked past him that morning, a pipe rack sat on the dresser and a stack of books rested on the bedside table. She crossed to the closet. Empty.

Nina looked surprised when she answered Diana's knock. "Oh, I thought it was Wallace," she said. "We're going out for dinner."

Diana took in the becoming new outfit Nina wore and the recently bronzed highlights in her hair. Nina had followed the diabetic guidelines the doctor gave her, losing fifteen pounds and greatly improving the condition of her feet.

"Nina . . . " Diana took her arm to guide her to the bed and sat down beside her. Nina didn't resist though her eyes grew wide, questioning.

"I have something to tell you." Diana sat down on the bed across from her. "Wallace is gone—bag and baggage."

"What?" Nina's hand flew to her mouth. "That can't be! He wouldn't—"

"But he did." Diana's voice was firm, leaving no room for doubt. "He fooled us both. He was behind in his rent, gave me lots of excuses. I shouldn't have let it go on as long as I did, but I wanted to believe him. This morning I told him I would need full payment by this afternoon or report the delinquent amount to the owners. I just now knocked on his door and unlocked it when he didn't answer. The room and the closet are empty."

Tears stood in Nina's eyes. "But he wouldn't . . . " Her voice quivered and trailed off.

Diana placed her hand on Nina's arm. "He liked you, Nina," she said. "I know he did, but he took advantage of your goodness and my inexperience."

"That's not fair. Wallace is a good person. I was in love with him." Her cheeks reddened, and Diana sensed her embarrassment at being taken in.

"That's not hard to understand," she answered. "I liked him myself. He was charming, and you had some good times together, but he's a con man, Nina. Pure and simple. He fooled both of us."

Nina's face crumpled. She covered it with her hands and began to sob. "Why didn't he tell me good-bye, or at least leave a note? I've been such a fool."

"I felt the same way when I realized he was gone," Diana told her. "Betrayed by someone I thought I could trust. But trusting someone you believe in doesn't make you a fool. Remember the good times and what you gained from them. You've got your life back, Nina. You can thank him for that."

"I'm so embarrassed. He gave me such nice compliments and I thought he meant them." Nina stood to pace back and forth and then sat down hard on the bed beside Diana.

"I'm sure he did," Diana assured her. "That's why he couldn't say good-bye. He would still be here if I hadn't given him a deadline. He's not a bad man, Nina, just a weak one. Isn't it best you found that out?"

"Perhaps you're right." Nina reached to snatch a tissue from the box on her bedside table and dabbed at her eyes. Tears still flowed, but she raised her head to face Diana. "I feel ten years younger than before Wallace came. I can't let his treachery take me back to what I was."

Diana hugged her, looking straight into her eyes. "I'm so proud of you, Nina. I know this is a terrible blow, but you've just proved that you can be even stronger because of it."

Nina clung to Diana for several moments. Then she sat back and straightened her skirt. "Don't worry about me, Diana. I'll get over this. I have to."

Diana set the table for dinner. She prepared herself to pour out the whole story as soon as Ted came home from work. Might as well get it over with and admit how gullible she had been to believe Wallace in the first place.

When Ted stepped through the door, she crossed the room to give him a quick kiss before she began. But Ted had his own news.

"Guess who I saw today. Joshua Toos!"

What seemed so important just minutes ago now fled her mind. "Joshua?" she asked, her eyes wide. "How? Where?"

"On my way home I stopped at Safeway for razor blades." Ted shrugged out of his sport coat and laid it over the back of the wing chair. "Forgot to tell you I'm out of them. Anyway, been in that store only a couple of times, so I looked for a clerk to tell me where to find them. You know how I hate to hunt for things."

Yes, Diana knew. She set her foot tapping. What did that have to do with anything?

"I saw a young man in the produce department unpacking a crate of apples. It's right there to the left as you enter from the parking lot."

As if she needed to know that. At her sides, Diana rubbed her fingers and thumbs together to control her impatience.

"He looked up and saw me heading his way. When he stood, I saw his badge with his name on it: Joshua Toos, Assistant Produce Manager."

Diana's eyes widened. "Joshua? It was really Joshua?"

"I don't know what I expected. Shows how stereotypes take over. I thought he would be an errand boy, doing menial jobs for minimum wage. Shows what a jerk I am. He couldn't have been politer or more professional."

Diana forgot Wallace Churchhouse. "What happened?" she asked.

"He said, 'May I help you, Sir?' and I stumbled around like a dummy and finally asked what aisle razor blades were on."

"And?"

"He said, 'I'll show you, Sir' and led me across the store to the right aisle where he pointed them out. He walks very erect, has broad shoulders, a great physique and a wonderful smile. The only way he looks handicapped at all is in the wide set of his eyes. He must be a responsible employee to have a manager's position in such a big store."

"Was that all?"

"No. I'm getting there. He walked very fast ahead of me down the aisle. I asked him how he kept in such good shape and he apologized. Said his boss tells him to slow down. He gave me this huge smile over his shoulder and said, 'I guess it's 'cause I work out every day after work.' I asked him where and he told me his basement is full of weights and other equipment—a treadmill, recumbent bike, and a couple of other things I've forgotten."

"He uses all that by himself?"

"I asked him, and he said he has several friends, one named Sam, I think, and some others who work there at the store who come by and work out with him."

"Really!"

"Then—here's the corker! He said, 'After we work out, my foster mom sets out cold drinks and we have a Bible study.'"

"Oh, Ted, that's beautiful!"

"I wanted to stay there and talk longer, but he said, 'Nice talking with you, Sir. I should get back to work.'"

"Then?"

"I thanked him again and he gave me another big smile and walked away. I just stood there—stunned."

"I wish I'd been there."

Ted picked up his coat and took the small package from the pocket. "Did you start to tell me something?"

Wallace Churchhouse seemed less significant now, but Diana related the story. "I feel so stupid, Ted. You warned me, and I was so gullible."

"I'm not going to say, 'I told you so,'" Ted said as he hung the coat in the closet. "Wallace Churchhouse was a charmer. I wanted to believe him myself. Hands down you're not his first victim."

"But what do I tell the Tooses?"

"The truth. I doubt if they'll be that shocked." Ted turned to the sports page, subject closed.

After clearing the table, Diana picked up the phone and talked to Emma, leaving out no details of the deception and the resulting loss of income for the hotel.

"Live and learn," Emma told her. "Next time you won't be so easily deceived. Require payment up front. And remember, the law is on your side."

"But I feel like such a fool. And poor Nina . . . "

"She'll get over it. Better that she learn the truth now than later."

James Toos called the district attorney, who sent a detective.

"Got any ID?" the detective asked. "License? Picture? Social security number?"

Diana felt the hated blush. How had she been taken in so completely? Worse than Nina because she wasn't emotionally involved.

Then she remembered. "Laurel took a picture one day when he and one of our guests were leaving together. Laurel told Nina how nice she looked and snapped their picture on her cell phone. I have it on my computer."

She printed out the picture and handed it to the detective. Wallace Churchhouse looked pleasant, relaxed—his arm around Nina's shoulders.

"A cool customer, wasn't he?" the detective remarked. "Probably minus the mustache by now." He pocketed the photo. "I'll check the computer and give you a call. It's a felony—innkeeper's fraud. But don't hold your breath. He sounds like a pro. Won't have the same name. That's for sure."

Would someone else be as gullible as she? How many lessons must she learn before she could think of herself as a competent businesswoman?

CHAPTER 26

MARIO PREPARED THE FLOWER BEDS for planting and edged the garden paths. When the representative from the guidebook agency conducted his annual inspection the first week in April, he restored the hotel rating to three stars.

Emma was overjoyed. "That's wonderful, isn't it, James!"

The old man's eyes twinkled, but Diana had to strain to hear his hoarse reply.

"Deserves a bonus, don't you think?" He winked at Diana.

"Absolutely," Emma agreed. "It's miraculous what you and Ted have achieved in such a short time, Diana. We know the many challenges you've faced, besides putting up with that good-for-nothing Hattie."

The amount James wrote out on the check was not only generous but came at just the right time. Now they could afford a nice reception for Brad and Charlotte.

Diana seized the moment. "Speaking of maids," she ventured, "I'd like to give Margie a raise. If it's all right with you. She goes above and beyond to make up for Hattie's shortcomings."

"Of course. You have full authority to make such decisions."

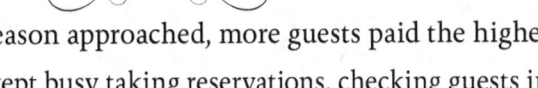

As the tourist season approached, more guests paid the higher nightly rate. Diana kept busy taking reservations, checking guests in and out and completing the redecoration of number one.

She took away the heavy maroon velvet draperies and replaced them with shutters and floral tie-back curtains. Then she added a matching king-sized bedspread and a soft beige carpet. The bedspread was fresh out of the package the morning Helen Wells checked in.

Helen and Douglas Wells paid annual visits to Hartwick House. "We make it a tradition to stay here," Helen told Diana when she returned to the desk after they carried in their luggage. "It's so out-of-the-ordinary and not that far from Cherry Creek, where we like to shop. This big suite has always been our favorite and now just look at what you've done with it. Douglas agrees that it's lovelier than ever!"

Over the course of the next week, the couple came in with packages from Neiman Marcus and Saks Fifth Avenue. As they left one evening, Helen shared with Diana their plans to eat at The Broker to celebrate her birthday. She held out her wrist for Diana to admire the lovely bracelet Mr. Wells had purchased to surprise her. Real sapphires sparkled in the intricate setting.

Now, two days after their departure, she called about that very same bracelet. "I can't think where else it could be. I haven't worn it since and I remember taking it off and putting it in the desk drawer. Hugh never wants valuables lying about in plain sight, so I left it in there. Forgot about it, I'm afraid. Dumb me."

"Don't worry. I'll check and call right back." Diana's stomach muscles tightened. Nothing like this had happened before. She tried hard to sound confident, reassuring. "It's probably right where you left it."

But after a thorough search, it wasn't.

"I'm so sorry," she told Helen Wells as she gripped the phone. "I searched the entire room. I'll check with the maids, but any items left behind are to be turned in to me the same day."

The woman thanked her, but Diana sensed an element of doubt and it deeply disturbed her. She questioned Margie and Hattie, but both claimed not to have seen the bracelet.

"Don't know why folks leave things like that laying around, anyways," Hattie remarked. "Just askin' for trouble."

"She didn't leave it laying around," Diana replied, appalled as always by Hattie's assumptions. "She put it in the drawer."

"Still her fault, I'd say." Hattie held her lower back as she straightened from her assigned job—scrubbing between the posts of the stair railing. She no longer mentioned the rash, arthritis being the new complaint. "Rich folks are spoiled from not having to work hard like I do."

Diana bit her tongue to keep back what rested on the tip of it. As the week went by, the missing bracelet continued to trouble her. She knew how she would react herself, the suspicions it would raise. The fact was, she had immediately suspected Hattie, but what good did that do her?

On Saturday Diana left Ted to watch the desk while she did the weekly grocery shopping. She enjoyed strolling the aisles at King Soopers without any need to hurry.

Today, however, she decided on impulse to shop at Safeway. Perhaps she would encounter Joshua herself. Upon entering the unfamiliar store, she saw Kate Danson in the checkout line and waited until Kate finished paying before catching her attention.

"Hi, Diana," Kate responded. "I didn't know you shopped at Safeway."

"I don't usually, but it was convenient today."

"You mentioned at Bible study that you finished redecorating that apartment just off the lobby," Kate said. "I can't wait to see it."

"Number one? Stop by any time and plan to stay for a chat."

Just then Diana thought she saw Hattie rounding the end of an aisle. Well, it was possible. She knew Hattie's address was only a few blocks away.

"I will. You have such a gift," Kate said. "I need to redecorate our bedroom. Maybe you could take a peek at it when you come to Bible study next week. Give me some suggestions?"

"Sure. I'd love to."

"Great!" Kate changed the subject, telling Diana a funny story concerning her small grandson. Then she said good-bye and left with her cart for the parking lot.

Diana got a cart of her own and steered it left to start down the outside aisle. That's when she spotted Hattie again and came up behind her as Hattie studied the contents of the ice cream case.

Diana decided to greet Hattie as just another shopper. Away from the hotel and the boss-employee relationship, perhaps they could achieve just a friendly conversation.

But when Diana spoke her name, Hattie jerked back and looked at Diana as though she had been struck. "Whatcha' doin' here, Boss?"

Diana started to reply, but then she saw the bracelet on Hattie's wrist gripping the handle of the cart. She stopped, mouth open, staring as Hattie reacted and flung her arm behind her back.

"What are you hiding?" Diana demanded. "That's Helen Wells' bracelet. You stole her bracelet!"

"This thing?" Hattie flashed the sapphires on her wrist before swiftly hiding them again. "I bought it last week at Target."

Anger rose, and Diana let out a curse. She never swore, and it shocked her as she did so. "That's Helen Well's bracelet and you stole it out of their room!"

Hattie stood her ground for several silent seconds, then peeled off the bracelet and held it out between thumb and forefinger like a piece of rotten fruit.

"Here," she said. "Don't much like it anyways. Too heavy."

Diana snatched the bracelet away from her. "You know what this means," she said, her voice shaking with rage. "You're fired!" She moved toward a teenage girl who had stopped to watch the altercation. "Don't try to wriggle out of it. I have a witness. Any trouble and I'll call the police."

Hattie's lower lip protruded. For several moments she held her ground, her eyes hard. Then she shrugged. "It's too hard at Hartwick House, anyways. And you're too mean. I'd rather be on unemployment."

"Forget that! Stealing is ample grounds for dismissal. The Tooses won't pay you another cent."

Hattie abandoned her cart and fled, her flip-flops slapping the floor as she ran.

The teenage girl remained, seemingly fascinated by the altercation.

"May I have your name and phone number?" Diana asked as she fumbled in her purse for a pen and paper. Her hands were shaking. "Just in case I need a witness."

The girl nodded.

"I'm so embarrassed," Diana told Helen Wells on the phone. "It was a miracle I caught her with it on."

"I understand," Helen Wells replied. "We have a wonderful house-keeper, but I hear horror stories from some of my friends."

"I'll send the bracelet on Monday by registered mail," Diana promised. "Again, please accept my sincere apology. I do hope this won't prevent you from coming back to Hartwick House."

"Of course not. It taught me a good lesson. After this, I'll make a thorough search before we leave any hotel room."

When Diana replaced the phone, the adrenaline drained away, and reality sank in. She was once again without a weekday maid.

She found Margie scrubbing out the bathtub in twenty-five as if potatoes had sprouted in it. When Diana entered the room, she started to scramble to her feet.

"Don't get up," Diana told her. "I came to tell you I just fired Hattie."

"Oh, my goodness!"

"It was for good cause, believe me, but now I need someone to replace her. I don't suppose you know anyone looking for work?"

If Margie wondered what had happened—or thought it was about time—she hid it well. Her forehead wrinkled in thought. Then she broke out a wide smile. "I know just the right person."

Diana realized she had been holding her breath. Now she let it out, lightheaded with relief. "That's wonderful. Who?"

"A young woman at my church. I know she's lookin' for something part-time. Her name's Magdalena—from Ecuador. Married a history teacher travelling down there one summer. Doin' some sort of research she said. Don't know if she's done this kind of work, but she seems like a wonderful Christian girl and I'd be glad to help get her started. She could follow me around for a day—learn what I do and where things are."

"Could you ask her to stop by Monday morning?" Diana asked.

"Actually . . . " Margie paused, keeping her eyes on the floor. Then she spoke in a rush. "Would you consider me for Hattie's job?"

"Consider? I'd like nothing more! But what about Sam?"

"Sam's older now, manages on his own when he needs to. Needs to know I trust him." She looked down, twisting her scrub rag in her hands. "Besides, I can use the money."

"Oh, Margie! You're an answer to prayer."

"And you are to mine. And maybe Magdalena's. I know what she wants is weekends when her husband is home to watch her little brother. They brought him back with them from Ecuador."

It would be a story Diana would want to hear, but right now things were falling into place and she could hardly wait to call Laurel and tell her about Hattie. Laurel had been the one to say Hattie would go too far someday.

But, of course, Cousin Fanny had the last word. "All's well that ends well," she reminded them.

CHAPTER 27

ON FRIDAY, TED LEFT WORK early to meet Diana on the steps of the county courthouse. They went in together to find the office where Hack and Fern waited to be married by the Justice of the Peace. Fern wore a denim skirt and plain white blouse and Hack looked uncomfortable wearing a sports coat over his open-necked shirt. Fern clung to his arm and he put a protective hand over hers.

"Guess we're as ready as we'll ever be," he told Ted and Diana. "Helps that I've got steady work now."

When he had finished the counter for Abe Feinstein, Abe referred him to the elderly couple who ran a mom-and-pop grocery store three blocks over. They needed additional shelves.

"I can see I'll have to call ahead when we need you at Hartwick House," Diana had teased.

"Naw," Hack had replied. "You'll always come first."

The clerk called them into the Justice of Peace chambers and the brief ceremony began. Diana fought back tears as she realized she was here for Hack and Fern but had missed Brad and Charlotte's wedding altogether.

Had Charlotte looked at Brad the way Fern looked at Hack? Was Brad serious the whole time or had he smiled as Hack did when Fern repeated the words wrong and had to start over? She was startled to hear Hack called by his real name—Elliot—and noted that Fern reacted to it also.

But her emotions stirred for other reasons as well. Standing there, she viewed Hack and Fern as good, hard-working, down-to-earth people, like Margie and Magdalena and others she had known throughout her lifetime, yet never took the time to care about. She remembered the men who unloaded furniture off trucks and wrestled it into the showroom and the cleaning lady who came as they closed the store each day. Yes, she smiled and spoke to them, but had she ever considered them as people with lives of their own rather than just as employees?

The short ceremony ended, and the bride and groom kissed. Diana hugged Fern while Ted shook Hack's hand and insisted on taking the newlyweds to dinner to celebrate. Fanny was at the desk, so there was no need to hurry back to Hartwick House.

They ate at the Cherry Creek restaurant James and Emma recommended for Brad and Charlotte's reception. It was only a few blocks from the hotel. "We've dined there often," James had told them. "Found Consuela there ten years ago, waiting on tables and helping in the kitchen. She's been with us ever since."

The hostess showed them to a table. Ted told her the occasion and she added her best wishes as she placed menus in front of them.

Hack stripped off his coat and draped it around the back of his chair while Ted loosened his tie and ordered a bottle of champagne from the approaching waiter.

Fern giggled. "We're really doing this up right!"

"Better be," Ted teased. "I'm doing this only once."

"Still can't believe I'm a married man," Hack said, pulling a long face.

"You'll get used to it," Ted told him, punching his shoulder. "It's not so bad."

Fern squeezed Hack's arm and turned to Diana. "I've been dying to ask. I thought Hattie was back and Margie worked on weekends. Now Margie's there during the week. What gives?"

Diana told her the story of the bracelet and the blessing that Margie wanted Hattie's place. "I'm learning God answers prayer if only we ask," she told Fern. "I can count on Margie all week long and Magdalena is a breath of fresh air on the weekends. The guests love her even though she's still struggling with her English. She has such a sunny disposition and is always anxious to please."

"Well, Hartwick House has certainly changed," Fern said. "There's a whole different atmosphere."

The food was good, the service excellent. Ted made one more toast to the couple's happiness before his handshake and Diana's kiss sent the newlyweds on their way. Hack told them with a certain swagger that he had reserved a room for two nights in the resort town of Vail.

Before they left, Ted booked a date at the restaurant for Brad and Charlotte's reception.

Charlotte's grandparents came, as did Diana's parents and her sister and brother-in-law. They all stayed at Hartwick House the night before.

Charlotte and Brad were already there when Mr. and Mrs. Swanson arrived. The elderly couple were all Diana had expected—gracious, sincere, and exceedingly proud of their granddaughter, as indeed they should be.

Ted carried in their luggage and Diana got them settled in number one, for easy access coming and going.

"The hotel is just what I pictured from Charlotte's description," Mrs. Swanson told her. "She's our joy, you know."

"And Charlotte often expresses her love for you," Diana said. "We could not have asked for a more perfect wife for our son than your granddaughter."

"We feel the same about Brad," Charlotte's grandfather assured her. "Her parents would have been very pleased."

"We had no idea Hartwick House would be this grand," he added. "We'll be very comfortable here."

"It's just lovely," Mrs. Swanson agreed.

As they closed their door, Diana thought what a shame it was that Ted's mother couldn't be with them as well. She had grown progressively weaker, her mind often confused. Ted and Diana visited her often at the nursing home. Occasionally it took a reminder for her to remember Diana, but she always knew both Ted and Laurel. When Brad and Charlotte had paid her a visit the day before, she recognized Brad as the small child she remembered and Charlotte as his neighborhood playmate. So sad.

The May morning dawned warm and sunny. At the restaurant, the hostess ushered them into the room set aside for the reception.

After the delicious luncheon, Ted whispered to Diana, "Everyone's having a good time." He linked his arm in hers and hugged it to his side as they watched the newlyweds open their presents. "You've done it again, Babe."

"Not without you." It was true. He was the perfect host.

She experienced a deep sense of peace that continued when they all were back at the hotel and Ted ushered them into the garden. Only the morning before, Mario had sculptured the flower beds to his satisfaction and placed pots of geraniums in the window box. Clumps of tulips graced the base of the huge oak and jonquils and daffodils bordered the paths. The scene was indeed the serendipity Diana had discovered for herself nine months ago.

Under the oak tree, a long table was set with crystal glasses on a white tablecloth. Ted proposed a toast and they lifted their glasses to the bride and groom. It was the end of a perfect day.

Later their guests retired to their rooms and Laurel scooted up to her loft. "Next year we'll be elsewhere, and this will seem like a dream," Ted commented as he and Diana retrieved the glasses to carry them back inside.

Was that true? Where would they be? She pushed the thought from her mind.

They prepared to sit down and relax as well, but when Brad walked into the apartment, Bible in hand, they sensed something else was in store. "Mom . . . Dad," he began, his expression serious, intent. "I want to take this opportunity to share with you what changed our lives."

"We're waiting, Son," Ted replied.

Brad opened the book to the Gospel of John to share the Good News. "When we believe in our hearts that Jesus died to save us from our sins and confess it with our mouths, we are saved unto eternal life with Him," Brad told them.

"I do believe," Ted told him.

"So, do I," Diana added.

"Then let's pray."

Later that night, Diana lay in bed reflecting on the struggles undergone as well as the blessings received. She often pictured Hartwick House as a giant beehive, of which their own quarters constituted only one of many compartments. The bees nested now, but in a few hours, they would stir again, then come and go, some entwining their lives with hers.

She thought of Nina who had made Hartwick House her permanent residence. The Tunisian pilots, Assad and Mosab, who sent postcards now and then as they travelled the globe. She thumbtacked them to the bulletin board above her desk and shared them with Nina and Emma, who remembered them from Christmas.

Vangie lived in a small, but trendy loft near the lower downtown restaurant where she was now top chef. She made it a habit to stop by Hartwick House, bringing samples of entrees to share on occasion. Even hard-to-please Mrs. Talbot had returned for her semi-annual asthma evaluation and cornered Ted to voice her approval of the improvements they had made.

Was her own desire to remain at Hartwick House a selfish thing—denying Ted the peace and comfort of a home in the suburbs? She knew her growing satisfaction with life at Hartwick House remained in conflict with Ted's stated desire to move on.

The phone shrilled on the nightstand, the sound creating instant alarm. Who would be calling at this hour? Ted groped for it as Diana reached to turn on a light.

"Ted?" Diana could hear the high-pitched tremor in James' voice. It brought Ted's feet to the floor. "Come right away—hurry! Something's wrong with Emma."

"I'll be right there." He hung up the phone and fumbled for his slippers.

"Should I go with you?" Diana asked, flinging back the covers.

"No, you'd better stay here. I'll call you." He struggled into the pants laid over a chair and pulled a sweatshirt out of the bureau.

Diana rushed to the window facing the Toos mansion. "I can see only a faint light," she told him.

Ted quickly switched into his shoes and hurried out the side door. Diana watched his shadowed figure run down the sidewalk and turn to climb the front steps of the mansion. James must have been waiting because Ted went right in.

"Something's terribly wrong." James' frail voice shook as he turned and beckoned Ted to follow. He wore silk pajamas, but no robe. His bony bare feet padded across the living-room carpet and down the hallway. "Emma always wakes up when I stir in the night, but when I came back from the bathroom, she didn't move. I've called her name, but she won't answer."

Ted felt the need to hurry, but James moved as if in slow motion.

"Maybe she took a sleeping pill." James sounded suddenly hopeful. "She worries about me so . . . " His voice trailed off as they entered the bedroom.

Never having been in this part of the house before, Ted now felt like an intruder. The large bedroom, dominated by a king-sized four-poster bed, was brightly lit by a crystal chandelier and twin lamps on the antique nightstands.

Emma lay with her back to them. Her hair was released from its twist and curled on the pillow like that of a young girl. For a moment both men stood still in the doorway as if expecting her to move. Surely, she would have heard their voices. Always proper, Emma would never let a strange man find her in bed.

Ted placed a steadying hand on his employer's shoulder. "Stay here," he said, and James relaxed slightly, as if relieved to do so.

As he circled the bed, Ted wished fervently that Diana had come along after all, but when he saw Emma's face, he was glad she hadn't. He knew without a doubt that Emma was gone. Her eyes were closed, but the lips drew back in a firm, unnatural line as if she had attempted some final effort to speak. There were no other signs of struggle. One hand lay unclenched beside her cheek.

Ted took a moment to collect himself before returning to James' side. "Come," he said in the gentlest tone he could muster. He guided James to put on the slippers left at his bedside, then took him by the arm and steered him to the doorway. "We'll call for an ambulance."

Relief covered the old man's face. "Of course," he breathed. "The paramedics. Such capable people. They'll know what to do." Then he stopped and turned back. "But should we leave her alone? Maybe I should stay with her while you call."

"We'll wait together." Ted kept his voice firm though he was shaking inside. Once back in the front parlor, he led James to the sofa and gently guided him down against the cushions. Then he sat beside him to reach for the beige princess phone on the end table and cradle it between his knees as he lifted the receiver and dialed 911.

They waited in silence. Ted recalled the verse Brad quoted about everlasting life for those who believe. Had Emma believed because of Joshua?

The old man was trembling—probably in shock. Ted took the afghan from the back of the sofa and tucked it around his shoulders. He offered to get him a glass of water, but James shook his head in refusal. Diana would do it better, but he refrained from calling her, afraid it would alarm James further.

"She wouldn't leave me." The certainty in his tone belied the tremor in his voice. "She wouldn't go first."

A siren pierced the silence that followed. Ted jumped up as the wail died in front of the mansion. "I'll let them in," he told James.

When Diana saw the ambulance arrive, she scribbled a note to leave at the desk and flew out the side door. She arrived on the heels of the paramedics.

Ted introduced himself. "In the back bedroom," he told the two men, motioning down the hallway. "I'll be right there." Then he turned to Diana, grabbing her by the shoulders. "Emma's gone," he told her. "Stay with James."

"What do you mean—gone?" Diana demanded.

"She's dead." Ted kept his voice low. "James is in shock."

Diana's hands flew to her cheeks. "Emma? Dead? Are you sure?"

"Yes, I'm sure." Then he left her and hurried down the hallway.

Diana remained in the entryway as if her feet were glued to the floor. Through the arched doorway into the parlor, she saw James seated on the sofa, dwarfed by the plaid shawl spread over him. He appeared to be studying its pattern in minute detail, his hands clasped together in his lap.

With a rush of compassion, she hurried to kneel in front of him and take his icy hands between hers. "I'm so sorry," she told him over and over.

At last he nodded and broke into dry sobs that wrenched from his chest without tears to ease them. Diana felt at a loss. What else could she say?

One of the paramedics came back down the hall and sat beside the old gentleman. He gently pulled the blanket away to wrap a blood pressure cuff around James' arm. The Velcro overlapped almost too far to fasten. "Mr. Toos, can you hear me?"

The old man nodded.

"Your wife is gone. It happened in an instant. She didn't suffer. Her heart just stopped."

James showed no emotion and the paramedic turned to Diana. "Are you family?"

Diana shook her head, unable to speak. The tears that stood in her eyes now spilled over and rolled down her cheeks.

"Mr. Toos?" The paramedic's voice was gentle, but firm. "We need to take care of you now. I'm calling for another ambulance to take you to the hospital." James still made no comment. Either he didn't hear or didn't care.

Taking his hand in hers again, Diana rubbed it gently with her thumb, murmuring incoherent words of comfort, as much for herself as for him. She stood to block his view as the stretcher covered with a sheet wheeled past them.

"I loved her so much," James blurted suddenly, the words so abrupt that Diana jerked backward. "I never meant to hurt her."

"Of course not. You didn't hurt her." Diana felt the tears reach her neck and trickle down inside her nightgown.

"I did. I made too many demands. I should have—"

Diana interrupted him. "She loved you. She wanted to take care of you."

"She loved the boy." His tone was flat now, void of expression.

The words stopped Diana's hands. Who would tell Joshua? It took a moment for her to find her voice. "You always came first."

James raised his eyes to hers. "I did, didn't I? But I didn't deserve it."

At last tears ran down the furrows of his cheeks. He pulled away from Diana and buried his face in his hands. Diana clasped her own hands together.

Ted retrieved an overcoat and muffler from the hall tree in the entry hall. He helped the old man stand, put his arms in the sleeves and tied the muffler around his neck.

"Where are you taking him?" Diana asked the paramedic who arrived with another stretcher.

"University Medical Center, Ma'am. Someone will need to accompany him to fill out the papers." He led James to the stretcher where James lay down without any protest.

"I'll go." Ted turned to Diana. "Call Nora to get his insurance information. I'll call you from the hospital."

"Oh, Ted!" Diana gasped. "He's so alone now. I think he has one living brother, but I'm not even sure about that."

"Nora will know."

Diana went to Emma's Rolodex and found the telephone number for Nora Weeks, and then Diana awakened her out of a sound sleep.

Nora told Diana she drove the distance in a daze. "I can't believe it," she said over and over as she wiped her eyes again and again.

"The hospital needs his insurance information. We didn't know where to look." Diana wondered if Nora would be able to function. Her hands shook as well as her voice.

"I'm sorry, I'm sorry," Nora said over and over as she hunted through the office desk for the information required. "I can't seem to think. I know it's here."

"It's all right," Diana soothed. "Take your time."

"I've been with them thirty years. I never married. The law firm is my life."

"I know. James and Emma always speak so highly of you."

Soon she found the information.

The papers in hand had a calming effect. "I'll take them to the hospital myself," she told Diana. "I must see James. Oh my, how can this be?"

Nora insisted on packing a suitcase and moving into a small spare bedroom—at one time the maid's quarters. "I'll be close to James if he needs me," she told Diana. "Their bedroom used to be a pantry and storage area, but they remodeled it when they got older and didn't want to climb the stairs. I don't know what will become of him. His mind is still sharp, and he has clients who depend on him."

She wiped her glasses with a handkerchief she removed from the waistband of her skirt. "Whoever would have thought Emma would go before James?"

Consuela agreed to come Monday through Saturday to cook and clean, as she always had. On Saturdays, she would leave a salad and casserole in the refrigerator, instructions taped to the lid. She showed no outward emotion regarding Emma's death, but her unwavering loyalty spoke for her.

Ted brought James home two days later.

"His condition remains fragile," the doctor had told him, "but we've stabilized his blood pressure."

Nora made the arrangements in consultation with James. Wednesday, the day of the funeral, dawned bright and clear. Nora laid out James' three-piece suit, but he fastened his own cuff links and tied his silk tie. Both looked pale and drawn as they prepared to enter the funeral home limousine for the ride to the cemetery.

James paused, then turned and walked back to Ted and Diana's car where they waited to pull out behind. "You and Nora are my family now," he told them. "Would you ride with us? My brother, Edgar, is coming directly from the airport. I haven't seen him in ten years. He's almost a complete stranger to me now."

Ted turned off the ignition. "Of course. We'd be honored."

Flowers banked the altar and clients and friends filled the pews. As she and Ted were ushered down the aisle behind Nora, Diana recognized some of the women who attended the Christmas reception.

They sat with Nora behind James. James sat alone with a vacant seat beside him on the aisle. To steady herself, Diana studied the stained-glass windows and prayed Emma found peace with God—eternal rest—and that James would find it also.

Laurel sat with Brad and Charlotte in the pew behind them. A middle-aged man slipped in beside Nora and introduced himself to Ted and Diana as John Conover, James' law partner. James turned to look back and acknowledge him.

Just as the organist started to play, a man younger and heavier than James—yet bearing a resemblance in his features—slipped into the vacant seat beside James. The two men exchanged nods and a brief handshake. Then the younger man settled himself, reaching with both hands to slick back the sides of his carefully coifed white hair. As he did so, gold cuff links glittered on the French cuffs before disappearing into the arms of the dark gray worsted suit coat.

James sat erect and unmoving throughout the brief service. The chaplain read a short obituary with no mention of Joshua. He quoted from John fourteen: "In my father's house are many mansions . . . " Emma would be pleased to find it so.

When the service ended, they followed James and the man she assumed to be Edgar Toos back up the aisle. Diana saw Hack and Fern on her right, Abe Feinstein on the left. Consuela sat in the back pew against the wall. She was dressed completely in black and stared straight ahead. No sign of Joshua or the Sheedys.

Edgar Toos took his brother's arm, leaning toward him in what Diana took to be a show of concern. When they reached the vestibule, however, James shook off Edgar's hand and turned to Nora instead.

Edgar turned back to Ted and Diana. His voice was loud and others assembling in the narthex turned to look. "You must be the Rutherfords. I'm Edgar Toos. On the phone, my brother spoke well of you, saying how efficiently you've run the hotel—Hartwick Hotel, I believe?"

"Hartwick House."

"Yes. How quaint."

Us or the hotel? He probably meant well, but already she didn't like him.

"Sorry to come in at the last minute," Edgar continued, ignoring people leaving the chapel who stopped to speak to James. "Couldn't be helped. Business prevented an earlier flight."

The funeral director motioned for them to follow him down the steps and back to the limousine. James kept his eyes trained on the casket as it was lifted into the hearse. He had yet to utter a word.

Beside him, Nora's face was drawn, her eyes red. Then they all reentered the limousine.

An attendant shut the door and Edgar Toos continued to speak, addressing them as if James wasn't present. "My brother doesn't appear at all well. I'm very concerned. As his only living relative, I intend to see that the right provisions for his care are made before I leave."

Diana felt Nora stiffen beside her. "We're all concerned about Mr. Toos," Nora said. "We've been concerned for both James and Emma for some time."

Edgar continued. "Of course, you have. But I'm here now to share that burden."

"It's no burden." Nora trembled visibly, her hands twisting the handkerchief in her lap and color rising above her lace collar.

When they arrived at the mausoleum, Edgar Toos got out first and strode after the funeral director, catching him by the arm to address him with some question or comment. Ted came around the limousine and offered his arm to James.

"Bloodsucker!" Nora hissed in Diana's ear. "I'll bet he smelled money all the way from Texas. Concerned, my foot. He knows he's the only living relative now."

Diana thought of Joshua. Would James accept him as his son now that Emma was gone?

Edgar planted himself beside James during the internment. Nora wept, and Diana twisted her handkerchief in her hands, thinking of all she could have done for Emma, but didn't.

The ride home was quiet. James appeared exhausted. He clutched the funeral bulletin in gloved hands as if by doing so he could somehow take Emma away with him.

Nora turned to him. "Emma's in a good place now. Such a saintly woman would go straight to heaven."

A flicker of his former spirit sprang forth as James turned and looked straight at her. "Quoting Lord Byron, 'Love is heaven, and heaven is love.'"

"Of course, but what I meant . . . " Nora, stopped, flustered.

Diana wondered what comfort she could share of her newfound faith, but the moment had passed. James turned away to stare out the limousine window, his expression cloistered by his grief. They rode the rest of the distance in silence.

Fanny had insisted she remain on duty at the hotel during the funeral. "I can't do anything for Emma by being there," she said. "It's the least I can do. I'll also keep an eye on the mansion. Sometimes thieves read the obituaries and know when a residence will be unoccupied. If I see anything suspicious, I'll call the police."

Ted waited for Laurel, Brad, and Charlotte and then went on to pick up pizza. Diana trudged back to the apartment where Fanny brimmed with questions: "What were the musical selections?"

"Just one song, 'Always.' An unusual choice, I thought, but Nora said James requested it."

"Of course. Emma once told me that Art Gow's orchestra played it for them at the San Marco room where they held their wedding reception. They were high society then. What about flowers?"

Diana sat down in the nearest chair. The adrenaline that had carried her through the day had seeped away. "I'm sorry, Fanny, but I'm beat. Can we talk tomorrow?"

Fanny turned to gather her things. Diana could tell she felt dismissed. "Anything I need to know?" she asked.

"No phone calls even. Like a tomb." Her hand flew to her mouth as she realized what she had said. "I mean . . . like the outside world was paying respect."

"I knew what you meant." Diana stood and hugged her. "Thank you, Fanny. I'll call you in the morning, okay? It's just that I'm bushed right now."

"Of course, you are." Fanny's features relaxed. "I think the teakettle's still hot. Make yourself a cup."

The door closed behind her. Diana went to the kitchen, found the Constant Comment tea bags, took down a ceramic mug and poured water from the teakettle. She noted without caring that it barely steamed.

Carrying it to the dining alcove, she sat down and twirled the bag in the water by its string. The lights along Humboldt flickered on as clouds gathered overhead and thunder clattered in the distance.

She raised the lukewarm liquid to her lips. "I'll miss you, Emma."

CHAPTER 28

FANNY STOPPED BY THE NEXT morning and handed Diana the obituary notice clipped from the *Denver Post*. "No mention of a son named Joshua," she said. "Do you think he knows? He would have expected his mother to come on Wednesday. Emma told me she always called if she wasn't coming."

"Who did she call? Do you know his foster mother's name?"

Fanny pondered, her forehead creased. "Sheedy," she said. "That's it—Sandra Sheedy. I remember because Emma said it's pronounced like Shady but spelled with two e's. She wrote down the name and number for me to call in case of an emergency."

Diana thumbed through the white pages. She never ceased to marvel at Fanny's memory—for quotations and other minutia as well. "Here it is—641 Clinton Street. Do you think I should call? Or tell her in person?"

"It's up to you, Diana, but a call seems pretty impersonal. Social services will do that in due time."

"You're right. It's not that far away. I dread it, but no use putting it off. Will you stay here if I go right now?"

"You know I will."

Diana parked at the curb in front of the red brick duplex. A car was parked in the driveway facing a separate garage. The sidewalk ran the length of the block as well as straight up to each of the front doors, but the house number 641 appeared only on the door to the right. The lawn was mowed and the bushes bordering the foundation were neatly pruned.

Diana stepped out of the car and took a deep breath. She had passed the bus stop at the corner. Had Emma looked forward to Wednesdays or had she dreaded the visits, viewing them as her duty? Joshua was a grown man now. Did he love his mother or resent her for putting him in a foster home? So many questions. She recalled Ted's description of Joshua. Was it possible he was at the funeral?

The doorbell rang deep inside and Diana heard footsteps approaching. She took a deep breath and prayed for the right words.

The woman answering the door was a tall, capable-looking woman in her late fifties. She wore a flowered apron over jeans and a long-sleeved denim shirt. Short curls framed the round face that had a streak of flour resting on its cheek. She broke into a warm smile when she saw Diana.

"Hello. May I help you?"

"I'm Diana Rutherford—the manager at Hartwick House."

Sandra's smile faded. She opened the screen door and stepped back. "Please come in. We've been so worried. I planned to call Social Services today if we didn't hear anything."

Once inside, Diana saw that the duplex was one house with a large living room and dining room extending across the front. The wood floors were so highly polished it seemed the comfortable furnishings would have trouble staying in place.

"Please sit down." Sandra's hands twisted in her apron. "Joshua is at work, so we can talk. He's fit to be tied without news of his mother."

Diana took the nearest chair, so Sandra would sit as well.

Sandra perched on the arm of the couch. "He works five days a week," Sandra continued. "Every day but Sunday for church—he wouldn't miss that—and Wednesday for his mother's visit. His boss says he's always so cheerful and punctual at work, but now he doesn't want to leave home, sure his mother will come in his absence. Is she ill? She always calls if she isn't coming."

"Emma Toos died in her sleep last Saturday night," Diana told her, relieved to have said it without breaking into tears. "It was a shock to everyone."

Sandra clapped her hand to her mouth. "Oh my! How can that be? Poor Joshua. I knew something had to be terribly wrong. She hasn't missed in all these years without calling to let us know." She slid off the arm of the couch onto the cushion. "She's looked awfully tired lately, but I never . . . of course she never complains, never talks about herself . . . always concentrates on Joshua—what he's been doing, what concerns him. What will happen to him now?"

"I don't know, Mrs. Sheedy."

"Please call me Sandra."

"It's really none of my business, Sandra. I just thought someone should let you know—let Joshua know." Diana took some deep gulps to hold back the tears. She hadn't realized she would get so emotional. "Is Joshua born again?" she asked. "Does he know Jesus as his Savior?"

Diana was shocked to hear herself ask those questions. She held her breath waiting for the answers.

"Oh, my yes!" Sandra answered. "He loves Jesus and shares Him with everyone he meets."

"Then he would have shared the gospel message with his mother?"

"Her more than anyone. They were very close."

"Would he have told you if she put her trust in Jesus?"

"Not necessarily. He takes it for granted that people need the Lord and will invite Him into their hearts once they hear the good news He offers them."

Diana stood and crossed the room to hug this warm-hearted person who would now assume an even larger role in Joshua's life. "You don't know how that blesses me," she told Sandra. "Emma Toos was such a good person, but I had no assurance of her eternal resting place. Now I do."

Sandra let tears spill down her face. "Yes, that's a blessing." Then her voice grew indignant. "You'd think his own father might have the decency to let us know, even if he wants nothing to do with his son—which is a crime in my opinion. None of my business, but Josh is so fine! I can't imagine his own father rejecting him as he has. Oh yes, he signs a generous check every month—Josh doesn't lack for anything. But I've always thought Josh capable of achieving much more, given the chance."

"Mrs. Toos was very protective of Joshua," Sandra continued. "She wanted him sheltered from the world as much as possible. Now he won't have his mother's love or his father's attention. It's a real shame." She cleared her throat and wiped her eyes with a corner of her apron.

"Mr. Toos is in poor health himself," Diana said, torn between defending her employer and agreeing with Sandra. "He's in his eighties. Right now, his secretary is staying with him. I can give you the number, so you can call him if you'd like."

Sandra didn't appear to be listening. She fingered the collar of her shirt and pushed her bangs back from her glistening forehead. "My concern lies with Joshua." Her voice cracked on his name. "He'll be devastated. I'll have to call the social worker—see what she says—see if she wants to tell Joshua or have me do it. Oh my."

Diana stood. "Is there anything I can do?"

Sandra stood also. "Please excuse me. I'm not usually so rude. I could have at least offered you a cold drink or something. I so appreciate you coming in person to tell me and don't worry . . . we'll work things out somehow. I'm glad we met. Emma spoke so highly of you."

"Please call me at Hartwick House if there's anything I can do. Do you have the number?"

"Oh yes—from way back—when Mr. and Mrs. Toos lived there. And yes, there is something you can do. Please pray for Joshua."

Edgar Toos went back to Texas two days later, much sooner than he said he would. He told Nora in his brother's presence: "James needs a trained night nurse. I know you do your best, Nora, but I won't feel right leaving until I know he's in competent hands round the clock."

Nora sucked in her breath. "Is that so!"

James eyed his brother with a slight smile. "My, my. You've gone years without being so concerned. Why the sudden interest?"

Edgar lit a cigar and puffed on it before answering. "You're a tough old coot, James. I suppose I deserve that. But people change, you know. I admit we've drifted apart, but now that I'm here, I'd hoped to make amends."

"By insulting Nora—my loyal legal secretary and friend? Amends come on the heels of understanding. I miss Emma." His voice broke. "I need time to grieve for her without someone hovering over me."

"But what if something happens?"

"Like what? Ted and Diana are next door. Henderson barks at any strange sound. Besides, I'm capable of managing my own affairs."

"I'm sure you are," Edgar said, his tone low and soothing. He looked around for an ashtray and finally stood up to flick the ashes into a vase of lilies brought back from the funeral. "I have pressing business to attend to, so I'll be leaving in the morning, but I'll stay in touch if there's anything you need . . . anything at all."

He did indeed leave the next day, voicing solicitude for James, but glorying in his self-importance. "Call me anytime. I'll do my best to be available."

"I'm glad he's gone," Nora confided to Diana. "I didn't trust his newfound concern any more than James did. I discovered him going through a drawer in James' desk. Said he was looking for paper clips, but I didn't believe him—looked mighty fishy to me, snooping around like that."

"James and I have come to terms," Nora continued. "He will stay in contact with me daily by telephone and two afternoons a week, Tuesdays and Thursdays, I'll come to open the mail and be on hand for his appointments with clients."

She patted her hair, having stopped by the hotel directly from the beauty salon. "He needs to feel needed, which he is. His body may be weak, but his mind is as keen as ever. Keeping busy is the best therapy for him. I don't ask if he's taken his medicine because he just glares at me and asks if I'm his mother. So, I guess I have to trust he will. He's still feeble, but he doesn't seem to get any worse."

Diana found her own excuses to check in on James . . . calling for advice on something she would have asked Emma regarding the hotel or taking over a loaf of banana bread and a thermos of hot chocolate after Ted got home. She wondered what, if any, contact regarding Joshua had been made with Social Services, but nothing was said.

His voice shook when James thanked her. "Emma often made hot chocolate when she'd been away on Wednesdays and wanted to make it up to me."

Always in denial dwelling on Emma's absence instead of where she'd been. She wondered if he was eating enough. He looked almost gaunt. She'd check with Consuela, or maybe Nora would know.

James changed the subject. "Will Laurel work after the wedding?"

Diana snapped back to the present. "Definitely. At least until she graduates, or they start a family. She has always said she wouldn't work while her children were small."

"Good for her. Things are so different today. Emma was a teacher before we married—gave up a career to be my wife, live under the same roof as her mother-in-law and run the hotel. She never said she regretted that role, but now sometimes I wonder . . ."

Diana listened, but didn't comment. Did James allow any thought of Joshua to cross his mind? Didn't he realize Joshua would also be missing Emma? She had heard nothing more from Sandra.

She voiced these thought to Ted when she returned to the hotel. The No Vacancy sign was on, for which she was grateful.

"I've been thinking," Ted answered. It had been a busy day for them both, but now the apartment was their cocoon again. "James needs us now. This just isn't a time to run out on him. He's helped us out of scrapes in the past and now he needs our support. So, if it's all right with you, I'll tell him we'll stay another six months instead of leaving it on a month-to-month basis."

Diana felt as if a heavy yoke fell from her shoulders. "I know how much you want a place of our own, especially now that you've earned a promotion, but James has undergone so much. Finding new managers for Hartwick House might be the last straw."

"I know. But remember . . . " Ted paused for emphasis. "It's only a postponement . . . until his health improves."

CHAPTER 29

THE FOLLOWING SUNDAY NINA ARRIVED to tend the desk while Ted and Diana went to church. Nina had come a long ways since Wallace left, who to their knowledge had never been found. For several weeks, she suffered through a rough patch—holed up in her room and losing more weight. Then one day she fired up her laptop to explore volunteer opportunities. Now she manned the book cart at Children's Hospital and read to the elderly at a nearby retirement home. She visited the hairdresser, had her nails done, bought some new clothes, and the pharmacy deliveries dwindled.

During the church service, Diana tried hard to concentrate on the pastor's message, but her mind kept straying to Joshua. She had missed Bible study because of the funeral, but when Kate called, Diana had told Kate of her concern for Joshua: "I haven't heard anything more from Sandra Sheedy. She actually has no reason to call me. It's just that we feel closer to Joshua now that Ted met him at the store. It feels as if he's had no closure for Emma's death. I suppose Sandra called social services to check on the status of things, but how cold is that?"

"Someone else cares," Kate had answered gently.

"Who's that?"

"Joshua's Heavenly Father. I suspect He's assigned angels to keep a special watch."

Diana had felt the tension in her chest drain away. "Yes, of course," she breathed.

Kate went on. "Corinthians chapter two, verse nine says, 'No eye has seen, no ear has heard, and no mind imagines what God has prepared for those who love him.'"

Now as they stood for the closing hymn, Diana gave thanks for that blessed assurance. After the funeral, Ted had announced they would stay another six months before moving on. What plans had God in store for them?

"It's such a beautiful day," Ted remarked as they drove home. "I wish we were going to a Rockies game or could at least take a walk over in Cheesman Park."

"I know." And she did know. Hartwick House was always a magnet pulling them back. "Why don't you change and go for a run?" she suggested. "Mario put the umbrellas out yesterday. I'll fix a picnic lunch and we'll eat on the patio when you get back."

She knew it was a poor substitute, but it was the best she could do. "We can take the Sunday paper and stay there as long as we want," she added. "I'll put a note at the desk and take the cell phone with me."

Ted shrugged as he parked at the curb. "Okay, Babe."

Nina told them things had been quiet except for a phone reservation. She picked up her purse and started out the door. Then she turned back.

"By the way," she said. "A rather strange thing happened. The front door buzzed, and I went out to see who was there—a young man, in his thirties I'd say . . . nice-looking and polite, though somewhat hesitant in his speech. He asked for Emma."

Ted was draping his suit coat around the back of a chair. Now he stopped and exchanged a look with Diana.

Nina continued. "I told him Emma Toos had passed on, but that she didn't live here anyway, but next door at the mansion. He asked where that was, and I gave him directions to find it. I hope I did the right thing. He thanked me and left."

Diana placed her purse on the desk, striving to act natural although her hands shook, and her heart came up in her throat. "Probably someone who stayed here years back. People still ask about Emma all the time."

"Maybe." Nina started to leave again and then turned back. "Oh yes, there's a phone message. A Mrs. Sheedy. Wanted you to call as soon as you returned. Left her number but hung up before I could get any more information. Sorry."

"No problem. I'll call her back. Thanks again for coming down on such short notice." Diana restrained herself to see Nina out the door, then came rushing back.

"It had to be Joshua," she told Ted. "Should we call James? Or maybe you should go over there."

"Call Sandra first."

Sandra answered on the first ring. "Diana! I hope I didn't alarm you. It's just that I was so worried, but it's all right. Mr. Toos just called and I'm on my way out the door to pick up Joshua."

"What happened?"

"Joshua couldn't accept his mother's death. He convinced himself that she was ill or that something else explained why she hasn't come. It's been a nightmare for him—he can't eat or sleep—and then today is his birthday. He pinned all his hopes on her coming, or at least calling. She's never missed."

Her voice broke and Diana waited for her to collect herself and go on. "I baked a cake," she continued. "We had presents waiting, but he slipped out so quietly it took a while to realize he was gone. Took the bus, I guess. Mrs. Toos talked about the hotel many times—he knows it's on Humboldt. I don't know how he found Mr. Toos, but that's where I'm headed now."

"Did Mr. Toos say anything else?" Diana asked, knowing it wasn't any of her business.

"No, but he didn't seem angry. Heaven knows what transpired between the two of them."

Yes, only heaven knows.

When the doorbell rang, James expected to see one of his elderly clients stopping by for a Sunday chat, or perhaps a friend of Emma's paying a condolence call. Probably bearing yet another casserole or loaf of homemade bread. He had dressed carefully, just in case.

Henderson bounded ahead, barking in anticipation, but when James pulled the lace curtain aside, he saw a stranger, a young man neatly dressed in khaki pants and a white polo shirt. He almost decided not to open the door. Yet something stopped him—something familiar—as if the person shouldn't be a stranger after all.

James unbolted the heavy door and cracked it open wide enough to inquire. The dog continued to bark.

"Hi, Henderson. There, Henderson. Good boy."

James drew back. This could be a trick, learning the dog's name to gain entry. "How do you know my dog's name, young man?"

"It's Henderson all right. Mother told me he's a German Shepherd." Henderson poked his nose through the crack and tipped his head up toward the stranger. He was panting now with his tongue hanging out and his hind quarters twitching.

"Emma Toos does live here, doesn't she?" The young man bent over to stroke Henderson's nose as he spoke. "The lady next door told me so . . . at Hartwick House."

The hotel? Diana? James tried to collect the information into something manageable but could not. Why did this young man's face seem somehow familiar? How did he know Emma? And what had he said about his mother?

He needed time to sort it out. Opening the screen door wider, he answered gruffly, "Come in, come in. What's your name?"

"Joshua. Joshua Toos. It's in the Bible, you know. My mother read it to me. Joshua was a great man who led many people for God."

James felt a jolt go through his body. Henderson continued to shiver and bark, straining on his collar. As if in a trance, James closed the door and struggled to turn the old brass key in the lock, grateful for the time it took. His heart pounded in his frail chest.

Henderson quieted and rubbed against Joshua's leg. Instinctively, James let loose of the collar. Foraging for a handkerchief, he swiped at tears coursing down his cheeks. He whispered in a barely audible voice, unaware he spoke the thought aloud. "You're as handsome as can be."

Intent on Henderson, Joshua didn't appear to hear him. "Mother came to see me every Wednesday, but she hasn't come lately, and I've been very worried. Is she sick?"

James led the way into the parlor, thankful to turn his back and fight for at least a measure of composure.

"What's your name, Sir," Joshua asked.

James found himself discombobulated by the show of good manners and his own sudden lack of them. "I'm sorry," he hurried to answer, his voice still not under control. "I'm James Toos. Please sit down."

"Of course. You're my uncle—Uncle James." Joshua's face broke into a wide smile. "I've heard so much about you. Mother talks about you a lot—what a fine lawyer you are and all. She said you lived with her because my father is dead."

Uncle. Not Father. But what had he expected? Hadn't he made it clear from the beginning that he didn't want to be a father to the boy? Yes, he had always thought of him as such. All these years he and Emma maintained a silent truce. He said nothing when she left on Wednesdays, leaving the slate clean. Emma was simply doing what she saw as her duty.

If he ever wondered about the child, he pictured him helpless, without character or personality. Inferior—isn't that what the word *retarded* conveyed? What do they call it nowadays? Mentally handicapped.

Now as he looked into the blue eyes, so like Emma's and so utterly without guile, he experienced a jolt of jealousy. What had he missed all these years?

With great effort, he broached the silence—one of many that waited to be filled. "Your mother is dead, Joshua. I'm sorry." The words echoed firm, as they must. "She didn't suffer. She died in her sleep of a heart attack."

Joshua covered his eyes with both hands. Henderson sat very still, looking up at him. Then the young man's chest heaved up and down, pumping out strangled words in place of the sobs James had dreaded. "I didn't believe it. I didn't think she would leave me."

The words struck a deep chord with James, forming a bridge with someone who understood his sorrow and shared his grief as no one else could. Struggling to his feet, the old man bridged the distance between them to place a gnarled hand on Joshua's broad shoulder. Henderson inched toward him as though torn between the two.

My son. James let the words take root. *The strong son I always wanted. Well-mannered and sensitive, if not brilliant in the ways I deemed important. Why didn't Emma tell me? Would I have listened? I'm an old man now.* But the truth would only cause Joshua further pain.

His eyes rested on the framed photographs displayed on the antique sideboard. Not one picture of this fine young man. "Come," James said. "We'll go to the kitchen and have some hot chocolate."

"I'm afraid it's instant," James told Joshua as he removed the cups from the microwave with an unsteady hand. "Your mother always made the real thing."

"I know. She told me. She told me everything." Joshua took the cup in both hands, bringing it to his lips. Over the rim, his blue eyes—so like Emma's—searched the old man's face. "Why did she have to die, Uncle James?"

Uncle. The word stabbed through James' very soul again. Looking directly into his son's face, he realized he must memorize it while he had the chance—Emma's eyes and high forehead, but his chin, his color of hair—what used to be his hair.

"I don't know why she had to die," he told Joshua. "I miss her, too. All I know, Son, is that she loved us both very much."

He had used *son* without thinking and the utterance of it jolted him afresh. But Joshua didn't react. Of course, he's probably been called that by doctors, social workers, and other kindly adults—including Riley Sheedy, who truly is like a father to him. Only when used by his mother did the word carry special significance.

"Mrs. Sheedy says my mother loves me just as she always has . . . that she's in heaven with Jesus and continues to watch over me."

"Mrs. Sheedy sounds like a fine person—someone who loves you very much. Does she know you're here?"

Joshua hung his head, like a young boy caught playing hooky from school.

James chuckled. It felt good. "Oh-oh. You're in trouble."

Joshua looked up with a shy smile—a conspiratorial bond formed between them.

"I shouldn't have worried her," he said.

Though it was the last thing he wanted to do, James reached for Emma's Rolodex. Then he realized Joshua would know it. "If you'll tell me the number, I'll call so she won't worry."

Sandra Sheedy answered on the first ring. "No need to hurry," he told her, trying to sound casual and hoping she would take him at his word. "We're having a nice chat."

He'd no sooner hung up the phone when Joshua asked, "Do you know Jesus, Uncle James?"

The question startled James and, for a moment, put him at a complete loss for words. "Of course, I do," he finally managed. "I went to church all my life. Jesus is the Son of God."

Joshua edged closer on his chair. "But do you *know* Him?" He pointed to his chest. "In here?"

James might have laughed at someone else putting it that way. Instead he felt tightness in his throat, an urgency that caused him to lean forward, searching for what Joshua meant. "What are you saying, Son?" he asked.

"Jesus loves you," Joshua told him, his eyes so tender that James wanted never to look away. "He wants you to be with Him forever. Here on earth or in heaven where Mother is. Don't you want that?"

"Of course, I do." The words were out before the old man realized how much he meant them.

"Jesus died on the cross for us," Joshua said. "He was buried, but he came out of the grave after three days to give the Good News that anyone who opens the door of his heart and invites Him in will have his sins forgiven and live with Him forever. Just bow your head and say this prayer . . . "

James had no wish to resist. "Dear Jesus, I love you . . . " Joshua prompted.

James repeated the words, his voice little more than a whisper. Joshua continued, "Please come into my heart and be my Friend forever. Amen."

It seemed so simple, yet James experienced a sense of peace that he hadn't known since Emma left him. He reached for his handkerchief and took off his glasses to wipe the tears from his eyes.

Joshua took a drink of his hot chocolate and went on to describe his job at Safeway and the rowing machine he kept in the basement. "It makes me strong, but it doesn't take me anywhere."

They laughed together. James asked about his time spent with Emma—where they went, what they did.

"Sometimes we went to the zoo or the art museum," Joshua told him. "Another time we saw a parade. That was fun. You should have come along."

The words stuck, but James forced them out. "Yes, I should have. I'm sorry I didn't. I was always too busy."

At what? What was so important? When the child was born—before the doctor's opinion was rendered—hadn't he dreamed of doing those very same things with his son? Now it was too late.

"I tried running the Boulder Marathon one time," Joshua confided. "I was terrible at it." He laughed, and James laughed with him, some of the pressure lifting off his chest. "I finished though. Mother was proud."

"I'm proud, too. That's a real accomplishment."

The doorbell sounded far away. It brought Henderson scrambling to his feet and renewed his barking.

"Hush, Henderson. Stay here, boy." James shut the kitchen door behind them as Joshua followed him back through the house to the entry hall. A tall, neatly dressed woman stood on the stoop, anxiety etched on her face.

"Mrs. Sheedy?"

"Yes. Are you Mr. Toos? Did Joshua . . . "

"Come in, my good lady. Joshua and I have had a good visit. He's sorry to have worried you, but he arrived here without incident."

"I'm so sorry . . . "

"Don't be, there's no need. No need at all. Everything's fine. Please come in."

Joshua stepped forward to hug her. "I didn't mean to worry you, Aunt Sandra. I had to find out about my mother. Uncle James told me. You were right. We can go home now."

Home. Would the hurt never end? This home he had shared with Emma would never be home for their son. The choice had been made long ago.

"Take good care of him, Mrs. Sheedy." His voice was steady now. "Would it be too much trouble to send me a monthly report—a simple statement of his activities and well-being?"

"Of course not, Sir. I'll see to it. Will we be seeing you again?"

"Perhaps. But I'm not well."

Sandra started to say more, but then appeared to change her mind. She linked her arm in Joshua's, a familiar action not lost on James. "Come then, Joshua." Her voice was gentle, yet firm. "Uncle Riley will be wondering what's become of us."

"Good-bye, Uncle James. It was nice meeting you. Thanks for the hot chocolate and please say good-bye to Henderson for me."

"I'm very glad you came." The old man restrained himself from reaching out to take Joshua in his arms. "Take care of yourself."

He watched them go down the steps. Watched as his tall son with the straight back walked down the sidewalk and climbed into the car. But before they drove away, he closed the heavy door and leaned against it, pressing his forehead against the hard wood as the tall clock ticked and Henderson continued to bark far away in the kitchen.

At last he turned back to cross the room, walk down the hall and open the kitchen door. Henderson reached to lick his hand. "I'm sorry, old friend." James stroked the silky fur. "It's not your fault. It's all mine."

CHAPTER 30

TED WAITED UNTIL LATE AFTERNOON the following Sunday to have his weekly visit with James. It allowed time for the nap Nora said was now the old man's practice. The neighborhood remained quiet and stately on this May afternoon, the Sunday traffic subdued. Ted waited longer than usual for James to answer the door.

"Come in." The old man reached to shake Ted's hand. "Glad to have company."

They talked of Ted's work. James commented on the petunias Diana had planted by the side entrance. "They look lovely, but she could have asked Mario to do it."

"I know, but she enjoys the opportunity to be outside."

"Of course. And what do you hear from Laurel and David. I understand Laurel has an engagement ring."

"She does. They want to be married right away and it's something I need to discuss with you." Ted took a deep breath. "They both want a small wedding and Laurel has her heart set on the hotel patio. I know it's crazy, taking a chance on the weather and all, but you know Laurel."

The old man chuckled, a good sound Ted hadn't heard for a while. "That does sound like her and you know what? I'd say, go for it."

"Really?" Ted had expected James to state some reservations—not about the occasion, but sharing Ted's concerns regarding weather, traffic noise, interference with hotel guests, and countless other unpredictable things that could take place.

"From what I've observed," the old man continued, "Laurel will adapt to any situation and be a radiant bride—no matter what."

"Yes, but what about hotel guests?"

"Some of them will be your guests, right?" He actually winked. "I never complain when the No Vacancy sign lights up. Emma always said part of the hotel's charm was the unexpected. You may have some curious strangers peering out the windows or over the fence, but I doubt that will bother Laurel."

"You're right about that," Ted conceded. "Laurel never met a stranger. As for rooms, Diana said Laurel has already picked out twenty-four for her grandparents because her Nana will love the claw-foot tub."

"Will Brad and Charlotte take part?"

"Oh my, yes. Brad is David's best man and Charlotte will be Laurel's maid of honor."

"Hartwick House will be honored to provide the setting," James told him.

"It's very generous of you, Sir. And of course, you'll be an honored guest."

"I wouldn't miss it for anything. Let me tell you something, Ted." James sighed and passed a hand over his face. "Cherish your children. Keep an open mind toward all that they are and all they do." His voice caught, and he pulled a handkerchief from his back pocket and blew his nose. "Value who they are and refrain from making judgments. You won't regret it."

The tall clock ticked loud in the silence that followed.

How could it be that both of their children would marry within months of each other. Not quite a year ago, they lived predictable lives in their small western city with both children in college as their only real adjustment.

Yet Diana loved Charlotte and admired David, her future son-in-law. He appeared to unabashedly love Laurel and accept her spirited nature.

"She's talked me into writing vows," he told her one day when they stopped by on the way to shop for wedding rings. "That's not so bad, but now she has a plan for the guests to participate during the ceremony. Who knows where that will lead?"

"It will lead to something unique and wonderful that we'll remember the rest of our lives." Laurel's eyes snapped. "I'm glad the ceremony will be recorded so I can remember it always."

David flashed his infectious grin and Diana knew he would go along with whatever Laurel conjured up. Not that David was a pushover. She knew Laurel listened to and respected his thoughtful opinions.

"It's great that Laurel wants to include my sisters," he told Diana. "I'm proud that they're members of the Colorado Ballet Troupe, but isn't dance a little much for a wedding? Especially on a hotel patio?"

"King David danced before the Lord," Laurel reminded him. "How do you argue with that?"

Diana laughed. "I feel for you, David. Good thing you're such a good sport."

"What can I do? I love the girl."

Vangie agreed to prepare the food. "It's such an honor," she told Diana. "And I know I can do it."

She conveyed such confidence that Diana harbored no qualms as they sat down together to finalize the plan. The big day was exactly a week away.

"There's plenty of room in the lobby to set up a table," Vangie said. "We'll serve finger foods that the guests can eat standing."

"What a good idea." Diana pictured it in her mind. "We'll need only a few chairs along the walls for the older guests—my parents, Charlotte's grandparents if they come, Nora, Fanny and Mr. Toos. I guess other people can sit on the stairs if they want, as long as the fire marshal doesn't show up. We're winging this, Vangie, and you know what? I'm enjoying every minute."

Laurel walked into the lobby just then to leave with her mother for the final fitting of her dress. "Hi, Vangie," she said, giving her a big hug. "I'm so excited that you're doing this. I would have hated the old-fashioned cake and punch routine."

Vangie laughed. "Well, it won't be that!"

Leaving by the front entrance since Laurel's Bug was parked in front, mother and daughter encountered Magdalena polishing the staircase banister.

"I thought you did that yesterday." Diana laughed.

Magdalena ducked her head. "Just making sure."

"Margie's worked overtime all week," Diana told Laurel as they went on out. "She's so pleased to be invited and allowed to bring Sam with her. Magdalena will be helping Vangie, but the two of them will watch from the open window in the lobby."

"It's going to be perfect, isn't it?" Laurel's eyes sparkled with confidence.

"I hope so," Diana replied.

Laurel's dress was a simple, street-length linen sheath. A short veil attached to a circlet of orange blossoms would hold back the golden curls cascading down her back.

"You'll be a gorgeous bride," Diana told her, fighting back tears.

"Go ahead and cry, Mom. You're going to anyway and it tells me how much you care. Just remember, we'll always be best friends."

With Fern's supervision, Hack constructed the trellis under which the bride and groom would say their vows. The ivy entwined on it was artificial, but Mario could replace it with clematis later and make it a permanent part of the garden. "Hack counts it a privilege," Fern told Diana. "It will be our gift."

Mario insisted on grooming every vine and bush on the patio. "It's my job," he insisted as he pinched off dead blossoms and scrubbed the flagstone path on his hands and knees. "Miss Laurel very nice to me. Must make sure everything perfect."

Diana wore the cornflower blue dress Laurel helped her choose. "It brings out the amber glints in your eyes," Laurel had told her.

Now she slipped into the chair beside David's mother in the front row of the thirty assembled chairs. Reba Miles had flown in from Phoenix the day before and was settled in twenty-one. Tall like David, she was warm and friendly—down-to-earth like her son.

Reba wore a salmon-colored frock and both mothers had white gardenia corsages. Diana's mother and father sat in the row behind. Her mother wore a red rose corsage, her father a single rose in his lapel. Charlotte's grandparents had declined the invitation and, sadly, Ted's mother was unable to attend, but Hack would videotape both the wedding and highlights of the reception.

Diana's hand strayed to her hair where her forefinger started to twirl, but she caught herself and clasped her hands in her lap.

Everything would be fine, she told herself. And, if it wasn't, Laurel would find a way to make it so.

The June morning had dawned bright and beautiful—the Colorado sky pure azure. A tent had been reserved in case, but it wouldn't be needed.

Situated to the west of the hotel, the patio remained covered in shade at mid-morning. Nora guided James to the seats reserved for them by maroon velvet cushions on the seats. On all three floors, open windows overlooking the scene held hotel guests who, along with Magdalena and Vangie, gathered to view the tableau below.

"The charm of Hartwick House!" one woman observed. "You never know what to expect."

Diana watched Brad as he waited at the south end of the patio to take his place as best man. She reflected on his attitude that day almost a year ago when he had helped them move into the hotel. Then he would have been highly critical of his sister's plans, embarrassed by something so unconventional. Everything changed after he met Charlotte and grew in faith. Now he could take the day in stride, even enjoy it. After all, Laurel was Laurel.

David motioned for Brad to follow as he stepped up to the trellis archway with David's roommate following Brad as groomsman. All three wore light-colored suits with a single white gardenia pinned to the lapels.

The recorded chamber music began and David's twin sisters, dressed in matching ballet costumes, performed a graceful prelude as they scattered rose petals from wicker baskets on the flagstone path. The young girls looked radiant as they turned and stepped to the side. Marsha followed down the aisle, then Charlotte. Both wore street-length dresses in some kind of soft print of water-colored flowers. Diana saw Charlotte smile and wink at Brad as she took her place. Did she regret not having a formal wedding herself? No, Diana didn't think so.

She jolted herself out of her reverie to stand and face the guests. They followed her lead as Ted and Laurel entered through the garden gate and walked down the short aisle. How right they looked together, their coloring so similar, their smiles tilted in the same self-assured direction.

Ted wore a light tan suit with a blue tie and his own gardenia boutonniere. Laurel carried white lilies, her favorite flower. The yellow centers brought out the depths of her brown eyes and matched the blonde highlights in her hair under the short veil that seemed just right with the simple dress.

As Ted joined Laurel's hand with David's and stepped aside to sit beside her, Diana assessed her husband's expression as peaceful, matching her own. Whatever God had in store for David and Laurel, it would be for good.

Laurel and David spoke the vows they had written, pledging their love for each other, but putting God first. Then the pastor addressed the guests, encouraging them to add their own advice, whether humorous or profound. Laurel and David turned to receive it.

At first there was silence. Then Nina stood to her feet. "Someone has to start," she said. "My advice is to not dwell on past mistakes. Look to the future and what you can make of it."

Diana's friend, Dorothy Miller, who drove over Vail Pass to arrive that very morning, followed Nina. She quoted Galatians chapter six, verse two, "Bear one another's burdens. They're much lighter that way."

Cousin Fanny voiced a quote from Shakespeare's *Sonnet Sixteen*, "Love is not love which alters when it alteration finds, or bends with the remover to remove. Oh no, it is an ever-fixed mark that looks on tempests and is never shaken." Laurel gave her a thumbs-up. What would the day be without Fanny and Shakespeare?

The crowd hushed as James took several moments to push himself up on his cane and address the young couple. "Don't be quick to judge," he advised. His voice was surprisingly strong, reaching back to those standing at the open windows. "It will harden your heart," he told the bride and groom, "and you will regret it."

The serious tone created a pause, but then others took their turn before at last the young pastor pronounced the young couple man and wife and David leaned to kiss his bride. Then the pastor asked everyone to stand, join hands with others beside them, and sing "Blest Be the Tie That Binds." The service ended without a recessional as the radiant bride and smiling groom turned and thanked their guests for coming.

"Refreshments are served in the lobby," Laurel announced. "Not the usual wedding fare, but specialties of Vangie Emerson, head chef at La Feastiesta."

The bride and groom led the way, guests following amidst much excited chatter. Diana dabbed at her eyes with the handkerchief wadded in her hand. As Ted rejoined her, he shook his head in wonderment. "We've come a long way, Babe," he said. "Remember the day we moved in here and you cried tears over some trays of pansies? Now we just expect the unexpected."

The long table in the center of the lobby was covered with a white cloth and strewn with rose petals. It held Vangie's specialties—beef flautas, chicken gorditas, egg salad on pita chips, and a Mexican wedding cake constructed of almond cookies dusted with powdered sugar and piled high in a pyramid.

First the bride and groom crossed arms to feed a cookie to each other, then Vangie served them to guests on white napkins. Margaritas were available in glass flutes with soft drinks and coffee available as well and Vangie, dressed in a chef's hat and frilly white apron, invited guests to help themselves to the rest of the food.

James pulled Diana off to one side. "I felt Emma here in spirit. She would have been so pleased and so proud. Thank you, my dear, for carrying on what I believe was her vision for Hartwick House—a place of welcome and surprise. I'm very tired, so I must go now. God bless you."

Diana placed her free hand over his thin one and felt the roped veins that stretched over the rigid bones. "Thank you." Her voice was barely a whisper as she fought back tears. "That means so much to me."

He leaned heavily on his cane as well as Nora's arm. Diana watched them leave. "Will he be all right?" she asked Ted.

"I don't know. He's so frail. And so alone without Emma."

Once back inside the mansion, James insisted that Nora leave. "Go on back and enjoy the festivities," he told her. "I need to rest and be alone."

"At least let me help you to a chair," Nora pleaded. "You look very pale. I can bring you a glass of water."

"Don't hover. I hate it when people hover."

Reluctant, but knowing better than to argue, Nora left. Henderson whined and nosed the palm of his master's hand.

"Good boy. You've been a faithful friend," James told him. Then he sat on the edge of the sofa and slipped slowly to the floor, where Henderson stood guard over him.

CHAPTER 31

DIANA CALLED SANDRA. "DO YOU know about Mr. Toos?"

"I saw the article this morning. He must have been an important attorney to get a big write-up like that."

"Will you be at the service?"

"It will be up to Joshua. I'm sorry, Diana, but it hurt that after all this time, Edgar Toos was listed as his only living relative."

Diana choked back tears. "I know," she answered.

"James Toos, 80, a prominent Denver attorney, died at his home on June 15th," the article read. "Graveside services will be held at Crown Hill Cemetery on June 19th at 2:00 P.M. He was preceded in death by his wife, Emma Wilcox Toos." A long list of professional and social affiliations followed.

"Somehow I had hoped for something more after Joshua's visit with him. I guess not."

"It seems contrary to Mr. Toos' strong sense of duty, his commitment to principle," Diana answered. "Let alone any personal bond he and Joshua might have established between them. Does Joshua know yet?"

"I told him this morning. He took it rather hard. Didn't say much but went off to his room and shut the door. Probably sees it as the last connection with his mother."

"Will you come to the cemetery?"

"Would we be welcome?"

"Of course. It might bring some closure for Joshua."

"Thank you, Diana. I'll leave it up to Joshua."

The faithful Nora rode with Ted and Diana to the cemetery. To Diana, Nora appeared to have shrunk in size in just the three days since Laurel's wedding. Her black hat sat low on her forehead.

Once again, Fanny insisted on staying at the hotel. "I've come full circle with James and Emma now," she said. "It's the last favor I can grant them."

A sizable crowd gathered. Diana saw Consuela dressed in her customary black. Brad and Charlotte were there, but David and Laurel were still in Jamaica on their honeymoon.

Edgar Toos pulled up in his rented Cadillac just minutes before the service began. He acknowledged Ted and Diana with a brief nod and shook hands with both John Conover and the funeral director. Then he crossed to stand close to the presiding pastor.

John Conover approached to shake hands and acknowledge his sadness at his partner's passing. "James Toos was a good man—an honest man. I learned so much from him," he said.

The simple ceremony followed James' stated request. Nora found the written instructions in his desk: *"No church rites, no eulogy. Just short readings from the Book of Common Prayer."*

"However," Nora had confided to Diana, "I was floored to find an open Bible at his bedside and a listing of Scripture references in his shaky handwriting."

The huge basket of roses looked oddly out of place, as Nora had tried to tell Edgar it would. "That man didn't care a hoot about his brother," she complained to Diana. "It's all for show."

Diana tended to agree. Nora bore the brunt of the pompous oil-man's grievances. When Nora notified him of his brother's death, she told Diana he berated her for leaving James alone following the wedding and informed her that he would be making all the decisions from now on.

"He's such an arrogant fool," Nora complained. "Not a word from him since Emma died, but now he waltzes in, prepared to take over. Well, we'll just see about that."

Diana nudged Ted and nodded toward the young man standing with the Sheedys near the rear of the assembled crowd. "Is that Joshua?"

"Yes, it is," Ted replied. "This must be hard on him to lose the person he thinks is his uncle so soon after losing his mother."

Joshua carried a Bible against his chest and stood erect with head bowed during the short service. When the service ended, the three turned and walked away.

"I wish we could have spoken with them," Diana said.

The crowd dispersed and walked back to their cars. Ted waited to pull out behind the Cadillac that Edgar Toos rented at the airport and drove alone behind the hearse. Edgar paused beside their car and Ted rolled down the window.

"I have to fly back to Dallas tonight," Edgar said without preliminaries—his tone brusque. "I'll be in touch with John Conover, whom I'm told is the executor of the estate. It would have simplified things if my brother had named me to that position, but perhaps it's some unique Colorado law that requires local residency. Regardless, I'm sure our mutual concern is for an orderly transition. I'll keep you informed so you can proceed with your future plans." With a brief, unsmiling nod, he returned to his vehicle.

"Well, I never. The nerve!" Nora sputtered. "Future plans. Sounds like Mr. Texas Big-Shot can't wait to get his hands on what he's sure he has coming. Talk about arrogance."

Ted squeezed Diana's arm. "Sounds like a moving van for us, Babe—a decision we didn't have to make after all."

Diana didn't answer, and Ted started the ignition to follow Edgar's car as it pulled away. The line of cars following theirs did likewise. Diana felt numb, as if this couldn't be happening. Her thought lingered on Joshua. What would the future hold for him now?

"I happen to know James made a new will after Emma died," Nora told them. "His partner, John Conover, drew it up and had his own secretary type it."

Diana reached for her handkerchief. "I still can't believe they're both gone," she said, turning to look at the cars following behind. "So much more could have been said about James today—his wit, his loyalty, his fierce dignity. I'm glad so many came to pay their respects. That in itself is a real tribute."

Ted parked at the hotel behind Nora's gray sedan.

"John Conover told me the estate will go through probate," Nora said after giving Diana a tearful hug. She fished for her keys in her black purse. "He asked me to stay with the firm to assist in the transfer of Mr. Toos' clients. After that, your guess is as good as mine. I'm old enough to retire, but it's been my life. As for you two—well, it's tragic. Just tragic."

Ted was first to reply. "God has a plan, Nora—a plan for good. We'll wait on Him to reveal it."

"Thanks," Diana whispered after Nora got into her car. "I needed that." She reached for Ted's hand and squeezed it. Still, she couldn't help but wonder. What would happen to Hartwick House? They could move on, she supposed. Ted's job would qualify them for a loan to buy a house in the suburbs. At the moment, that sounded very dull to her.

So many loose ends remained, as she supposed often happened at the end of a life. Henderson, for instance. She hated to think of him shut up in a kennel. Maybe if they bought a house. Her thoughts trailed off as she opened the door to face Fanny's questions.

At the barber shop a week later, the barber asked Ted about the rumor that Hartwick House might go up for auction. One of his patrons heard it would be torn down to make way for a Walgreens.

"I'm not surprised," Ted told Diana. "When Edgar Toos came for Emma's funeral, I overheard him tell James that the hotel constituted a liability and should be sold off. Mr. Toos just laughed and said something I couldn't hear, but things are different now. I don't suppose the hotel was ever a big money-maker compared to the law practice. More of a family treasure as far as James and Emma were concerned."

The certified letter arrived on Saturday. Diana signed for it. The return address read "Toos and Conover, Attorneys-at-Law." Slitting open the envelope, she hurried out to the patio where Ted sat reading the *Denver Post* in the shade of the arbor Hack built. How could it be that Laurel and David had been married in that very spot only two weeks to the day?

"You read it. I can't," she said, handing Ted the letter.

Ted unfolded the typed page and read the contents aloud: "The presence of Theodore and Diana Rutherford is requested at the downtown office of John Conover on June twenty-first at ten a.m. for the reading of the Last Will and Testament of James T. Toos, Deceased."

"What on earth?" Diana asked.

"It means we're named in the will," Ted said. "That sounds like James. If Hartwick House is to be sold or torn down, he would want to leave us something to remember it by."

"Maybe that antique chest in number twenty-one, or the doorknockers. I'll bet that's it—the doorknockers!"

"Whatever it is, life goes on, as Emma would say. For months we've been torn between staying or leaving. Now everything will be spelled out and we can make our plans."

A gentle rain moved the windshield wipers as Ted drove their gray Honda Accord into the downtown parking garage. In late June, it was one of those mornings when Diana often saw joggers on the sidewalk in front of the hotel enjoying the cool and the splash as the mountains loomed hazy to the west—luring city dwellers to weekend getaways.

Diana felt at peace. She and Ted had prayed together, acknowledging God's goodness and trusting His care over them. Now Ted came around to open the car door for her and Diana tipped down the mirror for one last look at her hair, which hadn't combed out to suit her that morning.

"You look fine, Babe," Ted teased. "We may land in the street, but you'll make a gorgeous homeless person."

That set the mood. With a lightened heart, Diana rode the elevator to the seventh floor and walked into the spacious offices of Toos and Conover. A young receptionist greeted them, checked their names on a list and ushered them into the wood-paneled office.

Diana assessed John Conover to be somewhere in his late forties or early fifties—around Ted's age, thereby falling into the young category by James and Emma's standard. "Good afternoon," he said, shaking their hands and giving them a warm smile. "Please take a seat."

The office was nicely appointed without being ostentatious. Nora already occupied one of the five leather armchairs arranged in a semi-circle in front of John Conover's desk. Consuela sat in another. Nora fidgeted as she greeted them—crossing and re-crossing her legs and jerking at the hemline of her suit skirt to keep it over her knees. Consuela wore a plain black dress and sat unmoving, her expression as unreadable as ever. Henderson had been removed to a kennel.

Ted and Diana took two of the remaining chairs. Diana felt more relaxed after John's warm greeting. If James had the confidence to make him a partner, he had to be someone she could trust.

Edgar Toos bustled in last. With a solemn nod to the others, he pulled the remaining chair to one end of the desk, sat down, and placed a yellow legal pad on the surface, a gold pen atop it. Then he leaned back, tugged at the points of his gray, pin-striped suit vest, and clasped his hands on his ample stomach.

"So like James not to leave anyone out," he commented, his tone condescending. "I hate to hurry this, but I have another appointment after lunch. Hope to wrap things up and fly back to Dallas tomorrow morning."

Diana wanted to look at Ted, but she didn't dare. She sensed the shift in his chair and imagined the frown on his face.

"I'm expecting one more person, Mr. Toos, and then we'll begin," John Conover said. Then he thanked each of them for coming, took off his glasses and positioned them on the desk pad in front of him. Taking a manila folder from the center drawer of the desk and placing it to his right, he leaned forward and clasped his hands together on the desktop, his smile one of genuine pleasure.

"I'm so pleased to have finally met all of you," he began. "Nora and I, of course, are long-time compatriots, but I feel as though I know each one of you personally from many conversations with James over the years."

A soft knock announced the arrival of the sixth person. John Conover called, "Come in, come in," and stood to introduce the newcomer. "This is Lawrence Grimes from the State Department of Social Services. He's here as a court-appointed legal representative." He motioned to the remaining chair. "Please have a seat, Mr. Grimes."

"Why is he here?" Edgar demanded, grasping the arms of his chair and rising halfway out of it. Diana glanced toward Ted, but Ted didn't react.

"The document before me will answer your questions," John answered as he settled his glasses on his nose. "Please make yourselves comfortable. It's quite lengthy."

Edgar sat back with an impatient grunt and twirled the gold pen round and round between his thumb and forefinger. John Conover opened the manila folder and began to read:

> I, James T. Toos, being of sound mind and disposition, hereby revoke all prior wills and codicils by me made and do make this my last Will and Testament.
>
> Section One
>
> I hereby direct that my remains be buried at a simple graveside service beside my beloved wife, Emma Wilcox Toos, in the mausoleum owned by my estate in Crown Hill Cemetery, Denver, Colorado.
>
> Section Two
>
> In the event she succeeds me, to my faithful secretary and longtime friend, Nora Weeks, I bequeath the sum of fifty

thousand dollars to assist her in enjoying the retirement years she so richly deserves. Also, Ms. Weeks has upon occasion expressed admiration for my wife's Persian lamb jacket and heirloom ruby necklace and earrings. These items I also bequeath to Ms. Weeks.

Nora drew in a sharp breath and groped in her purse for a handkerchief to dab at her eyes.

Section Three

To Consuela Diaz, my loyal cook and housekeeper, in the event she succeeds me and is still in my employ, I bequeath the sum of ten thousand dollars in appreciation for her longtime service.

Consuela looked up for the first time and nodded her acknowledgment.

Section Four

In appreciation of his brotherly concern, however tardy, I bequeath to my brother, Edgar Toos, any personal effects and items of furniture in my home that he would care to retain for their sentimental value.

Edgar paused in his note-taking. Diana glimpsed his frown as he looked up.

Section Five

This day I have established a trust for the remainder of my personal estate—including stocks, bonds, and property—in the name of my beloved son. This trust may be known hereafter as the Joshua J. Toos, Esquire Trust.

Nora made a small outcry. As for Diana, her breathing ceased, and she felt Ted stiffen beside her.

Edgar Toos roared to his feet. "Impossible!" he cried.

The attorney held up a restraining hand and continued reading. Edgar slumped back into his chair.

> This trust, and the assets thereof, is to be administered under the able direction of Theodore and Diana Rutherford, who—if they accept this position—are to be subsequently known as Trustees, drawing an annual salary of forty-thousand dollars for said services, in addition to commissions from Hartwick House, should they choose to retain their managerial position.

> In the event Theodore and Diana Rutherford should choose to refuse the trustee position, all remaining assets of the estate are to be sold and the monies invested under the guidance of a guardian appointed by the court, to be used to benefit the Joshua J. Toos, Esquire Trust. I also bequeath my dog, Henderson, if still living, to my son if so approved by Sandra and Riley Sheedy, Joshua's foster parents.

> As trustees, Theodore and Diana Rutherford are to have full power and authority in matters of use, investment, disposal, or management of same. I trust them to keep the welfare of Joshua as their primary concern and act accordingly, consulting with my able and trusted partner, John Conover, executor of this estate, on matters in which his advice would be beneficial. He, of course, may bill the estate for such services.

Should Theodore and Diana Rutherford choose to refuse this position within thirty days of their appointment—or by giving written notice effective after thirty days at any time in the future, Theodore and Diana Rutherford will be granted a one-time gift of sixty-thousand dollars as a token of my esteem, to assist them in pursuing a new course for their future. The decision is theirs without predetermination on my part as to what that choice should be. They have my blessing and gratitude regardless of the decision made.

In the event of my son's death, the remaining estate will be granted to my alma mater, the University of Colorado, with the stipulation that Diana and Ted Rutherford, provided either or both are still living, be allowed to occupy or manage Hartwick House as well as the mansion my wife and I owned and occupied next door to it, making all decisions pertaining to either or both, in consultation with John Conover, Attorney-at-Law. Otherwise, the entire estate will be turned over to the university to do with as the Regents see fit.

John Conover removed his glasses and addressed the group directly. "A list of assets follows," he told them, "along with a detailed explanation of the legalities involved in the trust, but these I can pursue later with Mr. and Mrs. Rutherford should they choose to accept the Trustee position."

The magnitude of the document and its implications simply staggered Diana. She turned to Ted and saw that his expression mirrored her own state of shock.

John Conover continued, "I realize this document is unusual in nature, but I have conferred with respected colleagues who assure me it is fully legal. If Mr. and Mrs. Rutherford elect within the next thirty days to decline the position, guardianship of the trust will revert to Mr. Grimes, court-appointed legal representative for Joshua Toos, to await disposition following probate of the estate."

He nodded to Ted and Diana. "I'll await your decision. You'll have questions, so feel free to call or come here to see me."

He then addressed Nora and Consuela, neither of whom had moved. "Again, I thank each of you for coming. It's been my great pleasure."

Edgar Toos was on his feet again, his face as red as his tie. "I've never heard such nonsense. James and Emma's only son died in infancy over thirty years ago. I don't know who duped my brother into doing this, but I intend to see this travesty of justice fully disclosed in a court of law!"

His loud diatribe continued as the others filed out of the room. Mr. Grimes asked the receptionist if he could use the phone and Ted, Diana, Nora, and Consuela walked down the hall to the elevator without a word spoken among them.

The elevator passed the fifth floor before Nora broke the fragile silence. "He never mentioned his son to me in all those years. Of course, I knew about him. I made out the check to the state every month and James signed it along with all the other accounts payable." Tears coursed down her cheeks. "All those years . . . "

Consuela's expression remained unreadable. When the elevator stopped, she walked out ahead of them.

Diana stood unmoving until Ted took her arm and guided her out of the elevator and toward the entrance of the building. Her mind felt frozen in a state of confusing questions and emotions.

How does one measure the love of one human being for another? By its duration, its sacrifice, its willingness to admit mistakes? Did

Emma love Joshua more because she never denied him her faithful presence? Or did she fail Joshua when she gave in to James and kept to herself the true extent of Joshua's handicap?

Was James' belated sacrifice greater because he kept his real identity from Joshua, sparing his son the pain of another loss? Was the burden of Emma's silence nobler than today's public act of recognition and generosity? The questions jumbled in Diana's mind as Ted guided her out the door into the light rain still falling on Seventeenth Street.

Nora had not ceased wiping her eyes. "I'm so overwhelmed by what James did for me that I can't even imagine what the two of you are experiencing," she said. "What a huge decision for you to make. I only hope James knew what he was doing, and why." She walked away with her head down, collar turned up against the rain. It hid the expression on her face, but her voice had given away her confused emotions—gratitude perhaps mixed with hurt at not having earned the confidence of her long-time friend and employer. When they reached the parking garage, they exchanged hugs before parting. Who knew when they would see each other again?

Alone at last, Ted let out a long, low whistle. "What a bombshell! Who could have imagined James would come through for Joshua like that? Let alone put such huge confidence in the two of us. I still can't believe it. I'll have to hear it again from Mr. Conover before it soaks in."

Diana's response came out slow—almost dream-like. "I think back to last August and our interview with James and Emma—how eccentric we thought they were. I thought Emma condescending and felt that James disregarded me completely, acknowledging my worth only through you—the man of the family. But over this past year, he and I became friends, especially when he got sick and after Emma's death.

Still, I had no clue he would put such complete trust in us. It would be a huge responsibility."

Ted pulled up to the booth and handed the ticket to the parking attendant. "Do you realize sixty-thousand is twice what we've made so far this year in commissions from Hartwick House?"

"With a ton more responsibility," Diana reminded him.

Ted merged into the traffic. "If we took the lump sum, we could get a new car. This one's nearing a hundred thousand miles, you know. And you could open your own decorating business."

"Laurel says I should design my own website. Something like *Decorating Disasters? Ask Diana.* I could do that from the hotel."

Each remained in his own thoughts. "I can't begin to fathom what this means for Joshua," Diana mused. "What does he need or want that he doesn't have now?"

She paused, still lost in thought, and then continued. "Sandra says Joshua is capable of achieving much more, but I don't know what that means. We know almost nothing about his interests, his capabilities."

"I'm sure the Sheedys know. They raised him."

They rode in silence except for the swish of the windshield wipers. Diana's mind veered in a different direction.

"What will happen to the mansion? Would it be sold? Laurel mentioned once that it would make a wonderful conference center in connection with the hotel—perhaps a Christian one."

"Joshua likes to stay fit—work out. Maybe it could be some kind of a fitness center for Christian youth groups."

Diana felt excitement rising in her throat. "He could help run it! Just think . . . " She stopped, turning to face her husband. "Do you realize we don't really know Joshua, Ted? I've never even met him."

"First priority, I'd think."

Ted's profile was erect—shoulders back, hands firm on the wheel. Diana relaxed. A long, unhurried pursuit of answers lay before them. "It's in God's hands, isn't it?" she asked, a sense of awe overtaking her.

"If we put it there," Ted answered. "If we trust Him for His direction and pray until we have His peace. Remember what we chose as our life verse: 'Trust in the Lord with all thine heart; and lean not on thine own understanding. In all thy ways acknowledge Him and He will direct thy paths.' James gave us the gift of time—time to seek God's guidance, as if he had prayed about it himself. Perhaps he was closer to God than we knew."

"Of course, he was! He spent time alone with Joshua. Remember?"

The raindrops fell faster now. Ted turned up the wipers and leaned forward to peer beyond them. "Let's find somewhere to eat," he said. "I'm famished."

EPILOGUE

AS DIANA LOCKED THE OUTSIDE door to the remodeled garden level of the mansion and climbed the short flight of cement steps, she saw Joshua wheeling his motorbike out of the garage in the alley. "Hi, Mrs. R.," he called, his huge smile gladdening her heart as always. "Been busy today?"

"Yes. Two new customers."

"Way to go!"

No wonder so many of his Special Olympic friends had memberships at his fitness center. But others had joined as well. Word spread of the Christian atmosphere—Christian music playing in the background and Bible studies and prayer groups meeting on the second floor, often led by Joshua.

Over the past five years, the interior of the mansion had undergone major remodeling. The grandfather clock still stood in the entry hall where the Persian rug, rosewood paneling, and marble fireplace continued to create a welcoming atmosphere. Beyond that, however, the wood plank floors, tall curtainless windows, and state-of-the-art workout equipment extended beyond the parlor into the dining room. The wall between the dining room and kitchen was removed and replaced with a long counter. Behind it stood a young lady named Lydia who wore a leg brace and ably dispensed cold drinks and healthy snacks.

"Off to work," Joshua told her as he wheeled past her toward the street.

"Take care," Diana said.

"You sound like Aunt Sandra," Joshua laughed, and Diana knew she did. Joshua still worked two nights a week at Safeway, taking side streets for the four-block ride. He liked his job and the fellowship among his co-workers, many of whom were now his customers. Riley Sheedy installed a big headlight on the bike and Joshua wore sneakers that sparkled as the wheels turned as well as reflective tape on his helmet. "They see me coming and going," he had told Diana.

At the top of the short flight of cement steps, Diana patted the artful sign with its arrow pointing downward: Diana's Decorating Den. Steady business came mostly from word of mouth as well as from local guests of the hotel who came for weekend get-a-ways and commented to Sandra Sheedy on the décor of the room they occupied.

After James died, they stayed on at Hartwick House two more years before Riley and Sandra took over. Hack remodeled both of the bathrooms with the latest fixtures and updated the kitchen. Sometimes he worked nights because he had so much work otherwise as word spread on Capitol Hill of his handyman talents. Fern would come along and often either Ted or Diana brought them soft drinks and lingered awhile to visit.

Then, three years ago, Ted saw the For Sale sign on a charming old house two blocks away. There was a small yard in back where grandchildren could play, tall windows and brick-a-brac trim. Best of all—"We can afford it," Ted said. "We've made it, Babe. Just as I said we would."

So they moved out and the Sheedys and Joshua moved in. Margie and Magdalena stayed on so the transition was relatively seamless and Sandra's warm smile and homemade cookies were an instant hit with the guests.

Number thirty-two became Joshua's domain, but he made Laurel's former cubbyhole his study after Laurel showed him the mountain sunset as the lights of Denver came twinkling on.

"Awesome," he said. "But the Buffaloes poster has to go. Denver Broncos for me."

Now Diana buttoned her coat for the walk home. This was her Bible study night. Nora and Fanny would join her at Kate's house. Fanny had new quotes of her own now, Proverbs nineteen, verse twenty-four being one of her favorites: "A man that hath friends must show himself friendly; and there is a friend that sticketh closer than a brother." Fanny had found that Friend and Diana rejoiced for her.

As she followed the sidewalk to the front of the mansion, she could almost hear Emma's voice: "Welcome. Welcome to Hartwick House."

THE END

In 1898, Alex Meissen, son of a wealthy Austrian bureaucrat, falls in love with beautiful Katy Thannen, the household maid.

Forbidden to marry, Alex devises a plan for them to sail to America to begin a new life together. When the plan fails, there is no turning back. Alone in New York City, Katy faces a devastating dilemma.

If Alex finds her, can they start over considering the secret she now bears?

No Turning Back is a lovely old-fashioned historical love story. It is an action packed, thought-provoking and entertaining page turner.

For more information about
Joanne Wilson Meusburger
&
Starting Over
please visit:

www.facebook.com/noturningback2013
@JMeusburger

For more information about
AMBASSADOR INTERNATIONAL
please visit:

www.ambassador-international.com
@AmbassadorIntl
www.facebook.com/AmbassadorIntl

If you enjoyed this book, please consider leaving us a review on
Amazon, Goodreads, or our website.

More Fiction from Ambassador International

For decades, the Reverend Sammy Milton was a force in American politics.

Scott Addison was a product of his time.

On the day Milton died, Addison was assigned to write an in-depth story meant to bury the fundamentalist preacher in vitriol. He expected the piece to bc an easy one.

Far from a simple assignment, the story would take him to places he never thought possible.

A Spiral into Marvelous Light
by Michael Gryboski

A Hollywood bad boy. A pastor's daughter. What could possibly go wrong?

Mission Hollywood is an inspirational story about love, faith, and second chances.

Mission Hollywood
by Michelle Keener

Can grace and love be found amongst coffee grounds?

Sonja Parker is about to find out.

Libby's Cuppa Joe is a riveting tale of second chances, forgiveness, and not living on borrowed faith.

Libby's Cuppa Joe
by Rebecca Waters

What am I going to do, God? Who am I?

Running for her life, Charlotte boards a bus to escape her pursuers and wakes up the next morning in the woods of Jennings, Georgia, without a memory of how she got there or of who she is. All she knows is an underlying fear she can't seem to shake.

Clear Confusion
by Kathy M. Howard